Other books by the author:

Caveman Politics
Ice Time
Legends of Winter Hill
City in Amber
Paradise Road
Tauvernier Street
Memoirs of a Rugby-Playing Man
Massacre on the Merrimack

THE
TREE STAND
Stories

JAY ATKINSON

LIVINGSTON PRESS

The University of West Alabama

UWA
The UNIVERSITY *of*
WEST ALABAMA

first edition
6 5 4 3 2 1

THE
TREE STAND

Whatsoever thy hand findeth to do,
do *it* with thy might; for *there is* no work,
nor device, nor knowledge, nor wisdom,
in the grave, whither thou goest.

Ecclesiastes 9:10

Contents

For my siblings Jodie, Jill, Jamie and Patrick. I'm a lucky guy.

The Tree Stand

Goodreault woke up on the couch when his wife Eloise came downstairs. It was quarter past six. Under normal circumstances, Joseph "Goody" Goodreault would have already finished his ham and eggs at the White Spot diner and been working by now. But he'd had only two paying jobs in the last six months—building a screen porch over in Jaffrey, and Mike Hargreaves' gambrel roof. And the only thing on his schedule for the next six months was a two-day Sheet-rocking job a hundred miles away in Jackson Village. It was so bad that Goody had to lay off all three of his employees, even Tom Futch, who'd been with him for nine years.

Eloise passed through the living room without speaking and turned on the kitchen faucet and ran the water for her coffee. Tossing off the quilt, Goody stepped into his dungarees, then his work boots, and went into the tiny bathroom in the front hall. He took a piss, washed his hands and face, shaved, and brushed his teeth, rinsing off the bone-handled shaving brush and inserting his soft gold bridge with the left eyetooth protruding from it. Worried about his overflowing septic tank, Goody closed the lid on the toilet, recalling something that his grandfather used to say: *"If it's brown flush it down—if it's yellow let it mellow."*

The lower floor of the house filled up with the smell of brewing coffee. He heard Eloise calling up the stairs, and then Joey and the fraternal twins, Lynn-Marie and Ben, their voices thick with sleep, rumbled along the hallway above him and descended to breakfast.

Goody took his old woolen hunting jacket from a hook by the front door, buttoned it up, and went outside. Dawn was still half an hour away, but the gigantic pines across Beech Hill Road were silhouetted against a sky that was turning crimson by degrees. It was cold, nearly freezing, though the first real frost hadn't yet arrived and there'd been no snow except far to the

Jay Atkinson

north, above Lincoln. A squirrel chittered from a leafless maple as Goody crunched over the stiff edge of his lawn. Once again, someone had thrown the "For Sale" sign into the ditch across the road, and he wandered up and down in the gloom until he found it.

After choosing a stone from the tumbled wall beyond the ditch, Goody pushed the green-and-white Sullivan Realty sign back into its hole in the ground. Holding the stone with both hands, he raised it overhead and gave the top edge of the sign four or five good whacks, driving it deep into the semi-frozen lawn. The concussions from this activity resounded against the house in a series of loud, dry reports. Facing that way, Goody noticed the sash drawn aside, and Eloise's face, pale and disapproving, showed itself for a moment.

Goody threw the stone back into the woods and, coming along the driveway, he stamped the mud from his boots and glanced at the house. It was a small, untidy cape, two rooms up and three down, shingled in cedar except for the lower, southern-facing half where it was wrapped in pink insulation. Like most tradesmen, Goody never seemed to have time to work on his own house. The upstairs bathroom was unfinished; the kitchen was stripped to the studs and sub floor; and the back porch, which faced Sportsman's Pond to the west, lacked a set of stairs. In his real estate advertisement, Tim Sullivan had called it a "quaint work-in-progress," listing the price as $152,900 or "best offer."

Now that the economy had bottomed out, Goody had plenty of time on his hands, but no way to buy the materials he needed to do these jobs right. In the fourteen and a half years they had lived on Beech Hill Road, the house had always been under construction, in some form or another, and he had grown accustomed to the half-tiled floors and Sheet-rock walls and exposed wiring. It was a quiet, secluded area and he would miss living there. Although they were on a dirt road and the house was built on a paltry half-acre, the nearest neighbor was almost a mile away and Goody's property abutted more than two thousand acres of state-owned wetlands and the 152-acre Sportsman Pond, which was also protected from development. Bow hunting and muzzle loading were permitted in season, and the local fishing was excellent. Last winter, Goody had taken a four-pound largemouth through the ice.

Eloise's little sedan was parked behind his truck. When he'd had money coming in, Goody had installed a large, walk-in tool cabinet in his pickup. Fully loaded it was so heavy he had to reinforce the truck's suspension, and he hired a body shop in Rindge to paint it jet black, imprinting *Jos. Goodreault & Sons*

Construction. Home Improvement and Remodeling along with his phone number and *metal and shingle roofs (snow plowing)* in smaller letters, along both sides.

These improvements, including the paint job, the tool cabinet, which was used, and a dozen power tools, also used, had cost him eighty-five hundred dollars, which he'd paid in cash. Although he sorely needed that money now, he was still glad he had done it. When Tim Sullivan finally sold the house, he and Eloise would pay off the mortgage and their credit cards, split whatever was left over, and then file for divorce in county court. His wife had already said he could keep the children. He was going to rent half a duplex in Winchendon for $250 per month less than what he was paying now.

Goody climbed into the front seat of his truck and began idling the diesel. Before long, Joey came out of the house with his school bag, followed by his mother and the twins. Having forgotten something, Joey ran back into the house. Dressed in a black leather jacket and high-heeled boots, Eloise walked by the truck without a sign of recognition. But the twins, who were six years old, stopped beside his door and Goody motioned them back so he could open it.

Lynn-Marie was wearing pink rubber boots and carrying

a stuffed giraffe under her arm. She had her mother's fair skin and light-colored hair and Goody could smell the maple syrup on her breath when he leaned down from the truck to hug her. "'Bye, Daddy," said the little girl. She presented the toy giraffe. "Give Isadore a hug."

Goody pressed the inert giraffe to his chest for a moment and handed it back. Her boots slapping the pavement, Lynn-Marie traipsed in the direction of her mother's car, the giraffe looking back at Goody with its lifeless black eyes. Ben wore green-brown camouflage pants, sneakers and a hooded coat; he looked like a tiny hunter who'd forgotten his bow. While his teenage brother exited the house, slamming the door behind him, and then opened the passenger side door of the truck, climbed in, and slammed that, young Benoit exchanged a complicated progression of fist bumps, taps and handshake grips with his father and then glumly walked away.

Joey had gone back into the house to retrieve his MP3 player, and he had the headphones on when he snapped his seat-belt into place; Goody could hear the percussive thump of the hip hop music that was playing. His son's hair hung over his face and the music was turned up so loud that Goody didn't bother speaking. He put in the clutch and joggled the truck into reverse but had to step on the brake and wait for Eloise, who was fixing her hair in the rearview mirror. After dropping the twins off at school, his wife would drive over to Sullivan Realty in East Rindge. Eloise had been working there as a receptionist for three months. It didn't pay very much but the job provided their only reliable income for the time being, as well as health insurance for the kids. Goody was grateful to Tim Sullivan for that.

Eloise finally backed out of the driveway, revved her tiny engine, and turned left. Goody went in the opposite direction; Joey was a sophomore at the regional technical high school, nine and a half miles away in Jaffrey. Like a lot of kids his age, he was interested in computers and the Reg Tech was the best place to learn about them. Joey's math and conceptual skills weren't strong enough for programming, his counselor had said. But he had an uncanny mechanical ability and had shown a lot of promise assembling computers—building them from kits, as Goody had once been proficient in making birdhouses and intricate wooden cabinets at the same school.

The sun was up now, but hidden in a seamless bank of clouds, which meant a raw, overcast day, typical for November. At the end of Beech Hill Road, Goody crossed a narrow bridge over a chattering stream and turned west onto Route 119. Along that stretch, the county two-lane passes through a forest of maple trees, oaks and pines that eventually gives way to the pond. Goody rode along in a comfortable silence; he never said much on their mornings together and neither did Joey, so he was content to have his fifteen-year-old listen to Kanye West and 50 Cent, mulling over whatever problems were waiting for him at school. Goody had attended the Reg Tech starting the year after it was built. He had learned how to make things, all right, but he wasn't athletic or popular, doing just enough to graduate with his class. Although they had never spoken of it, he was fairly certain that his eldest son shared the opinion that school was hell.

Beyond the local rod and gun club, the trees opened up and he could see the pond, irregularly shaped, pushed into the surrounding countryside like a coin. The wind ruffled the surface of the water, blowing it into shifting patterns of gray and black; there were mostly pines ringing the shoreline, mixed with oak and maple trees dressed in shredded coats of russet and burnt orange.

As the crow flies, Sportsman Pond is located four miles from the center of Fitzwilliam, New Hampshire. Founded in 1764, this tiny hamlet lies just beyond the Massachusetts border, not far from Mount Monadnock. A short drive from the pond, the grassy, half-acre common features a small Civil War memorial, and a plaque dedicated to Brigadier General James Reed, a native son who served honorably in the French and Indian War. A dozen massive Colonials surround the well-maintained patch of lawn, which is marked off by a low iron fence. Down one of the streets just beyond the common is the White Spot diner, fronted by a pair of gas pumps. As he went past, Goody noted Tom Futch's rusty old Jeep parked in the lot but he had to get Joey to school.

The Reg Tech was a massive brick building, three stories high, with a steep, sloping lawn and a quartet of tall white columns flanking the entrance. Kids in blue shop clothes and leather jackets were milling about the crescent drive when Goody pulled up.

A teenage girl with blue hair waved to Joey but he ignored her. "Angela's giving me a ride home," said Joey, referring to the girl. Then he slammed the door and walked away.

Goody waved to Angela and put the truck into gear and drove off. He had met Eloise on that same driveway twenty-seven years earlier, when he was a shy junior with bad skin and she was a freshman in the cosmetology shop.

Within a few minutes, he was back at the White Spot putting five bucks' worth of diesel fuel into his pickup. Tom Futch's Jeep was still parked outside, and on the dirt apron just beyond the lot, Miriam and Louie Daignault had set up their card table and were selling apples. The Daignaults were retired and every year after the harvest they bought several bushels of Macouns and Empires and Cortlands from a commercial grower in Rindge, selling them at a small profit.

This morning they were bundled up against the chill in parkas and woolen hats, sitting in lawn chairs with the apples in white-handled paper bags on the table between them. Goody nodded in their direction and Miriam called out, "It's our last day," her teeth chattering in the wind. She was in her late sixties, small and slender, with narrow pointed features and gray hair she wore in a ponytail. "Too cold for apples," she said.

Her husband was a robust, white-bearded man in overalls and a camouflage parka. "Too cold for Eskimos," he said, with a grunt.

Goody reached back into his vehicle for the plastic travel cup that was lodged between the seats. It represented the best investment he'd made in recent memory—fifteen dollars for a bottomless cup of coffee, good for a year from date of purchase. Jamming the cup into his pocket, he screwed the gas cap shut, replaced the handle inside the pump, and stomped up the wooden stairs into the diner.

When Goody entered the restaurant, Tom Futch, a large, balding man dressed in camouflage with his archery license dangling from its plastic case, was standing at the register where he had just settled his bill. The head of a ten-point buck looked out solemnly from there, and two giant largemouth bass were mounted on wooden plaques to either side. A pair of middle-aged men in hunting clothes sat at the counter by the windows, talking and drinking coffee. Otherwise, the place was empty.

Tom Futch greeted his former boss by lifting an eyebrow comically, while Goody handed his coffee cup and the money for the diesel fuel over to Mary Comeau, the waitress. A tall, pleasing brunette just beyond forty, Mary had full lips, even white teeth, and a dynamic figure that she somehow managed to squeeze into the pink skirt and coffee-stained blouse that made up her uniform.

"Goody, take him with you," she said, indicating Futch. She pivoted to fill the travel mug from the urn behind the counter, offering up her heart-shaped rear end for inspection.

"Don't move," Futch said, winking at Goody. "I think I'm having a religious experience."

Mary turned around with the cup in her hand, steam rising from it. "Watch out, Tom, or I'll baptize you right here," she said.

The men laughed and Futch drew out his wallet, extracted

a single dollar bill, and laid it on the counter beside his empty plate. "Last of the big spenders, too," said Mary, shooing them out the door.

On the wall behind the cash register was a large pin board containing over a hundred items that customers of the diner were trying to sell, most of them hand-printed on 3" by 5" cards—snow mobiles, plows, oil burners, wood stoves, shotguns, nickel-plated target pistols, fiberglass boats, canoes, kayaks, snow shoes, horse trailers, even a set of *Shakespeare's Compleat Works*, bound in calfskin, for $199. Goody had pinned up a card listing Joey's All Terrain Vehicle back in September, marked "best offer." He had paid $2,400 dollars for it a year earlier and had to settle for $650, not even half his mortgage payment.

Setting off the bell over the door, Tom Futch and Goody went outside, pausing at the bottom of the stairs. The Irishman was a head taller and fifty pounds heavier than his former employer, but Goody had wrists and forearms the size of a cartoon strongman, heavy round calves, and a low center of gravity. His body was suited to the work that he did, and he was restless now, eager to be doing something, anything, while Tom Futch withdrew a cigar from his jacket, searched his pockets for a match, and then struck it against the granite post, leaning his bulk there.

"I'm an Irish millionaire," said Futch, expelling a plume of smoke. "Nothing to do."

The wind had picked up. Over on the common, the uppermost branches of the trees were swaying back and forth, clattering together like sheaves, and there was a frosty dryness to the air that was more ominous than the damp chill of early morning. Goody and his hired man contemplated the wind for a few moments, scanning the trees off toward Jaffrey and the low brown hills beyond Mount Monadnock. When they were busy working, installing gutters on a house, or tacking in pieces of a hardwood floor, Goody and Tom Futch could spend an entire day with only a remark or two passing between them. They expressed themselves in what they did, going home afterward with just a wave of the hand.

While they were standing there, an abrupt *pop-pop-pop* carried over the trees from the rod and gun club out on Route 119. "Good white-tail weather," said Futch, tossing aside his cheroot.

Goody nodded, and the two men shook hands and walked off to their vehicles. His engine had been idling the entire time, and Goody shifted into gear and raised his hand to the Daignaults, who waved back. They looked cold, huddled together now with an old Hudson Bay blanket spread over their laps.

Back home, Goody kept busy for a couple of hours, shingling the side of the house closest to the driveway. He had a few bundles of cedar shakes left over from the Hargreaves job, not enough to do very much, but he worked slowly, using a chalked line to set the shakes plumb, lapping each one a half inch over the next. He nursed his coffee until it grew cold, then pulled off the top and dumped the last bit onto the lawn. After using up the shakes, Goody crossed the road into the underbrush and scoured the ruined wall for a half dozen flat, rectangular stones, each one nearly identical. Taking a spade from his truck, he measured out a small trench in the backyard, four feet long, a foot and a half wide, and ten inches deep, placing the stones into it, flat side up. This way, he made a solid footing for the porch stairs, which he would build when he could afford the pressure-treated lumber he'd need outdoors—if that day ever came.

Goody stayed outside past noon, working and sweating in the chill. He had always preferred the outdoors in the best of circumstances and now, especially, the house was foreign to him, almost hostile, a wreck he could never hope to fix. It wasn't the heap of unfinished repairs that troubled him. It was the scads of memories, of the children and their baptisms, of Christmas and Easter and the Fourth of July, opening days of hunting seasons and

Jay Atkinson

fishing seasons; of the myriad happy times he could never return to, at least not in this house. He remembered dragging Joey on a sled through the woods when his first-born son was a year old, coming up through the trees from the pond, a twist of smoke rising from the chimney and his wife in the kitchen window, smiling at them. It was their first house, and at that time he believed they'd live there forever.

Stepping onto the back porch, Goody knocked the mud from his steel-toe boots and went inside. There was an answering machine on the telephone stand in the hall; the little red light blinked three times. The first two messages were from a debt collection agency; and the last one was from Eloise, in a flat weary tone saying that Joey needed a ride after all, and since she was going to Jaffrey anyway she'd pick him up before fetching the twins. They would be home by two-thirty.

It was almost two ·o'clock now. In better times, Goody would return home after work and find half a dozen messages from customers and prospective customers—replacement windows, hardwood floors, finished basements, sometimes a large scale framing or commercial job. He'd work six days a week and spend his Sundays driving from Winchendon to Hillsdale, giving out estimates. Joey would ride along to keep him company, though not as often since he'd started high school.

In the kitchen, Goody made himself a peanut butter and jelly sandwich and felt guilty about it. For more than twelve years, he had been the only wage earner in the house and had never begrudged Eloise or the kids a single thing—her new car, Joey's ATV, a computer for the twins' bedroom. Now, with all of Goody's ladders and other equipment stored in the basement, Joey had moved upstairs to share a room with Ben, and Lynn-Marie slept in the master bedroom with Eloise. Goody sat up every night worrying about their unpaid bills before catching a few hours' sleep on the couch.

The sandwich tasted like ashes in his mouth. Working thirty-two hours a week as a receptionist for Sullivan Realty, Eloise took home $298.74, which was enough to cover electricity, propane, and groceries. Back in September, when Goody's work had dried up, they had canceled their Internet and cable TV subscriptions, cut up their credit cards, and started eating a lot of macaroni and cheese. They were two months behind on the mortgage, and if Goody didn't do something about his septic tank real soon, they would be swimming in raw sewage by Thanksgiving.

He opened the refrigerator to pour himself a glass of milk. On the bottom shelf was a six-pack of beer, with one of the plastic rings stretched out of shape where the lone missing can had been. It was on a Saturday in late August and sticky hot; he had finished with the Hargreaves' job, and begun to fret about landing something that would keep his guys working. He had just popped open the can of beer when his wife came into the kitchen and said that she didn't love him anymore. Simple as that. She hadn't loved him for quite some time, she said. Her voice was shaking a little but she had continued to look into his face with hard, glittering, triumphant eyes. She was going to move out as soon as possible and get a job and start living what she called her "own life."

That day, Eloise wore a pair of tight black pants and low heels and a red silk blouse. She'd just had her hair done and it was frosted into a blonde beehive-type arrangement. The smell of cigarettes lingered in the messy kitchen after she left, though Goody had never known her to smoke.

He hadn't said a word during or after his wife's speech. He had dumped the beer into the sink, ran water after it, and leaned back against the counter with his arms folded over his chest. There was nothing to say. That she didn't love him hadn't come as much of a surprise, because his own feelings were so muted they hardly registered; dulled by time, he supposed, by hours and hours spent together, in lines at the Wal-Mart, in doctors' waiting rooms, in the principal's office, and at the DMV. The routines of the marriage had worn them both out. When he wasn't working, Goody liked to hunt and fish. He loved to be outside, in warm weather or cold, crossing fields in the bright sun or kneeling in his tree stand in the waning light, studying the forest floor. He had no idea what his wife loved as much as he loved these few, simple things. But he was sure that it didn't matter, now.

The gritty sub floor beneath his feet was as white as the milk in his glass. When he ran out of paying jobs, Goody had used some leftover primer to put two coats over the plywood that was supposed to lie beneath the kitchen tiles that he couldn't afford to buy. It was just busy work, which gave him such a hollow feeling that he gave it up. It was worse than not working at all, and he swore to himself that he would never waste time on that sort of thing again. When archery season began on October fifteenth, he got into the habit of sitting in his tree stand from a half hour before Eloise and the kids got home until well after dark. He had seen a couple of deer in that time but had not used his bow, as he hadn't been able to get a clear shot.

Goody rinsed out his glass and left it in the sink. Then he opened the little cutaway door beyond the refrigerator, the flimsy cellar stairs bowing under his weight. When he reached the bot-

Jay Atkinson

tom he tugged on a beaded chain that hung down, illuminating the space. The odor of sewage was powerful here, leeching back through the old mortar in the foundation. Shadows projected from the single light bulb threw the elongated shapes of a table saw, ladders, and other objects against the cellar wall. His camouflage jump suit was balled up in his game bag under the stairs, and he put it on over the clothes he was wearing and pulled the web covers over his boots and snapped them into place, like gaiters. Taking down his bow, six razor-tipped arrows, and his bag, which was decorated in the same, gray-green camouflage and packed with his knife, a length of nylon rope, and a sewing needle and thread, Goody switched off the light and returned to the main floor of the house.

In the kitchen he took a bag of suet from beneath the counter, and going outside, he left his hunting gear on the back porch and dragged an old crate out from under it. The sky was low and dark and he could smell the rank odor of his septic tank penetrating the lawn, which was mushy in several places. In the far corner of his yard he overturned the crate and stood on it to restock the bird feeder that was hanging from the branch of a pine tree. Earlier in the month, Goody had found sign from a black bear around the feeder, including tracks and large piles of scat. The plastic cylinder hung eight feet above the ground and must have tantalized the poor bear.

When Goody was through loading the feeder, he opened the little windows at the bottom of the cylinder, allowing the device to swing by its cord. With most of the leaves down and food scarce, there was a lot of game in the area. Tom Futch had taken a nice, six-point buck in Greenville the previous Sunday. Goody had seen a lot of sign in the nearby woods and figured the hunting would be good over the last month of the season, though he hadn't taken a shot at anything in almost two years.

Goody had been hunting since the age of eight when his maternal grandfather, Benoit Joubert, bought him his first bow and a dozen toy arrows, at the Five and Dime in East Rindge. Under his grandfather's steady encouragement, he had practiced for hours on end, shooting at a target hung from a willow tree behind his grandparents' house. At eleven, Goody killed a rabbit; three years later, using a fiberglass bow purchased from a catalog, he shot a doe in the woods near Mount Monadnock. The doe was gut shot and he and Pepere Benoit tracked the spoor for over a mile. They found it lying beneath a hackberry tree, breathing red foam through its nostrils. His grandfather taught him to kill, drawing the blade of his knife across an artery in the doe's neck.

Jay Atkinson

The bow he was using now, made of composite materials and ultralight, had cost him $1,200. Goody was afraid that, before long, it would be for sale on the pin board down at the White Spot. He stored the crate beneath the porch and returned the suet to the house. It was 2:15 by the wall clock, prompting him to go right back outside. Slinging the bow and game bag over his shoulder, he passed around the side of the house and down his driveway. He walked a short distance along Beech Hill Road, and turned onto a fire road that ran parallel to his land before angling westward in the direction of Sportsman Pond. A loud honking broke the sky above him and he looked up to see an arrowhead of geese, their echo coming off the flat, still disc of the pond.

The dirt road was simple and rough, blocked by a heavy chain strung between two metal poles just a short way along. Out of towners had been dumping junk there of late and Goody was dismayed to find an old camp refrigerator, two beat-up kitchen chairs, and a rusted bicycle, all of it left since his last visit to the tree stand the day before. While he paused, trying to decide whether to haul the junk out now or on the way back, a gleaming new sport utility vehicle eased up the road toward him, stopping a short distance away. The door to the Kelly green SUV opened, displaying a white shamrock imprinted with *Sullivan Realty*, and a tall, wide-shouldered man emerged, smiling with his top and bottom teeth. He reached back and stubbed out his cigarette in the ashtray.

Tim Sullivan was in his late thirties, powerfully built, with a sweep of dark hair that he pushed back with a large be-ringed hand. Dressed in a green sports jacket, khaki trousers, and duck boots, Sullivan was a conspicuous figure—a one-time lineback-er at the University of New Hampshire, and the most successful realtor in the area, with offices in Winchendon, Jaffrey and East Rindge, where Eloise was working.

"I thought that was you," said Sullivan. He was several inches taller than Goody but their handshake was a standoff. "I bet you'll miss hunting around here when we sell your house. Then you'll have to start buying your food at the grocery store like the rest of us."

Sullivan roared at his own joke but when his laughter died out among the trees, the realtor took on a more serious tone. "Your house has been on the market for almost two months, Joe, and we haven't gotten a single inquiry," Sullivan said. "I think you should come down to one forty-nine-nine, and Eloise agrees with me." He took a piece of paper from his pocket, and showed Goody his wife's childish looking signature, right above the space where he would sign.

"Put your John Hancock on the form. I'll take an ad in the *Ledger-Transcript* for the price reduction, and we'll have an open house next Saturday, before we get too close to the holidays."

Sullivan took a Kelly green pen from his pocket, clicked the top, and with a flourish pointed toward the hood of his SUV. While Goody read over the price change form, Sullivan talked about the number of unsold houses he was renewing agreements for, but also how the low mortgage rates had stimulated sales lately. So the news wasn't all bad, the realtor said.

With his tradesman's knack for arithmetic, Goody had already figured out that such a price change on his house would eliminate most of the profit he and Eloise had hoped to make from selling it. And that was only if the change garnered a full price offer; now they'd have to get pretty lucky just to get out of debt. But Goody signed the form. In such a bear market, he'd take a shot at getting even. He had no choice.

"I'll get on this right away, and you can try to scare up something for supper," said the realtor, taking the form back and folding it into his coat pocket. He motioned for Goody to keep the pen. "If you don't kill a moose or a bear, at least you can fire off a stern letter."

The realtor waved goodbye and climbed into his vehicle.

Throwing gravel, he backed out of the narrow lane, disappearing around a bend and between the trees. Goody looked down at the cheap pen in his hand and tossed it into the empty refrigerator that was lying there. He knew that Tim Sullivan was fucking his wife. When that activity had commenced, it had a vague historical importance to it, although deep down, Goody didn't care. He and Eloise had not been intimate for well over a year, and when he looked at his wife none of those old, tender feelings were present.

Setting his bow aside for a moment, Goody knelt among the leaves and picked up a fistful of gravel and began "washing" his hands with it, trying as best he could to remove the other man's scent from them. Satisfied that most of it was gone, Goody picked up his bow and began walking.

There was standing water among the pines off to his right, and the wind had brought down most of the maple and oak leaves that were lying in bunches over the road. Of course, he still thought about women. He was only 44 years old and after his annual checkup, Dr. Comtois had told him that he was in very good health. When he fantasized about a particular woman, it was Mary Comeau, the waitress at the diner. She was divorced with two kids, a girl and a boy. Her son, Gerald, went to school with his twins. There was something in Mary's dark brown eyes that

Jay Atkinson

charmed him—a special glint of friendliness and warmth. Neither of them had ever spoken of it, but there was definitely a mutual attraction. Whatever it was, as Goody went deeper into the woods, he could feel himself moving farther away from it.

After the little swamp, the road ascended over dry ground, through a stand of tall, straight pines, then curving away into a birch forest. The crackle of riflery carried over the timber from the rod and gun club, and tendrils of mist drifted across the road. It grew darker beneath the trees, though it was only three o'clock, with a low-lying blanket of cold air emanating from the swamp. Goody had to look straight up to see the sky, which was sealed with heavy gray clouds. The weather was perfect for deer hunting, and a tiny chill of excitement began to steal over him.

Before he left the road to make way for his tree stand, he shortened the strap on the game bag, cinching it tighter so it wouldn't flop against his hip. Reaching in the pocket of his jump suit, he withdrew a pair of metal garden clippers. It was critical that he not leave any of his scent on the overhanging brush and, using a technique that Pepere Benoit had taught him, he started cutting away pieces of the undergrowth as he went along, letting them drop to the ground.

Putting on the soft, camouflage boonie hat that was

crushed up in his bag, Goody departed from the gravel road and headed off among the pines. At the top of a long, gradual hill, puffing from the effort, he reached a fork and chose the path on the left, which was grassy and flat, dropping into a copse of trees. Along here the canopy was tightly woven overhead, the thick gray branches marked by a few patches of gold and red leaves. A pee-wee called from the top of a massive pine up ahead, and a quartet of tiny sparrows had landed on the forest floor and was parading ahead of him.

At the conclusion of another long hill, the pond showed itself, smooth and silvery between the blackened trunks of the trees. His hunting spot was less than seventy-five yards away but he was coming to it indirectly, to keep from scattering his scent. On a pine needle-laden bluff overlooking Sportsman Pond was a dilapidated old cabin the size of a tool shed, with the windows busted out and an iron bedstead and sagging springs inside. Passing by with a quiet step, the hunter glanced at the broken whiskey bottles and old newspapers covered with droppings. The cabin, long abandoned, was the single blot on the landscape; it looked like a hideout for bandits.

Goody picked up another trail just beyond the cabin, which led downward to the pond through waist-high bushes. It took him five minutes to travel a short distance, as he was forced to clip the bushes along the way. Down at the bottom of the hill, he had a commanding view of the pond—the dense, tree-lined shore interrupted only by an overturned canoe and an abbreviated pier a quarter mile distant. From here, Sportsman Pond appeared as broad as it was long, with a slight chop perpetuated by the wind and not a soul in sight.

Weaving his way among the trees, Goody arrived at heaps of deadfall where someone had logged off a patch of ground at the foot of a small, round hill. Here, Goody was afforded a wider perspective on Sportsman Pond—the opposite shore nearly half a mile away, its humped-up pine forest dotted with red and gold patches of foliage. The wind had died out, flattening the surface of the pond, and the sky was low and leaden, marked only by a trio of Canadian geese flying just above the water. Their plaintive cries echoed over the landscape, and then the pond grew silent again.

The tree stand was less than twenty yards away, on a slight rise that contained three old fir trees and was screened off by a thick hedgerow. Goody stowed the garden clippers in his pocket, withdrew an arrow from his quiver, notched it on his bow, and walked alongside and around the end of the hedgerow. He paused for a long interval at the edge of a small glade, looking right-left, his arrow pointed at the ground. Nothing stirred.

At the base of the fir tree that contained his stand, again he waited for several long moments, scanning over the ground that lay before him. The trunk of the tree, more than a yard in diameter, slanted out from the grassy embankment at a sharp angle. Its gigantic roots were exposed on one side, and after swinging his right leg and then his left over the roots, the angle of the trunk allowed him to walk partway along, until he reached the lowest branches.

The tree stand was fifteen feet above the ground, just two old planks resting between level branches and a yard of gauzy camouflage fabric suspended in front of the planks. After laying aside his quiver to allow his arm freer play, Goody rested on one knee behind the fabric, his bow held in front of him. As a child, he had imitated Pepere Benoit—arrow pointed downward, eyes bright and steady, holding himself as still as a monument. His grandfather could remain that way throughout an afternoon, which was a skill that took constant practice.

To Goody's right, the logged off patches allowed him sight lines of thirty yards or so. Ahead was a small glen of knee-high grass and a few juniper bushes, and to his left was a thicket of scrub pines and undergrowth where deer came and went. He had fully explored the thicket in the off-season, discovering several spots where the animals had bedded down. Though he had never taken a deer from this particular tree, he knew it was a good spot. Sign was scattered everywhere.

It was close enough to day's end that target practice at the rod and gun club had ceased. Goody stayed motionless for more than half an hour, nose breathing in a slow, steady rhythm. The darkness was almost complete. What remained was the last, best minutes of light, when deer were still foraging but their poor eyesight was at its worst. Every nerve in Goody's body was tuned to the half-acre of ground in front of him. He smelled the watery chill of the pond; heard every branch that swayed, every chirrup.

Something moved on the far side of the glen. Rising into a half crouch, Goody drew his arrow back partway, feeling the tension of the bow. Thirty seconds went by, a minute. Then a buck emerged onto the grass. It was approximately a year and a half old, with a small, four-point rack. Goody estimated the animal's weight at one hundred-thirty pounds; the distance was twenty-five yards. He drew a slow breath, let it out, and waited.

The animal slowly moved across from left to right, halting again, its ears pricked up. Even in such low light, Goody could make out the animal's eyes, large and black and watchful, and its hide, luxuriant with feeding, rippling over the musculature beneath. It had survived one winter, and if the animal made it through another, it would have an eight-point rack in the new season. The buck would also have acquired more scent-wisdom in its second year, making it harder to kill.

It had a scent now, however faint. The perplexed animal began circling, never coming closer to the tree stand, but not moving away, either. Making an almost complete circuit around the glade, the animal paused, looked back the way it had come, and then moved on a little ways, halting alongside a juniper bush. It was less than forty feet from Goody's perch and at an advantageous shooting angle—a magnificent young buck, well proportioned, with a fine, sloping neck and sturdy antlers.

Goody drew the arrow back and straightened up, all in one motion. At the first sign of this movement, the animal broke for the hedgerow but Goody had let fly. The arrow whizzed downward at a steep trajectory. Though it was aimed a foot or more ahead of the buck's front shoulder he leaped right into it. The sound was like that of striking a gourd. The tip of the arrow entered a spot between the buck's shoulders and thrust outward from his chest, impaling him. The animal fell over.

Goody scrambled down from the tree and found the buck on its side, panting hard, its upturned eye already glazed and dimming. Taking his knife from its scabbard, he plunged the blade into the animal's neck, drawing it across to sever the major arteries. The animal had stopped breathing by the time he withdrew the knife.

Goody worked fast. Taking the rope from his game bag, he fashioned a rough bridle that he looped beneath the animal's front legs, crossed over its breast, and up behind the head, tying it off there. He slung his bow over his shoulder, took out the needle and thread to sew up the buck's throat wound as well as its anus, and used his knife to cut off the animal's musk glands, one pair at the inside hind leg at the hock and the other on the lower hind leg. Pepere Benoit used to say that leaving the glands in would taint the meat; Goody threw them over his shoulder into the underbrush, wiping the knife on his leg to remove any trace of the musk.

Taking the free end of the rope, he made a kind of harness that went under his arms, over his back in each direction, and fastened just below his chest. He'd have to drag the animal back to the house to butcher it. He would prefer to do it in the field but he didn't have a meat saw or hatchet, and, by hunting without a partner, he would lose what he left behind to scavengers if he attempted to make the haul in two trips. The best way of doing it, given the circumstances, was to get the animal out of the woods as quickly as possible, more or less in one piece.

Goody's heart was beating rapidly, but the understanding that he had to drag one hundred-thirty pounds of dead weight for almost a mile muted his excitement. He could save a little time by choosing a more direct path to the road. But satisfaction lay in the fact that, despite his troubles of late, Goody now had enough venison to last out the winter—over a hundred pounds of stewing meat, steaks, brisket, and delicacies like the heart and liver. He could make use of the entire carcass, just about. He'd even be able to sell the offal to a pig farmer over in Wilton, for twenty cents a pound. In the past, though he had only hunted for sport, his family had eaten the meat after giving some of it away. Now, in a season when he had not landed a single paying job, Goody had saved the household over five hundred dollars on their grocery bill. At least that was something.

Getting the heavy, inert bulk of the animal around the hedgerow and past the lots of deadfall was a challenge. Three times, Goody had to double up the rope and carry the buck over and around a huge pile of timber. It reminded him of carrying his wife over the threshold of their room at the Old Stone Inn. Almost nineteen years had passed since he and Eloise had gone to Niagara Falls on their honeymoon. He had drunk champagne for the first time in his life, and they had dined on lobster and jumbo shrimp and fillet mignon. They even sailed out from the tiny port on the Maid of the Mist, dressed in clammy rain suits. It was the only vacation they had ever taken in the course of their married lives.

The buck moved a bit more easily over the trail, though once or twice the antlers caught on tree roots or bracken. At one point Goody stopped to fish a headlamp out of his bag and slipped it over his hat, training the beam of light on the path just ahead. He was sweating, and his boots and the cuffs of his pants were sticky with the animal's blood. Once back on the road, he pulled the deer along the grassy center strip, its legs dragging behind in the dust. Going uphill left him breathing through his mouth, but he took long, quick strides on the descent, the carcass sliding along on the moss.

When he reached the chain stretched across the road, Goody angled off through the woods, reaching his backyard as the clouds broke up and a few stars appeared overhead. Just beyond the porch a motion detector set off the floodlights, and his oldest son, who was washing the dishes, looked out the window at him. Goody left a foot-wide trail of blood over the dried lawn and, bending down, he grasped the heavy, lifeless animal beneath its withers and about its neck, thumping it down on the porch.

The back door opened and Joey and the little ones tumbled out. "You got one, Dad," said Joey, kneeling to examine the buck's head and antlers. "He's a beauty."

"You're all dirty," Lynne-Marie said. Her hair was down about her shoulders and she was still carrying the toy giraffe. "I think it's dead."

Ben was kneeling beside his older brother now, feeling the truncated antlers and stroking the animal's fur. Emerging onto the porch, Eloise took Lynne-Marie by the shoulders and spun her around. "Get back in the house, missy," she said. "*Now.*" Clutching her toy, the girl made a set of bloody footprints going across the planks.

For several moments, Eloise remained by the door to the house while Goody cut through the animal's hide from the anus to the head. To eviscerate the buck, he started by cutting down through the leg muscles to the skin over the pubic bone. Blood was everywhere—soaking the boards of the porch, matted on the hide of the animal, and covering Goody's arms to the elbows. He turned the knife over and cut through the skin over the abdomen, using two fingers of his left hand to keep the intestines and stomach away from the tip of the knife. He worked slowly; if he were to puncture the intestines, the microbes in there would taint the meat. Still, the smell of the rumen was overpowering and even the open air did little to dissipate the stench.

Eloise had never objected to venison and, in the early years of their marriage, she had hunted with a muzzle-loader and participated in the field dressing of animals. But when Goody took the meat saw from his oldest son and hewed away at the breastbone and then upward, nearly severing the buck's head, his wife reached for Ben's hand and directed him inside. The boy didn't complain; he had seen enough.

Lingering for a moment, Eloise watched with an apologetic expression on her face, like she regretted what her husband and son had been compelled to do. As she looked down on the butchering, a series of changes came over her face. Beneath the tint of annoyance in Eloise's gimlet eye passed the emotions of pity, fear, abject disapproval, and then something near to acceptance, or even, understanding. It was like a dumb show of their lives together, and just as quickly it was extinguished and her eyes took on the dim, lusterless cast of the butchered animal.

Eloise was wearing a short black leather jacket over a purple skirt and shiny, high-heeled boots, being careful where she stepped to avoid getting any of the blood on them. Her throat worked up and down like she was going to say something, then she turned into the house and said, in a quiet, almost tender voice: "Somebody's gonna have to clean that up."

In the glare of the spotlights, Goody and Joey stood in the yard disemboweling the animal with sure, steady movements. Pepere Benoit had learned how to gut a deer from his father in northern Maine before the war, and Goody had taught his own boy what to do the summer before last. Goody severed the throat to the spine, tying a length of string around the spongy tube of the esophagus to keep from contaminating the meat. Next, he cut through the paper-thin diaphragm muscle that separated the heart-lung compartment from the main digestive tract, pulling it away from the rib cage. He removed the heart and liver, setting them in the grass at his feet.

He and Joey picked up the animal and laid it on its side. Most of the guts fell out of the open cavity, and Goody reached in to remove the last of the intestines, making a few cuts with the knife along the backbone to free the attached organs. The stomach was divided into four segments; in the first, known as the rumen, was a large ball of undigested grasses and other vegetation, which indicated that the buck had been feeding. Goody dumped the stomach and the intestines onto the ground, and then tied the nylon rope around the animal's hind feet. He left the hide intact to keep the outer layer of meat from drying out during the aging process. With Joey's help, he raised the buck into the air and suspended it, head toward the ground, from an eye-bolt driven into one of the beams extending from the porch. This would drain the blood from the carcass while allowing air to circulate around the body to cool it. Propping the cavity open with an old hockey stick, Goody wiped the inside of the rib cage with a damp rag and tipped the head forward, opening up the exposed throat. Already, gobbets of black blood soaked the ground beneath the animal.

Joey went into the house to fetch plastic bags for the heart and liver, while Goody shoveled the offal into a large pail that his son brought out. When that was completed, Joey washed down the porch with several buckets of soap and water from the house. Then he took a lawn chair from beneath the porch and unfolded it beside the carcass and sat down. The thermometer attached to the kitchen window marked the temperature at 39 degrees Fahrenheit, perfect for aging the meat. Joey and his father would stay up half the night, safeguarding the kill from predators while the blood drained sufficiently to leave the carcass in the cellar for a few days to tenderize it.

Cataloging his equipment, Goody realized that he'd left his quiver of arrows back at the tree stand. He stripped off his jumpsuit and without a word, reattached his headlamp and passed back over the ruined lawn and into the trees.

The beam of light jumped over the path ahead of him, illuminating the tangles of undergrowth. Soon, Goody's boot soles met the gravel of the road and he was able to travel more swiftly, heading for the western corner of the pond. The night sky had opened up, glittering with stars, and a three-quarter moon had risen, silvering the fir trees and throwing their pointed shadows onto the road. Departing from it, Goody found the path he had taken that afternoon but at the top of the hill chose the right-hand fork, which led to the pond.

Goody used his familiarity with the terrain to descend among the thorn bushes without slackening his pace, the flat black acreage of Sportsman Pond gleaming in the moonlight.

There was an opening along the shore, a grassy embankment ringed with boulders, and Goody dropped into a gully, passing through a hedge before emerging there. Squatting by the water's edge, he chewed on a spear of grass and contemplated the moon, floating on the pond's surface a hundred yards off shore. The only sound was a tiny lapping noise where the wavelets met the underside of the bank. Nothing in his life seemed important now, and he had little concern for what the future might bring.

Jay Atkinson

Rolling his sleeves past his elbows, Goody leaned over the bank and plunged his forearms into the shallow water. The cold numbed them almost instantly. In the beam of his headlamp, he saw the animal's blood seep into the yellowish water, the particles scattering among the tiny fronds. His wife and Tom Futch and the Daignaults and Mary Comeau, even his beloved children, felt like they were a great distance from him, living among the stars perhaps, and looking at the still black water of the pond, Goody knew that they would be all right.

After a while, he rose from the embankment and shook off the pine needles and the chill. Winter was a certainty now, and everything that walked and crawled and flew was intent on that fact.

Bergeron Framing & Remodeling

Whenever the guys finished a job and got paid—especially if it was a Friday—Hank Bergeron drove over to the stadium projects in Lawrence and bought a huge packet of cocaine. While his two older brothers, Charlie and Rick, went home to shower, change clothes, and pack up their wives, Hank cut two-thirds of the coke with baby laxative, pinched it into tiny, quarter gram baggie points, and sold as many of those he could for twenty-five bucks apiece. Then he swung by to grab Tammy and one or two of her friends, and with whatever coke was left over they went bombing up to the cabin. It was always a party when Hank Bergeron was around.

Hank and his brothers worked just as hard as they played. Mostly they framed houses, one at a time, with a crew of just five guys, and occasionally they built a garage or a deck or re-modeled someone's kitchen. The old man, Henry Sr., was pretty much retired by then, sitting up at his cabin on the family land, thirteen acres overlooking Mount Chocorua near Ossipee, New Hampshire. He had driven his boys like rented mules ever since they were teenagers, and all these years later, just a word hinting that his sons weren't doing enough to satisfy him whipped them into a frenzy on the job.

Although at 29 he was the youngest, Hank ran the crew and made all of the decisions. He answered whatever calls came in from their advertisement in the *Lawrence Eagle-Tribune*, priced the jobs, ordered the materials, and supervised the work. The old man used to say that Hank got two percent of his brainpower and the other boys got nothing. But they just laughed. All Charlie and Rick wanted to do was pound nails, drink beer, and get high. The current arrangement was fine by them.

Hank had blond hair halfway down his back, light blue eyes, and stood over six feet tall. In high school, he sold pot and used to skip out nearly every day after his first period class. He'd sneak through the woods to his girlfriend Marni's house and they'd spend the morning smoking joints and fucking in her parents' bed. During senior year, Marni began taking a friend along and Hank was happy to oblige; he'd simply bring more weed and stay through the afternoon, fucking both girls.

Tammy Taylor dated the quarterback on the football team at Carter High. She despised Marni Poulin and thought that Hank Bergeron was nothing but white trash. But in the drift that followed high school, T.T. got into cocaine and heard the rumor that Hank always had some. T.T. was a green-eyed dish with light brown hair, long, well-tanned legs, and a high, round ass. All the boys wanted to fuck her. She and Hank started making out down the beach one night and did a few lines in his truck. They had been together ever since.

Now they were driving up Route 16 through Dover, Somersworth, and Rochester with Guns N' Roses blasting out of the T-tops.

"How much blow you got?" Tammy screamed, tendrils of hair whipping her face. She was wearing a microscopic pair of terrycloth shorts and a yellow bikini top. Hank squeezed her thigh, his rough fingers leaving their impress on her skin. "*Oww*. Quit it," said T. T., slapping him. Hank laughed.

Tammy's friend, Sherry Piantigini, was wedged into the

back seat of the Firebird, also wearing a bikini top and shorts, deafened by the music.

"How many times can I fuck Sherry?" Hank asked T.T.

T.T. slapped him again, then squirmed over and pressed herself against him. "Can I have a taste?" she asked. "Pretty please."

Sherry heard this and leaned up, with one hand on Tammy's shoulder and the other caressing the back of Hank's neck. "I'll have a taste," she said.

"You sure will," said Hank, and the three of them laughed. He gestured that the open roof wouldn't allow him to break out the coke, and said, "I'll give you a face full, when I'm ready."

T.T. and Sherry began dancing in their seats, waving their arms out the sunroof and undulating against Hank's bucket seat. "Me first," said Tammy, rubbing her hand over her boyfriend's crotch.

It was a pig roast weekend. The old man had dug a pit for them the day before, using a backhoe he kept on the property, and Rick had been instructed to build two fires as soon as he got up there—one in the bottom of the hole, and another beside the pit. Of course, when Hank arrived with the girls, the eight-ball, and three thousand dollars in cash, Rick and Charlie and their wives were sitting on the front steps of the cabin drinking Heinekens, with the empty fire pit just a short distance away. It looked like a freshly dug grave.

Hank slammed the trunk of the Firebird. "What the fuck," he said, coming around the nose of the car. "Why isn't the fire lit?"

Rick hoisted his beer. "We ain't eating the fuckin' thing till tomorrow. What's the hurry?"

His brother Charlie stood up as Hank approached, but Rick stayed where he was, whispering something to his wife, Brenda, a chunky redhead with enormous freckled breasts. Brenda laughed, and then moved away when she realized that Hank, who was much bigger than her husband, had a twisted look on his face. He raced up the steps, grabbed Rick by the neck and threw him, sprawling, onto the hard packed dirt of the yard.

"Light the fuckin' fire," he said.

At that moment, the old man turned the corner of the house with the slaughtered pig dangling from one hand and a pitchfork in the other. Henry Bergeron Sr. was a small, compactly built, gray-haired man of 68. He was dressed in a pair of dirty jeans, a sun-faded denim shirt, and steel toe boots, with a red bandanna tied around his head. His neck was ropy with muscle and he moved with the energetic bearing of someone half his age.

"I lost my balance," said Rick, looking up from the ground.

Henry laughed in a sinister burst, heaving the pig carcass over the railing, where its small hooves clattered against the porch. "The best part of you ran down your mother's leg," said the old man, aiming a kick at his laziest son, who rolled out of the way. "You really are sorry as last week's meatloaf."

Rick went back for his overturned beer bottle, saw that it was empty but for an inch of foam, and pitched it into the hole. "Get that out of there, and do what Hank told you to do," said the old man, stomping up the stairs and going inside.

The "cabin" that occupied the grassy rise at the center of the Bergeron's property was actually a modified cape, shingled in dark, reddish brown cedar and trimmed around the windows in local hardwood, with a steep, gabled roof. The front door opened onto a spacious hallway laid out with flagstones, and the rest of the main living area was all white pine—the floors, cabinetry, and broad-board wainscoting that ran halfway up the walls. The upper half was painted a dark Colonial green, and the fireplace that dominated the room was built from fieldstone that Henry had dug out of the ground.

In the kitchen, ladder-back chairs surrounded a white

pine table and the polished granite island that contained the sink and butcher block. Recently made a widower for the second time, Henry had occupied himself over the two years of his wife's illness by digging the cellar hole, setting the wooden frames for the foundation, and constructing the chimney and hearth. Over the past few months, living in a smaller, more rustic cabin fifty yards behind the house, the old man had made every stick of furniture except for the sofa—the pine table, chairs, bedstead, the whole works. His sons had framed and finished the house.

Arriving in the kitchen, Henry ransacked the cabinets for the spices necessary to season the pig; a tiny canister of salt, black pepper, oregano, a knobby head of garlic, crushed parsley, and cumin. When these were assembled on the island, he reached into the stainless steel refrigerator for a bottle of beer, snapping the top off by laying it against the counter top and jerking it downward.

"Stop doing that," said Hank, coming into the room. "It chips the granite."

The old man turned up the beer, emptying half of it. "It's my fucking house," he said.

"You gonna put the pig in the ground?" asked Hank, retrieving a beer of his own.

The old man shook his head. "Everything's right here," he

said, indicating the spices. "I told Charlie what to do. You don't need me."

"Have a couple beers with us."

The gray-haired man pitched his bottle into the trash. The top of his head rose only to his youngest son's ear, but he fixed Hank with his cold blue eyes, raised the index finger of his right hand, and stabbed Hank in the chest with it. "I don't drink with whores, sonny boy," he said.

Hank laughed. "They're not whores," he said. "It's my girlfriend and her friend, Sherry."

"And it's my fucking house, so I'll drink with whoever I feel like drinking with," the old man said. With that, he turned the knob on the back door and sauntered out.

Henry Bergeron had taught his sons woodworking at a young age; just small things at first, sconces and cobbler's benches and three-legged stools. When their mother was still alive, he had them making coffee tables and chests of drawers in the basement, and as each of the boys turned 15, he took them on job sites and taught them how to frame houses. Giving his sons a trade and the roof over their heads was all Henry ever did for them. He had been a heavy drinker in his youth, an inattentive father, and a lousy husband. Until his sons were old enough to work, he had little or nothing to do with them.

Henry had once built a sailboat from a load of teak that was delivered to his house by someone who owed him money and couldn't pay. It was a racing sloop and he drew the plans up himself. The job took three and a half weeks, and he sold the boat for twenty-four thousand dollars; the old man told his second wife it was like stealing, and he laughed when the fellow drove away with his sailboat on a trailer. Henry was more skillful than any of his sons, which was a source of pride for him. It was also an excuse to belittle them, even now, in the face of their—Hank's— successful expansion of the business. He had that over them.

His youngest son was better at ass kissing than he ever was, schmoozing the customers, turning a kitchen-remodeling job into a full-fledged addition, or a two-stall garage into a three-car garage with an in-law apartment above it. The kid was quick with a joke, easy for people to talk to, good at payroll and billing and keeping up with the taxes and Workman's Comp. But the old man never let Hank forget that he was a superior craftsman, or that it was his fucking house—his land, his business, and his name.

The Bergerons were doing all right. Each of the brothers owned his own place, a three-bedroom ranch situated on a nice plot of land; they all lived within a mile of each other in Carter,

Jay Atkinson

Massachusetts, on the New Hampshire border. Twenty years earlier, the old man had purchased the lots for a song but had never done anything with them; he sold them to the boys for $21,000 each the same year he unloaded the family house on Tauvernier Street, using the money to buy the land up in Ossipee.

Henry lived in his little house on the compound year round, and took fifteen percent of the business in exchange for his sons' use of the cabin and his land. That was the deal they had made, and it was working out pretty well as Hank took on more customers. The old man was shrewd that way; he rarely missed the opportunity to better his situation, and he was good at taking his sons' measure, each and every one. Thirty-four year old Charlie was the oldest—a large, dark-eyed man with thinning hair and a walrus mustache. He was just smart enough to know a good thing when he saw it, and had never objected to Hank running the show. Charlie was a steady worker, solidly built, and could read a blueprint—a perfect lead carpenter. His wife, Raquel, did the company bookkeeping and handled their two children, Sara and Charles Jr., without any trouble. After work, Charlie liked to drink beer and smoke pot. He wasn't much of a father, but the old man didn't hold that against him.

All Rick was good for was banging nails and pounding

beers. At 31, he had no more sense than he did at nine years old, when Charlie and his friends lured him down to the brook that crossed behind the house, saying they had captured a snapping turtle. It was Sunday and because Henry's first wife, the boys' mother, was a churchgoer (he always stayed at home, making furniture in the basement), little Rick was wearing a neat brown suit, patent leather shoes, and a red and white bow tie. The brook was running high that spring and when they pushed him in, guffawing like idiots, the boy came up sopping wet, a hole through the knee of his pants and one shoe missing, carried away downstream.

Howling with anger, Rick pursued each of them in turn, but they outran him, closing back in like jackals when he quit, taunting him and laughing. The boy was splayed on the muddy lawn, kicking his feet and screaming, when his mother came out of the house.

Two nights later, when Charlie was asleep in the lower bunk, Rick crept down the ladder from above, drew out a staple gun he had taken from his father's workbench and stapled his older brother, twice, on the side of his face. The four little scars were still there. That was the type of kid he was—sneaky, vengeful and weak—and the kind of man he became. Later, at 19, he married a girl, Brenda, who drank like a sailor and fucked around on him.

Jay Atkinson

The old man knew that if it wasn't for Charlie and Hank, Rick would be homeless, or in jail somewhere.

Hank was the pick of the litter—a real whore-master, with a natural talent for making money. The other two boys took after their mother, which meant they spent it.

The old man knew that Hank supplemented his income by selling cocaine but never said a word about it. He was all right with beating the government out of a few bucks, and if he had been born later, he probably would've done the same thing. The old man recognized, too, how Hank controlled everyone around him with the coke; by when he bought it, how much he sold, and how much he gave away. He was the only one who wasn't a slave to it. And the only one of the three boys who hadn't been in a hurry to get married, either. Yeah, Hank was the sharp one.

By ten o'clock that night, the pig, salted and seasoned in its cavity, double-sheeted in aluminum foil, and wrapped in shrouds of burlap, was buried in its hole near the bottom of the stairs. A brazier of smoking hot coals lay underneath it, followed by fresh pine branches; then came the carcass, another thick layer of charcoal embers over that, topped by a half yard of raked over loam. Two lengths of one-inch copper pipe had been driven into the fire chamber, allowing it to vent, and a pair of burning torches marked either end of the sunken hearth, lending it the air of a burial ground. After darkness came, with soft curls of aromatic smoke rising from the pipes, the mosquitoes grew thick, driving the party inside.

Someone had gone out for pizza and the tangled remains were scattered over the butcher block like entrails. Empty Heineken bottles littered the island and when Rick's wife, Brenda, cranked up the stereo, dancing over the cushions of the sofa in her bare feet, Charlie swept all the dead soldiers into the trash and dumped a good-sized bag of pot onto the counter top.

"Who wants to get stoned?" asked Charlie.

His wife, Raquel, sitting at the kitchen table, raised her hand. Rick and Brenda, lurching in a drunken tango between the island and the refrigerator, also volunteered. Over in a corner of the sectional, Hank and T.T., their limbs entwined, were enjoying a private conversation.

Charlie produced a wooden pipe he had carved from a stick of maple. After fitting it with a new screen, he thumbed the pipe full of the dark gold marijuana and handed it to his wife. The bowl, fashioned from a knurl at the end of the stick, resembled the head of an Indian chief. Charlie had made the pipe one afternoon while stoned, sitting in view of Mount Chocorua, a half mile away.

Using a little jackknife and an awl, it took him a couple of hours to hollow out the stick. Charlie said that the Indian was Chocorua, chief of the Pequawket, for whom the mountain was named. Legend had it that Chocorua fell from the top of the mountain in 1686, choosing to jump rather than be shot down by the white men who pursued him. As he plunged to his death, Chocorua uttered a curse on all those who lived in the valley.

One thing was for sure, Charlie said. The Indians only smoked the good shit.

He cupped a match, lighting the bowl for his wife. The pot was Acapulco Gold, and went for fifty bucks an ounce. He'd purchased it from a Puerto Rican dude just a few hours before the guy got busted, which was a shame, Charlie said, because it was righteous weed and he had arranged to buy half a pound the next day. Now he'd have to find another connection, while the Acapulco Gold was still around town.

"Statesboro Blues" played at full volume and Sherry Piantigini was talking over the music, hitting at the bottle of vodka on the kitchen table, and glancing across at Hank and T.T. every few seconds. The first time the pot was offered Sherry shook her head no, but when Charlie filled the bowl again, she grabbed it from him and took a deep inhale.

Crossing the room with the Indian-headed pipe, she called out to Hank and T.T., "Let's get high." Sherry held the pipe over her head like a totem, undulating toward the corner of the sectional where her friend was sitting. Hank laughed, waving her off. But Sherry continued forward with a mean little smile on her face, rotating her hips and shaking her ass for all it was worth. "C'mon, Tammy," she said. "Let's party."

T.T. barely glanced at her. "I don't wanna," she said.

The sexy little brunette stopped dancing. "I thought this was gonna be fun," Sherry said. "It's like a fuckin' morgue around here. I shoulda gone to the beach with Chris and Lisa."

Hank said something to T.T. in a low voice, and she laughed.

"Don't laugh at me, you bitch," said Sherry, grabbing T. T. by the hair. "You said there'd be lots of coke."

She still had the pipe in her hand, and Rick came over and took it from her. Gesturing toward Charlie and laughing, Rick sat down Indian-style and smoked while the two girls writhed on the floor, clawing at each other.

"Hey. *Hey!*" said Hank, pulling them apart. He lifted each of them in the air with the strength of one arm—their shorts rode up, and their hair flew in every direction. "Easy," Hank said. "The party hasn't started yet."

Rick had acquired a pinch of weed and a match from Charlie, and stood on a figured rug in the middle of the room and lit the pipe again. He took a big hit, gagged, and dropped the pipe on the floor, coughing in a prolonged horse laugh, his face turning crimson, hands flailing at the air. It started out comically, but soon took on the mien of some sort of attack.

Brenda ran over and switched off the music. Charlie began pounding his brother on the back, and Hank flung T.T. and Sherry onto the sectional and came over.

The fit continued for several moments. At the end of his oxygen supply, Rick made a dry, choking noise, almost a sob, ending in retches that sounded like a wild animal.

"Are you okay, Rick?" Brenda asked. "You sound like you're fuckin' dying."

Charlie called over to Raquel. "Bring some water," he said.

Rick staggered over to the sofa, covering his face with his hands and then running them through his hair. "I'm fine," he said. "Leave me alone."

"Can I get you something, honey?" asked Brenda, taking the glass of water from Raquel. Her infidelity was old news. Currently, she was dating a Lawrence fire fighter.

"Get me a beer," said Rick, pushing away the glass of water.

Charlie laughed. "Tough guy," he said.

Hank moved off and was standing in the entranceway to the master bedroom with T.T. clinging to him. He had not mentioned the cocaine all evening, but now, with Sherry sitting alone at the end of the couch, he took out the plastic bag and motioned to her. It looked like the bulb of some exotic plant.

"Want some?" he asked.

Sherry nodded her head. Hank gestured toward the bedroom while T.T. nibbled at his ear. "Well, let's party, then," he said.

*

The next day, Brenda and Rick got up before nine AM and drove home. Charlie slept until noon, when Raquel coaxed him out of bed by making some coffee. They smoked a joint at the kitchen table and left to pick up their kids. Hank and the girls remained in the master bedroom all day, watching porn on video-cassette and drinking Bloody Marys. Finally, at six o'clock, they took showers and began gathering their things.

Hank stood on the porch drinking coffee while the girls

loaded up the Firebird. They had their hair in ponytails and wore baggy sweatshirts and leggings. The tiki torches had long since burned out and the pig was moldering in the pit, forgotten. Wearing a pair of acid washed jeans, Hank descended the stairs just as the old man rounded the corner on his tractor. He rode over one of the blackened tiki torches, crushing it to the ground, and then switched off the engine. Behind the tractor was a small trailer filled with various garden tools and the old man unlatched the trailer and removed a spade and a rake.

"You look like a fairy in those pants," he said.

Hank gazed at him with mild eyes. "Got a match?" he asked, reaching into his pocket for another cigarette.

The old man tossed over a cigarette lighter, and stood regarding his youngest son. "Another wasted day," he said, shaking his head.

Hank laughed. "What are you doing today?" he asked.

"Doing? It's done, hotshot," said the old man. "While you nitwits were sleeping, I dug out the stumps in back of my place, sunk the posts for my new fence, cleared away two tons worth of boulders, and graded it all with the tractor." He took out a canister of tobacco and packed his lower lip. "Maybe you can get your hair done, or something."

The old man indicated the spot where the pig was buried. "What are you gonna do with that meat?"

Hank flung away his cigarette and upturned his coffee mug, dumping the remainder on the lawn. The girls were sitting in his car with the engine running, T.T. in the front seat and Sherry in back, mouths set in a grim line and arms folded over their chests.

"You can have it," said Hank. "We're cuttin' out."

"You bought the pig, made a fire, and sunk it into the ground," the old man said. "Now you're too lazy to eat it." He shook his head. "That's beautiful."

Hank stared into the distance with a faint smile. To the west, the rocky dome of Mount Chocorua was windswept and menacing, strips of fast moving clouds running just above the peak. Their shadows played back and forth on the broad flank of the mountain, and the wind increased as the sky grew darker, blowing cold and steady from the north.

The old man took up the spade and began digging at the bald patch on the lawn. Passing over the flagstones without another word, Hank climbed into the driver's seat of the Firebird, slammed his door shut, and pushed in a Rolling Stones cassette, which came blaring from the speakers.

"Hank—turn that down," said T.T., curled up in her seat.

Jay Atkinson

"I have a headache."

"Shut up," said Hank, throwing the Firebird into reverse.

The tires spun against the gravel, thrusting them backward until he shifted and the treads caught and shot them along the entrance road. Up by the house, the old man looked like he was exhuming a grave, throwing spadefuls of loam over his shoulder.

*

On Monday morning Hank priced a new job, framing a house abutting a golf course in Dracut, Mass. It was the first phase of a proposed forty-home development, which would mean a year's work for Bergeron Framing & Remodeling, if the job ran to completion. The general contractors were out of East Boston, and were interested in hiring as many as three framing crews. They had connections to the Anguilos but Hank marched right into their office on Bennington Street and talked to "Fat Sal" Tagliamonte, who ran close to three hundred pounds and had a face like mashed up pizza dough. Invoices were piled on his desk. He wore overalls and a pair of construction boots, but his small pink hands indicated that he didn't really work for a living.

Hank said that Bergeron Framing & Remodeling was a non-union crew, five white guys, and that they would frame the first house, in two weeks, for $3.75 a square foot. Total cost: $11,250 for the three thousand square-foot colonial.

Fat Sal told Hank to get the fuck out of his office. Nobody with a five-man crew would be able to finish that job in two weeks and besides, he was only paying $3 a square-foot.

Hank sat in a chair next to Tagliamonte's desk and lit a cigarette. "I ain't doing 'em all that fast, just this one," he said. "And the lowest I'll go is three-fifty a square foot."

"Put that out," said Fat Sal, pointing at the cigarette. "And get a haircut. You look like a fucking broad."

But when Hank returned home there was a phone message from Tagliamonte. He'd done some checking around. Bergeron Framing could have the first house, for three-fifty a square foot. He'd see them at the job site at six AM the next morning.

Hank called everyone with the news. Brenda said that Rick wasn't feeling well, and couldn't come to the phone. "I don't wanna talk to him, anyway," said Hank. "Just tell him to show up tomorrow morning."

But at quarter to six, when Hank arrived on the lot, only Charlie and the two hired guys were there, drinking coffee and inspecting the foundation. Huge pallets of two-by-fours and two-by-eights were stacked up on the muddy ground. Hank jumped out of the dented pickup with *Bergeron Framing & Remodeling* marked on the door just as Sal Tagliamonte drove onto the site in his Lincoln Continental. He was wearing a canvas jacket with a hardhat and boots.

"This is all you got?" he asked Hank. "Four guys? What is this, a fuckin' joke?"

Hank strapped on his tool belt. "There's five of us," he said.

"Yeah? Who's the other one? The invisible fuckin' man?" Tagliamonte shook his finger at him. "If you don't get this done, you're gonna be building fuckin' doghouses."

Tagliamonte clipped the wires on the bundles with a pair of red cutters from his pocket and then got back in the Lincoln and zoomed off. When he was out of sight, Hank kicked the side of the truck, flinging his coffee cup to the ground. "Where the fuck is Rick?"

Charlie and one of the hired men were already pulling apart the first bundle, sizing up the lumber and marking some of it with pencils. The smell of new wood filled the damp morning air. "Brenda says he's sick," Charlie said. "I tried to call you, but you'd already left."

"This is a big job. If he fucks it up, he's not gonna be working for me anymore."

Bergeron Framing & Remodeling

A man down, the crew worked straight through lunch, eating sandwiches that Raquel brought to the job site, while the first floor studs went up and they started on the second floor, saws whining, the chatter of hammers echoing over the park. By the time it got dark, the first floor was nearly framed in, and they had a platform down and were putting up the next set of studs. An hour after the last golfer had finished putting the eighteenth, Hank looked up at the stars glistening above the pines and called it quits. It wasn't a bad day's work for just four guys, but going vertical to the roof was the most difficult and time-consuming part, and they hadn't even started on the garage yet.

He and Charlie walked over to the pickup and Hank rummaged behind the seat for the six-pack of beer he usually kept there. It was getting close to seven o'clock. The girlfriend of one of the day laborers, who had been waiting for almost two hours, puttered away from the job site with her boyfriend up front and the other man in the back seat.

Charlie popped open two of the beers and they carved away the spewing foam with the flat of their hands and stood looking at the darkened golf course. Despite the briny wind harking over the fairway, they were still in their t-shirts and tool belts, and Charlie was bleeding from a cut on his elbow. Neither man was satisfied with their progress, but they drank the warm cans of beer with the sense of accomplishment that comes after a long day's work. Charlie dipped into a tin of loose tobacco, packing his lower lip, and Hank smoked a bent and wrinkled cigarette, admiring what they had done so far, with the wind dying away and the glint of fireflies beyond them in the tall grass.

"You want me to get another guy?" asked Charlie, when he had finished his beer.

"Most of 'em ain't worth shit that aren't already working," Hank said. "He'll be here tomorrow."

But he wasn't. Rick hadn't missed a day of work in seven years, rain or shine, and now, when they really needed him, he stayed in bed for three straight days. Brenda said it was the flu. On Thursday, Charlie found two new guys but one of them didn't bother coming back after lunch, and the other one was useless and Hank fired him. Fat Sal appeared every morning around nine o'clock, gazed up at the house with his hand shading his eyes, swore at Hank a few times, and then waddled over to his Lincoln and drove away. Two larger subcontractors, with crews of eight or nine men, were already framing on site and the Bergerons were falling behind.

Hank didn't say a word; he pounded nails like he was

driving them into his brother's skull and stopped talking altogether, even to Charlie, who never said much anyway. Hank didn't ask about Rick, or bother calling the house. Rick knew where they were. If he was enough of a pussy to let the flu keep him from working, then Hank had no use for him.

By Friday, the house was completed up to the second floor joist. They planned to work through the weekend, but a late storm blew in Friday night, cutting huge rivulets across the muddy lot. Because of the runoff from the fairways, which were pitched downward, the cellar hole filled with rain water to the cap, and a pine tree was knocked down; it landed square on the back end of the house, shattering the top half of the wall.

Hank met Sal Tagliamonte on the job site at eight-thirty on Saturday morning. The general contractor wore a yellow rain suit with a hooded jacket, smoking his cigar in short angry puffs and cursing the whole time.

"Cut this fuckin' tree up, and get it outta here," Fat Sal said. "You shoulda done that before you called me."

The trunk of the pine tree was three feet in diameter, fifty feet long, with thousands of branches that were sticky with pitch and radiating in all directions. Hank explained that the water level had to go down before he attempted to remove the tree. It was going to take three men at least half a day to dismember the pine tree with chain saws, and fixing the crumbled wall would take the rest of that day and into the next. The crew was shorthanded already, and this added delay was going to make fulfilling the original agreement impossible.

"Can you put an insurance claim in?" asked Hank. "I'm gonna need more materials to replace all this broken shit."

Tagliamonte stood with his feet apart, the stub of his cigar moving up and down as he spoke. "We don't have any fuckin' insurance." He threw the cigar into the mud. "You better fix this, or else," he said.

The next day, Hank threw himself into the job with renewed fury. On a gray Sunday morning that foretold hours of labor just to return to where they'd left off, Hank went bullshit when Rick didn't show up. That afternoon, Brenda called Raquel to say she was taking him to a doctor, an event in itself, since none of the Bergerons ever got sick. Vigorous good health was the principal trait that they had inherited from the old man, along with a near total disdain for every other living thing.

Dr. Pierce didn't like what he saw when Rick arrived at his office on Monday, and ordered a full course of blood work and some other tests at the local hospital. By the time Rick presented himself there the next morning, he was a pale, shivering wreck. He hadn't eaten any solid food for a week, and he was so unsteady on his feet that the charge nurse ordered a wheelchair the moment she saw him. The tests, lasting about an hour, exhausted him, and Brenda told Charlie afterwards that Rick was so sick he coughed up blood, promising his wife that he would quit smoking cigarettes and weed.

At lunch, Hank went down to the Wonder Bar and hired two more guys right off their stools—he had no choice. The next morning, he was compelled to do something he found even more disagreeable than that. He called the old man in Ossipee and told him they needed help. Two hundred fifty bucks a day, the old man said. That's a lot of fucking money, Hank said. Next time I'll think twice.

Next time I won't come, said the old man and hung up.

Although they hadn't worked for him in almost five years, having the old man on site pushed Hank and Charlie to new feats of endurance. Most of the old man's talent as a carpenter wasn't put to good use framing a house, but he had done it a thousand times as a young man and prosecuted the raising of the second floor, and then the roof, with ease—measuring the two-by-fours swiftly and surely, cutting lengths of two-by-eight with uncanny precision, and making the jack studs and door and window headers with a virtuosity that his sons could never hope to reproduce.

But it was his skill as the de facto foreman that hastened the pace of the job and earned the old man his money. Hank's latest hires had very little experience building houses but the old man adopted the two barflies as his crew, using one as a laborer to fetch tools and wood. After teaching the other one to measure and cut the studs, Henry concentrated his own energy on going up, putting the vertical weight-bearing studs in place, raising the ridgepole with a block and tackle, and attaching all the rafters with a nail gun, which increased the speed of their overall progress.

Hank and Charlie worked the opposite wall, sweating like devils in the awful humidity that followed the storm; they had trouble keeping up with the old man, despite having two good laborers and familiarity with this sort of work. By Thursday afternoon, the plywood was nailed over the second floor. They ate lunch with their legs dangling over the rim joists, taking stock of their diminishing supplies and eyeballing how much light remained in the western sky.

"We'll be shingling the roof tomorrow," said Charlie,

throwing down his empty lunch bag.

Hank lit a cigarette. "Save a couple of two-by-fours," he said. "One to shove up Fat Sal's ass, and one to smash Rick in the face."

By dusk on Friday, the crew had buttoned up the second floor and was enclosing the roof amidst a din of hammers when Fat Sal pulled onto the lot. All three Bergerons were up there— the old man, Charlie, and Hank—in various attitudes of labor and totally preoccupied with what they were doing, until, one by one, they left off driving nails and the cacophony died away. With tool belts girdling their waists and nail guns in hand, the trio of carpenters was silhouetted against the burning violet of the sky.

While they looked down from the roof, Tagliamonte came around the Lincoln, stuck his head in the front door to examine the interior studs, and passed alongside the garage, tiptoeing through the thick orange mud. At the rear of the house, he squatted by a window to make sure the water had drained from the cellar, and straightening up with some difficulty, retreated to his car. Fat Sal pulled a briefcase out the driver's side window, opened it on the trunk of the Lincoln, and then, leaning backward to attain the proper perspective, hailed the men on the roof.

"Are you gonna get it done?" Tagliamonte asked.

Jay Atkinson

Hank stood with one foot on the peak of the roof, his blond hair falling to the middle of his back. With his gauntlet and hammer, he looked like a figure in a storybook. Charlie was several feet lower on the slope of the roof, and the old man was straddling the peak of the garage.

"What does it look like?" Hank asked.

Other than a peewee calling from the treetops, silence reigned over the job site. The unspoken question that hung in the air between the nose of the Lincoln and the ridgepole was whether Hank and his crew were going to get the contract for the other twelve houses. Deep down, Hank didn't give a shit either way. He had gotten the job done, on time, despite an act of God and his worthless no-show of a brother. He had fulfilled his end of the deal, and he was waiting there on top of the roof to hear the man say it.

"Are you gonna come down for the check, or should I just leave it on the fuckin' ground?" asked Tagliamonte.

Hank laid aside his nail gun and dismounted the slope of the roof, signaling the crew to get back to work. Hidden from the general contractor for a moment, Hank glanced at Charlie and spat over the rim joist. "You know where you're gonna be workin' for the next year," he said.

An hour later, the crew had their wages, paid in cash, and the old man lit out in his truck for the ride up north. Charlie drove to the bank to drop Tagliamonte's check in the night depository, and Hank stayed at the job site with one of the hourly guys to pick up the stray tools and load the trash into the back of his pickup. When they were through, Hank dropped the hired man in front of the Wonder Bar, hovering at the curb as the laborer entered through the heavy door, his pay envelope sticking out of his back pocket. Playing his new Metallica cassette, Hank drove over to the stadium projects to buy an eight ball of cocaine. He wanted more than that, being flush with cash at the moment and because the eight ball was probably cut to shit already—his connection insisted it wasn't—but it was late for a Friday and six grams was all he could get. It was enough to party with that night, and he could phone a guy he knew in Lowell when he got back on Sunday.

Hank went home, took a shower and picked up Sherry a little after nine. He'd told Charlie that T.T. had been getting on his nerves lately, so he was phasing her out. They did a couple of toots in Sherry's driveway, heading north with a twelve-pack of beer and a hefty Dominican cigar for the ride.

All the lights were blazing when they arrived at the cabin around eleven thirty. Hank parked on the grass beside Charlie's

Jay Atkinson

van, and they did another line off the dashboard before heading inside. Rick's '72 El Camino was nearest the house, which meant that he and Brenda had gotten there first. It was a surprise to see it there, as Rick hardly ever took the fifteen-year-old classic out of the garage. It was his baby.

Hank had stopped in town for more beer, and with the case on his shoulder he went up the front stairs into the house. "Where's the fuckin' bed wetter?" he asked, blinking in the light. His blood was racing, the pulse squishing in his ears. "The candy ass of Mount Chocorua."

Hank flung the case of beer down on the kitchen table. Behind him, Sherry tiptoed through the open door, carrying a pair of sandals, her toenails painted fire engine red. She wore a pair of tight ripped jeans and a sheer white blouse that accented her shining brown hair, dark tan, and melon-sized breasts. "Hiya," she said.

Seated at the table were Charlie, Raquel, Brenda and Rick. Before them was a scattering of beer bottles and a pair of ashtrays, where both of the women had cigarettes going. The mood was solemn; no music played from the stereo, and Raquel looked like she'd been crying. Brenda's eyes were vacant, gazing toward the far wall, and Charlie was drinking his beer in a mechanical fashion, working over the tobacco that packed his lower lip.

At the end of the table, Rick was slouching in his chair, his face the color of dried concrete. His brown hair, usually combed straight back, was sticking out every which way. He wore that familiar guilty smirk, but there was another emotion as well, like he had just played a trump card, or delivered some sort of pronouncement.

"What's going on?" asked Hank.

The silence lasted seven or eight seconds. "Rick has leukemia," said Brenda.

From behind where Hank stood, Sherry uttered a gasp and sat down on the flagstones. Hank continued to regard his older brother while nothing stirred on his face. After another moment, he reached over and pulled one of the bottles from the case.

"That calls for a beer," Hank said.

Charlie raised his own bottle to his lips, speaking around it before he drank. "He refuses to do chemotherapy," he said. "We've been arguing about it all night."

"The old man know about this?" asked Hank.

Charlie nodded. "He was here."

Brenda spoke again, this time in a quavering voice: "The doctor said it's bad. The cancer's aggressive, and it's really advanced."

"How bad?" Hank asked.

"He's got a few weeks," said Charlie, looking Hank in the eye. "If he has the chemo, maybe three or four months, the doc says."

Rick pushed his chair out, and stood up. His legs looked thin beneath his dungarees and his arms were like sticks. In just two weeks, he'd lost more almost twenty-five pounds. "If I do the chemo, I'll be nauseous most of the time. Just to live until November? Fuck that."

He walked around the table before returning to his chair while Sherry Piantigini watched from the sectional.

"Rick, you gotta think about your health," Brenda said. "You shouldn't even be drinking that beer."

Rick laughed at her. "My health? I'm gonna be dead in three weeks. Then you can fuck Billy DeFiore all you want."

Raquel burst out crying again, and Charlie went over and kneeled beside her. "It's okay, honey," he said, stroking her hair. He raised his eyes. "Try not to be such an asshole, Rick," he said.

"I can be an asshole all I want," Rick said. "Besides, chemotherapy ain't cheap. Is Bergeron Framing & Remodeling gonna pay for it?" There was silence at the table. "I didn't think so."

None of the family had any insurance except the old man, who was on Medicare, and Charlie, whose kids had health coverage through their school. Raquel paid for it every month by doing the company books. That was it.

"No life insurance, nothin'," said Brenda, like she had been holding it back. "What am I gonna live on?"

"Ask Billy DeFiore," said Rick.

Brenda hurled one of the ceramic ashtrays at him but missed, shattering it against the granite island. No one said anything, until Hank returned his empty bottle to the case and opened another one. "So, what are we gonna do?" he asked.

"I'm gonna die, that's what I'm gonna do," said Rick. "Got any coke?"

Raquel wiped her eyes on Charlie's shirt. "Do you think that's a good idea, doing coke when you have leukemia?" she asked.

Rick's laughter echoed over the flagstones. "I don't think it's gonna make much difference," he said. "It should liven things up a bit. C'mon, Hank. Think of it as my severance pay."

Arms folded over his chest, Hank looked at his brother without expression. Then, abruptly, he got up from his chair, went over to the wall, removed a heavy, gilt-edged mirror and laid it on top of the kitchen table. "Fuck it," Hank said, reaching into his pocket for the cocaine. He dumped it on the mirror and fished in his wallet for a hundred dollar bill and threw it alongside the pile of coke, which was the size of a child's fist.

"Knock yourself out," he said.

Hank was grinding his teeth. His mouth was dry in spite of the half dozen beers he had drunk, and the baby laxative was running through his guts like a squirrel. Bent over the table, Rick used his driver's license to divide the coke, cutting it into lines, which were reflected in the mirror. Just then, the old man entered through the back door, his wispy hair standing on end, and his face dark and raw-looking in the harsh kitchen light.

"To my health," said Rick, flourishing the tightly rolled hundred.

He leaned over the mirror, hoovering up a line through his left nostril and another one through his right. He straightened up, blinking rapidly, a dusting of the coke on his upper lip. Tipping his beer bottle, he moistened his finger, swept up the crumbs of cocaine from the mirror and inserted the finger into each nostril and snorted. He returned to his chair with a satisfied gasp, smiling at the people seated around the table.

"I'm cured," Rick said. "It's a miracle." He gestured with

the rolled up bill to Hank, and then to Charlie. "Who's next?" he asked. "Who's gonna have a toot?"

Nobody at the table moved, or said a word. "C'mon, Brenda. For old time's sake," he said. Her gaze elsewhere, his wife refused to answer him.

The smile faded from Rick's face. He looked past the table to where Sherry was sitting, her legs pulled up to her chest. "You, there. What's-your-name. You look like a party girl."

Sherry stared over her knees at him, motionless. Rick held the hundred-dollar bill like a telescope, peered through it at Hank and Charlie, and then sniffed a few times and used the edge of his driver's license to stretch the lines of cocaine. "I'm dyin' of leukemia and nobody wants to party with me? Well, fuck you, then."

Before Rick bent to the mirror again, the old man circled the island and took the rolled up bill from his son's hand. Henry Bergeron, Sr. was not given to fits of anger, or loud demonstrations of any kind. He stood beside Rick's chair for a moment, the rolled up bill down by his side. He searched the faces of those seated around the table until his gaze settled on Rick.

Touching his son's shoulder, the old man said, "I've never done this before," and leaned over the island.

　　　　　　　　　　　　　　　Jay Atkinson

Lowell Boulevard

C handler the regular mechanic had weekends off. When one
of the fire department ambulances broke down on Saturday,
the driver, Glenn Garvey, asked a few of the guys to help push it
into the service bay. It was a bright, temperate, April morning,
and sunlight was pouring in the brick archways of the firehouse,
illuminating the rolled down boots and bunker pants lined up
along the wall. While Garvey jogged to his pickup truck to fetch
his toolbox, his partner on the ambulance, a skinny young EMT
named Gage Henry, kept busy polishing the fire pole and fixtures
with a can of Brasso and a chamois. Several of the older fire fighters sat out front in wooden chairs, and although smoking was not

permitted in the firehouse, the penetrating odor of a cigar meant that the chief was in the building.

Garvey returned to the ambulance bay, running hard despite the encumbrance of his toolbox, the muscles of his arms bulging from his t-shirt. After six weeks of boredom in the alarm room, answering the phones, he had completed EMT training and, like all the other rookies, he was spending a year on the ambulance before being assigned to a truck. His father, Jack, had recently retired from the department after putting in thirty-seven years on Engine 5.

Glenn unlatched the hood of the ambulance and opened his toolbox and set his portable radio on the apron. "You probably shouldn't do that," said his partner. Gage Henry indicated the half dozen fire fighters sitting out front. "It might piss somebody off."

Glenn had positioned the ambulance so the morning sun fell on the workings of the engine. "You worry too much," he said, testing the battery connections with his hand. The alternator light had come on when they were returning from their first call—a high school baseball player had been hit in the head by a pitch, suffering a concussion—and Glenn ran his dirty fingers along the belt, checking it like a fisherman testing his line. "Something ain't right."

One of the fire fighters out front, a large, bald-headed man with tobacco stained teeth, was shading his eyes and looking in their direction. "Oh-oh," said Gage.

Jerry Montefusco ambled toward them like an old circus bear, half on his toes, his short arms held out to the sides. "What the fuck are you doing?" he asked.

Ignoring him, Glenn tried to loosen the belt on the alternator with a socket wrench. Montefusco leaned over to shut off the radio. "You two are supposed to be on housework," he said.

Glenn pointed to the other ambulance bay, which was empty. "Tom Lyons and Jose are out on a call, and this truck isn't running," he said. "I'm gonna try to fix it."

"Leave it for Chandler," said Montefusco. "It's not in your job description."

Glenn Garvey turned to face the other man. The former University of Massachusetts fullback was two inches taller than his colleague, with wide, flat-boned shoulders and the arms, wrists, and hands of a stevedore. "Chandler's not gonna be back till Monday," he said. "I'm just trying to figure out what's wrong."

Montefusco looked over at Gage Henry. The narrow-faced EMT had stopped shining the brass and was standing there, mouth agape, with the chamois in his hand. "What are you looking at?"

asked Montefusco. "Do your fucking housework."

Montefusco leveled his gaze at Glenn Garvey. "You're in local eleven sixty-two, remember?" he asked. "Mechanic is *not* a union job."

At twenty-three years of age, Glenn Garvey could bench press 350 pounds; Jerry Montefusco was forty-five and regularly hoisted a beer mug. Without another word, Glenn turned around and resumed work on the stubborn alternator belt.

Montefusco glared at Gage Henry, who had returned to polishing brass but was keeping an eye on the proceedings. Then he stomped off, disappearing into the shadowy recesses of the firehouse. A few minutes later Montefusco returned, accompanied by Billy Ronan, a trim, intelligent-looking fellow with wavy gray hair. Ronan wore pressed blue work pants and a gray "CFD" polo shirt; with more than twenty years on the job, he was the representative of the seventy-eight Carter fire fighters who belonged to the union.

"Can I talk to you for a minute, Glenn?" asked Ronan.

"I'm right here, Billy," Garvey said.

The trim little firefighter nodded. "Leave that off a minute," he said.

The alternator bolt was refusing to yield despite all the

pressure Glenn was putting on it. "I know—it's Chandler's job," Glenn said, straining with the ratchet. "He's off today."

"It's a union rule," said Montefusco. "I can file a grievance against you."

Glenn Garvey threw the wrench against the bulk of the engine and faced his inquisitors. "It's a not a union issue, it's a public safety issue," said Glenn, directing his comments to Billy Ronan. "The ambulance broke down. We need two ambulances to cover the ward. End of story."

Montefusco looked over at Ronan. "I tried to fuckin' tell him, Billy."

Billy Ronan folded his arms. "He can write you up."

"So write me up," said Glenn.

He reached under the hood, groping among the mass of hoses and cables for the socket wrench. When he had closed his hand on it, Glenn turned back, resting the head of the wrench against Jerry Montefusco's shoulder. "Say a call comes in this afternoon that someone's having a heart attack on Tauvernier Street, and the other ambulance is busy somewhere else," he said. "Whatta we tell 'em?"

"We'll get there as fast as we can," Montefusco said.

"Your mother lives on Tauvernier Street, doesn't she, Jerry? Or your Uncle Tony on Durrell Street. Then whatta we do, Jerry? Tell 'em we'll get there as fast as we can?" Glenn Garvey spoke like he was trying to explain something to an idiot. "It's a public safety issue, Jerry. Pub-lic Safe-ty."

Montefusco's face had turned crimson but for the tips of his ears, which were as white as parchment. He made a grating noise in his throat, but Ronan preempted him with a glance, and the two fire fighters walked away. Straining, shifting his feet, and cursing, Glenn Garvey tried in vain to loosen the bolt on the alternator. Taking up a flashlight from his toolbox, he called to Gage Henry and his partner looked right and left, set his can of Brasso and the rag aside, and came over.

"You're gonna get me in trouble," said Gage.

"Shut up, you pussy. Hold this," said Glenn, aiming the flashlight at the appropriate spot. "I can't see what I'm doing."

Pushing down with both hands he tried to loosen the bolt but the head snapped off, remaining inside the socket attachment of the wrench. "Fuck," he said, throwing the wrench down. Now Chandler would have to drill out the bolt and replace it, sometime on Monday.

"Let's do things the hard way," said Gage, with a sigh.

Glenn Garvey was packing up his toolbox. "It's not an

easy job," he said.

*

Located just beyond the town square, the Central Fire Station was a massive brick building, four stories high, with a rectangular tower that rose another fifty feet above the gabled roof. By tradition, the "lines," or hoses, were hung inside the tower by means of a pulley system to dry them out after a fire. The giant bell was an oxidized green color, and the wooden fretwork within the tower was frosted with a thick layer of pigeon shit.

Erected in 1889, the firehouse contained four large bays facing Lowell Street and housed the town's only ladder truck, a combination engine, a pumper, the rescue truck, and the chief's car. The huge wooden doors to each of the bays, painted dark green, were forty-five feet high and thirty-two feet wide; each included another door within itself, large enough to accommodate a man leading a draft horse, as they were necessary equipment in the early days. The horses were used to pull the fire wagons, then taken round to the stable, which had been torn down in 1935, the empty space converted to a parking lot.

Men were housed in two dormitories on the second floor, between which was a common room for playing cards or watching television. On the floor above the dormitories, paneled in dark wood, was the chief's office, the alarm room, a storage area where the leather horse collars and bridles could still be found; alongside was a bunk room for the EMTs. Ambulance crews were called out more often than the trucks and had their own separate alarm: a low, persistent buzzer that sounded throughout the house and was easily distinguished from the ear-splitting klaxon of a general alarm.

Glenn Garvey hadn't yet grown accustomed to being awakened from sleep for an ambulance call; within seconds, his heart leaped from the resting rate of a well-trained athlete, somewhere in the fifty to sixty beats a minute range, to upwards of a hundred, propelling him from his bunk.

"I think I'm having a heart attack," he said to Gage Henry late one night, as they scrambled into their bunker pants and boots.

Sliding down the pole ahead of him, Gage said, "Wait till we get to the truck."

The town square was deserted when they came zooming from the bay, the siren going *wah-WAH, wah-WAH, blip-blip-blip-blip-blip* as they skidded over the cobblestones and turned up Lowell Street. It was just after one AM on a quiet night in June. The houses—most of them neat little cottages—were dark and silent as they ascended the hill, passing Tauvernier Street and the entrance to the old cemetery, which included the town's Revolutionary War dead and a trio of brothers who were killed at Antietam.

"Twenty-one," came the radio call. "A one-car accident on the boulevard, near the Dracut line. Roll over. State Police en route."

"Roger," said Gage into the transmitter. "Twenty-one, out."

Glenn Garvey was driving. In the six months he and his partner had been on the ambulance they had seen an ever-widening range of human misery. It came with the job, of course, and preparing for it had occupied a large part of their training. Together he and Gage had been dispatched to gory crime scenes; nursing homes that reeked of shit, urine, and cleaning solvent; elementary schools; shopping centers; parking lots; a myriad of private residences scattered across all four wards; even town hall on Saint Patrick's Day, when the mayor sprained an ankle after joining in with the Irish step dancers.

They had treated stab wounds and gunshot wounds; lice infestations; broken bones of every sort; dementia; drug overdoses and hallucinations; delirium tremens; stroke victims; elderly shut-ins awash in their own piss and covered in feces; a man impaled on a stockade fence; just about everything imaginable, although there were enough new and often amazing situations that these, too, became a matter of routine.

Of course, Glenn and Gage Henry had also encountered death: corpses in bath tubs, in reclining chairs, in parked cars, and a family of four strewn across an empty lot after a residential gas explosion; even a dead man at the local YMCA, slumped over the handlebars of a stationary bike. After work they went to the small gabled fire fighters' club, the Relief's Inn, leaning up at the high wooden bar. The walls of the club were stuccoed over with departmental patches and pins, brought back by vacationing fire fighters from all corners of the world, along with sepia-toned photographs of horse-drawn pumpers and old time firemen in double-breasted coats with brass buttons.

There in the smoky bar, amidst other men drinking bottles of beer, Glenn and Gage talked about things they had seen: Mr. Deschane, their eighth grade math teacher, who had hanged himself in his basement when Mrs. Deschane was out shopping; and the nine year old girl with the burst appendix who almost died on the way to Bon Secours; and Father Beauvais from St. Anthony's church, nipped on the hand by a fox terrier at something called the

"Blessing of the Pets."

Sometimes the young firefighters were amused by what they had experienced, like the time they were called to the home of Roland Gladstone, who owned Gladstone's Hardware store and had a wife and two kids; the respectable Mr. Gladstone was wearing his wife's evening gown and had a small can of peas lodged in his rectum. During the transfer from house to ambulance and throughout the entire ride to Bon Secours hospital, EMTs Garvey and Henry avoided looking at each other and then howled like banshees upon their return to the station.

On other nights, they sat on bar stools at the Relief's and said very little, drinking their beers and staring into the blue haze of cigarette smoke. Back in November, during what was their second or third shift on the ambulance, Glenn Garvey and his partner were dispatched to a house on Forest Street. The address was familiar to them both: Mary Constantine lived there. She and Gage had gone steady during high school, and he had taken her to the senior prom, double dating with Glenn and one of the Dixon twins. After Mary went off to Framingham State, Gage worked construction for a couple of years and then took the civil service test. He and Mary had diverging interests and different friends, and the soft-spoken former soccer player and his wisecracking girlfriend lost touch.

Jogging toward Mary's front door with the medical kit and a backboard, Gage and Glenn expected to find a household accident, or perhaps Mr. Constantine, a heavyset man who drove a forklift, had suffered a heart attack. But the man who had always been cordial to his daughter's friends jerked open the door, his face white as chalk, pointing their way down the carpeted hall toward one of the bedrooms.

Mary was on the floor, dressed in a pair of panties and skimpy T-shirt. She appeared to be in full cardiac arrest: limbs rigid, pulse infrequent, little evidence of respiration. It looked like an overdose of heroin, or some other opiate. They loaded Mary on the backboard and got out of there, the Constantines following them to Bon Secours in the family car. It was no use. Later, at the Relief's, an EMT from Lawrence bought them a round. "Tough night, fellas?" he asked. Gage shook his head, saying nothing.

Now, Lowell Street was dark and empty and Glenn Garvey drove the ambulance seventy miles an hour down the long slope past Forest Street church, straight through the blinking light, and halfway around the rotary that passed beneath the interstate. Merging onto Route 110, also known as the Lowell Boulevard, the ambulance flew over the deserted roadway with its turret light cleaving the darkness and the klaxon sounding in prolonged bursts. With the windows down, they could smell the marshy taint of the Merrimack River just beyond the trees, its banks overflowing with the late spring thaw.

The boulevard was a winding two-lane road that followed the contour of the river from Carter, Massachusetts to Lowell, passing through Dracut on the way. Large pines screened it off for a couple of miles, but glimpses of the Merrimack, one hundred-fifty yards across, were visible between the trees. Low-lying mist crept up from the riverbank, lying in pools over the boulevard. These were whipped aside by the hurtling bulk of the ambulance only to form again in its wake.

A series of deadly curves loomed in the road, and by long acquaintance Glenn Garvey anticipated each one, banking the ambulance to the right before leaning the weight of the vehicle toward the centerline as the boulevard unfolded itself and ran straight again. Beside him, Gage snapped his gum and beat a steady rhythm on his knees, eyes bright with adrenaline. Bad accidents occurred with some frequency on this stretch of the old Lowell road; it was a treacherous place.

They approached the Merrimac Park Drive-In Theatre, which occupied a long stretch of the riverbank and had been closed for three or four years. Suddenly there was a sandy clearing among the trees; the curved rows of speaker posts appeared, in the middle of which they could make out the concessions stand, made of cinder blocks painted white and sitting low on its plot like a bunker. Up front was a swing set and metal slide, flanked by a giant sandbox now overgrown with weeds. The magnificent canvas of the screen, blowing in tatters, stood fifty feet tall and was supported by an enormous wooden superstructure. It glowed like a specter as they went past, marked here and there by missing panels that revealed the night sky. Back in high school, they had come here with Colleen Dixon and Mary Constantine to drink beer and make out while second-rate horror flicks and westerns flickered in the darkness. Now, when Glenn was at the firehouse and couldn't sleep, he would imagine the great ragged screen, and merely by picturing it in his mind and lingering there, he would drift into unconsciousness. It was a neat trick.

A mile beyond the drive-in, they came upon the wreck. The victim had been traveling eastbound so Glenn took the ambulance past the scene, slowed to five miles per hour, and reversed direction with a sweeping U-turn, the klaxon's wail interrupting the stillness. A Massachusetts State trooper had arrived and was putting out flares to slow traffic, though presently there was none.

As Glenn brought the ambulance into the breakdown lane, Gage spotted the car, an old Chrysler, about twenty yards ahead and a good distance from the road. It had broken through the guardrail and was lying on its roof among the tangled weeds along the riverbank.

Gage leaped out with a medical kit while Glenn came around the ambulance and unsnapped the backboard from beside the rear door.

"He's down there," said the trooper, pointing to a spot among the trees. The victim had been thrown from the car when it overturned, he said.

The trooper was wearing an old fashioned motorman's cap, a pair of jodhpurs, and shiny boots that ran to his knee. He was a burly man about forty years old, with a ruddy face and close-cropped black hair.

"Any fire, sparks, gasoline smell?" asked Glenn, running past him.

The trooper shook his head. "Negative," he said. He ran to his cruiser and aimed the spotlight toward the victim.

Gage jumped over the guardrail, nearly losing his balance on the downward slope, before he went shimmying on his hip down the embankment toward the man lying there. Carrying the heavy backboard, Glenn ran to the break in the railing, and then worked his way around the car giving it the once-over in the glare of his flashlight. He had to be certain it wasn't leaking fuel or otherwise posing a danger to the rescuers.

"Anyone in the car?" he called to the trooper. "Anyone else on scene?"

"Negative," said the state trooper.

When Glenn was satisfied that the car was unoccupied, he joined his partner beside the victim. The man was unconscious; in his late twenties, clad in jeans and a flannel shirt; one of his work boots was missing. In the garish light from the cruiser, the man's face was purple and misshapen with his straight, thin lips pressed together; he had several broken bones, and while Gage checked his pulse and respiration, Glenn, who was wearing latex gloves like his partner, felt along the man's skull and rib cage. Beneath the victim's curly dark hair his skull was fragmented and mushy in the anterior portion, and his ribs had been pushed in close to his heart and other vital organs.

"He's hardly breathing," said Gage. The victim was a working man; his knuckles were skinned and grime was etched into the lines in his palms. Gage took out the man's wallet and checked his driver's license with a penlight: Thomas W. Moffat,

Jay Atkinson

D/O/B 21 March 1957.

Working in unison, Gage and Glenn rolled the man onto the backboard, fastening three straps to hold the twenty nine-year-old victim in place—*nipples, nuts, knees*. Then Gage fixed the Styrofoam blocks on either side of the man's head to stabilize his spine, running the strap through slots in the blocks and across the man's forehead.

The trooper scrambled down the embankment to join them, and all three men grasped the board by the handholds. "One, two, three," said Glenn, and they lifted him, waist high, and struggled up to the roadway where they laid the man on a collapsible stretcher.

"How's he doing?" asked the trooper

Gage shook his head. While they were examining the victim, the trooper had collected half a dozen beer cans from inside the car and the undergrowth nearby. He had them in a flimsy plastic grocery bag beside his cruiser, and now he tied the ends of the bag together, reared back, and threw the parcel into the river. His wedding band flashed in the light when his arm came around. There was a tiny splash, and the current took the parcel away.

The trooper removed his cap, wiped his brow with a shirtsleeve, and returned the cap to his head. "Won't be needing those," he said.

The squawk of his radio drew the trooper back to his cruiser while the two EMTs pushed the stretcher containing Thomas Moffat into the ambulance. Gage climbed in after it and Glenn raced around, got behind the wheel, slammed the driver's side door and sped away, the siren bleating.

Glenn radioed ahead to the emergency room and then informed the dispatcher of their route. When he signed off, he looked back at Gage in the mirror and his partner, who was taking the victim's blood pressure and had started him on oxygen, glanced at his watch and said, "Pulse is weak and thready. Pressure: sixty-five over forty. Dropping." A few seconds later, he added: "Agonal respiration. Cardiac event...no pulse."

Though it was apparent that Thomas Moffat had expired before they reached the old drive-in, Gage continued working on him all the way to the hospital, administering CPR with quick, steady chest compressions and bagging him with oxygen. Moffat never came close to regaining consciousness, and had not spoken a word or illustrated any sign of life. However, only the emergency room doctor could pronounce him dead, and every tiny event that unfolded during their nine and a half minute ride to Bon Secours, the words they uttered and the actions they performed—even their feelings about the accident, which were a precise but delicate admixture of compassion, detachment, empathy, and skill—were in keeping with what they had been taught.

*

By mid-July, Glenn Garvey had finished his stint on the ambulance and was assigned to Engine 5, where his father had begun his own career in 1948. Gage had another four weeks until his assignment changed and the two men occupied different shifts for the time being; unless they arranged a "swap" or took an overtime shift, when one of them was working, the other man was off.

Engine 5 had just returned from a kitchen fire on High Street and it was Glenn's job to unhitch the main line and drag it to the cellar, where it was rinsed off, attached to a pulley and hauled up the tower. But the line became snagged and Glenn was dispatched to the rooftop to shake it loose. On his way he stopped at the main floor, stuck his head into the clamor of the ambulance bay, and whistled between his teeth. Chandler rolled out from beneath the chief's car on a dolly; he held an acetylene torch in his hand and the unlit stub of a cigar in his teeth. The torch glowed like a spirit lamp in the dim, gasoline-smelling bay. Chandler lifted his safety glasses onto his forehead and extinguished the torch, going into his pocket for a rag.

"Rita wants to see you," said Chandler, wiping his face.

"Maybe she wants me to run for mayor."

Chandler lowered his goggles and relit the torch. "Maybe she wants you to quit," he said, rolling beneath the chief's car.

In the end, Jerry Montefusco had decided not to file a grievance against Glenn Garvey for working on the ambulance, although guys talked about it for weeks, ending conversations whenever Glenn walked into a room. The rumor was that Chandler had called in a favor, though he never said anything about it. Bounding up the stairs toward the door that marked the dusty shaft of the tower, Glenn stopped on the third floor to visit Rita O'Callahan, the chief's secretary. Passing along the corridor, he opened a green baize door on the left and went into a small office. Inside, a blade of sunlight fell through the window, exposing motes of dust in the air and making a dappled pattern on the floor.

The outer office, no more than twelve feet square, was paneled in vertical strips of dark wood and adorned with a broad-paned window that trembled in its casing when the wind picked up. The space reeked of Chief Ewing's cigar, which his secretary detested, and overall the office resembled a ship captain's billet; a bookcase ran chest-high across three walls and was stuffed with leather-bound manifests. These journals detailed every fire visited by the department, in three-month increments, marked by the year and running from 1899 to 1985, when fire department records were computerized.

Seated behind a large desk with CFD carved into the frontispiece, Rita O'Callahan, a squat, white-haired woman who was rarely seen apart from this historic item of furniture, greeted her visitor with a prim gesture. Mrs. O'Callahan removed the eyeglasses from her nose, suspended them over her bosom by a chain worn about her neck, and waved a small piece of writing paper in the air.

"This came in yesterday," she said.

Standing with his back to the window, Glenn Garvey took up the letter and read these handwritten lines:

July 15

To Who it May Concern:
Last month I got a bill for an ambulance ride and emergency services for $656.91. I'm putting a money order for twenty dollars in with this letter. It's all I have right now. I hope you'll let me make payments. My husband died with no insurance and I have a little girl who's only three.

Lynda Moffat

"That was your call, wasn't it?" asked Mrs. O'Callahan.

When it came to fire department business, not a penny was spent nor a gnat farted that Mrs. O'Callahan didn't know about.

Glenn replaced the paper on the desk. "The guy died on the way to the hospital," he said.

Invoices were stacked in a pile on Mrs. O'Callahan's blotter. The top one, which Rita had just printed from the computer, was addressed to Mrs. Lynda Moffat in the amount of $636.91 and included the notation "More than 180 days past due. Please remit." For a moment, the only sounds were the fan whirring inside the computer and a hornet that droned past the open window.

Then, clearing her throat, the ample-bosomed secretary chose a rubber stamp from the rack on the desk, inked it on a pad, and stamped "Abatement" on the bill with enough force to impress the carbons below.

"She's got enough trouble without that," said Mrs. O'Callahan, donning her eyeglasses and taking up the next invoice.

*

In late October, two months after he rotated off the ambulance onto Engine 3, Gage Henry fractured his right ankle leaping from the first floor window of a burning tenement on Kirk Street. The surgery to hold the shattered bones in place did not go well, and after three months in a hard cast Gage was forced to endure a second operation. An orthopedist at Mass General had to remove the five titanium screws, re-break the ankle, sever Gage's Achilles tendon, re-insert the screws in the proper position and sew the Achilles back on. Confined to a cast for an additional six months, Gage was placed on indefinite medical leave.

Glenn Garvey missed his old buddy and their shifts on the ambulance. One night in January, after not seeing Gage for a few weeks, they made plans to meet at the Relief's Inn for a beer. Glenn was working a second job, driving a truck for Feole Oil on his days off. Deliveries ran late that afternoon and when he finally arrived at the bar, stamping the snow from his boots in the tiny vestibule, he intercepted Gage on the way out. The slender fire fighter was coming sideways through the door, holding his crutches in one hand and hopping on his good leg. He wore an CFD baseball cap and his hair, usually kept short, was down over his collar. Beneath his canvas jacket he looked spare and bony, his face pale, on the verge of jaundice.

"I heard it was Cripple's Night," Glenn said. "Gimps drink half price."

Gage smiled. "That's 'cause assholes pay double," he said.

With Gage teetering on one leg, they embraced for a moment. A pair of Lawrence fire fighters and their wives barged in, the cold air following them, and Glenn and Gage pushed themselves against the wall to make room. When they began moving again, they were going in opposite directions.

"So I'm an asshole," Glenn said. "Let me buy you a beer."

Gage rested on his crutches, his head hanging down. "My leg hurts pretty bad," he said. "I just wanna go home."

On the ambulance, the two friends used to laugh at their good fortune, saying that they had it made. Pulling down thirty-six grand a year plus overtime and living at home was pretty sweet. Gage's mother was divorced; he really didn't know his father, who had remarried years earlier and lived in Texas now. Glenn had intended to tell his friend that he was dating Colleen again, one of the Dixon twins—Gage had never been able to tell them apart, insisting back in high school that Glenn was dating both of the blonde, athletic girls without realizing it. After six years, Glenn had run into Colleen at the Sands-a-bar on New Year's Eve. They danced to the B Street Bombers and then sat in Colleen's jeep and talked until the sun came up. But now didn't seem like the appropriate time to bring up his romantic adventures.

"How's your Mom doing?" asked Glenn.

"She stares at me, and I stare at the wall."

Glenn regarded his friend. "I'll come over and watch a football game or something," he said.

"Sure," said Gage. He stuck out his crutch, putting the rubber end against the door and giving it a shove. "Yeah, see ya, partner," said Glenn, and with a blast of arctic air, Gage stumped past him into the night.

Heaving on the door, Glenn entered the first-floor bar, which smelled of spilled beer and was hazed over with cigarette smoke. Van Morrison was singing from the jukebox, and several tables and every stool at the bar was occupied by firefighters and sanitation workers and postmen, their rumbling talk and the chink of bottles and glasses rising toward the ceiling. The pain that Gage Henry felt was genuine, all right. But it had little to do with the throbbing in his ankle or the Percocet he was chewing to take the edge off. Glenn had seen all of that in his face.

Glenn squeezed in next to the waitress station and ordered a Jack and Coke from the bartender, who was Jerry Montefusco's cousin. Glenn knew that Gage's discomfort had more to do with the vagaries of his situation than the jangling nerve endings in his ankle. There was a good chance he would stay out for a year on half pay and then take a buyout on the grounds of "physically unable to perform required tasks," as dictated by the collective bargaining agreement. *Fini*. End of career. Over before it started.

The pall of smoke had settled two feet below the ceiling, tinted bluish-green by the lights strung over the bar. The smoke, pooling or eddying here and there as customers disembarked for the rest room or stooped to play a song on the jukebox, moved up and down the aisles in thin, volatile, blue-green currents. Permeating the room was the odor of after-shave, liquor, sweat, cigar smoke and the Christmas tree air fresheners that dangled from the cash register. When the bathroom doors opened, there was the stench of toilets.

Ordering another drink, Glenn recalled the night a few weeks before Gage's injury when the two of them sat at the bar watching the Red Sox play the Mets in the World Series. They had been die-hard Red Sox fans their entire lives and as the level of shouts and cheers rose to a crescendo, men pounding on the tables and bellowing like savages, Gage's eyes remained fixed on the television over the bar. "My old man loves the fuckin' Sox," he said.

Then a little squib rolled down the first base line and got through Bill Buckner's clumsy feet and the dream of a world championship skittered away with it. A few of the patrons inside the Relief's Inn said "Oh" and then the bar fell silent. Some out-of-town fire fighters, drawn by the $7 buffet, kicked over their chairs and a glass pitcher was smashed against the tiles. A lot of people left in a hurry.

In the silence that ensued, Gage and Glenn finished their beers without looking at each other. Then, pushing up from his stool, Gage tossed a few bills onto the bar and hitched up his pants. "I don't know what I wanted more," he said, "the Sox to win or my old man to lose."

Now, alone at the bar, Glenn shook his head at his own ignorance. He never was very good at reading other people's hearts. Gage hadn't just broken his ankle when he jumped from that window. He'd shattered the route his life was supposed to take; an opportunity had skittered past him, somehow. Maybe his fractures would heal, and in a few months, a year, he'd be able to pass the department physical and they'd be working together again. But Glenn doubted it. There was a finality to everything that had occurred, like it had all been decided beforehand.

The reasons why Glenn Garvey was living such a charmed life had so far eluded him. Back in high school, Gage was in the National Honor Society and captain of the soccer team, yet Glenn was the one who got a scholarship to play football. And despite scoring 98 on the civil service exam, Gage had been on the fire department waiting list for nearly two years. As a "legacy," Glenn was admitted to the academy six weeks after dropping out of UMass—with only a 91 on the exam. In point of fact, Gage could've jumped out of that window a dozen times without breaking a sweat, let alone his ankle. He had, on this occasion, been unlucky, a condition that Glenn Garvey was not very familiar with.

Thus Glenn stood, a drink at his elbow, when a pal from Engine 5 mentioned his name, asking if anyone had seen him. Not in the mood to talk, Glenn paid his tab, hurried on with his coat, and proceeded, hat in hand, out the double doors onto the street. Moonlight gleamed on the embankments of snow, and the moon, rising over Broadway in the clear night sky, was huge and shiny and white.

Quickly, it seemed, the old Broadway moon went through its phases again, waning to a crescent and waxing full once more; a month passed for Glenn Garvey in the straight ahead routine of eating, sleeping, and working 70 or 80 hours per week. He called it "the work sprint." When he was on days at the firehouse, Glenn drove the oil truck for a few hours in the evening, making deliveries until eight or nine o'clock. In March, following a late snowstorm, he was looking for a particular address among a maze of small crooked streets that didn't appear on his map. Six Fairfield

Avenue was proving hard to find, for some reason.

With only the moon to guide him, Glenn found the sign-post for a "Fairview Street" and made his way along squinting at the house numbers. Presently he came upon #6, a faded yellow cape bulwarked by piles of snow. Glenn checked the work order and left the diesel running out front and went up the driveway, kicking the snow from his boots as he climbed the stairs to the kitchen door.

A young woman was sitting on the floor playing with a little girl. Glenn knocked at the door and smiled, pointing to the *Feole Oil* embroidered on his jacket. The woman rose and came to the door. "Yes?" she asked, opening it a few inches.

Glenn had already noticed the propane tank out back; they weren't oil customers. "Do you know where Fairfield Avenue is?" he asked. When the woman shook her head, Glenn said, "Do you mind if I use your phone? I have to call the office."

"All right," said the woman. "Come in."

In jeans and a man's flannel shirt, the woman was small-boned and plain, her brown hair reaching to the middle of her back. "Don't mind the mess," she said. "I just got off work, and had to get Ellie from daycare." The little girl, with dark curly hair and an expectant look on her face, played idly with her toys while staring at the visitor.

"I didn't mean to bother you," Glenn said.

The woman's face looked tired, her eyes crinkling as she indicated the telephone mounted on the wall. "Not a problem," she said.

The interior of the house was cold. Other than the kitchen, the rooms on the lower floor were dark, and though the kitchen table and counter tops were clean, there was a general untidiness. Lifting the receiver, Glenn punched in the number for the office, turning around to face the woman, who was playing with the child again. Dishes were piled in the sink and an array of grocery store fliers and assorted correspondence, most of it utility bills and the like, occupied the sideboard. Glenn reached the company secretary right away and agreed to hold while she confirmed the address on the work order he held in his hand. Aimless music played in his ear.

The secretary returned to the line, informing Glenn that the address was correct: Six Fairfield Avenue was indeed where he was supposed to deliver the oil, and if he had something to write with, the secretary would give him directions.

Removing a pen from his breast pocket, Glenn stretched the cord over his shoulder and leaned down to copy the informa-

Jay Atkinson

tion. As the voice on the line began to recite the directions, Glenn cast his glance up and down for a scrap of paper. His gaze fell on an envelope from Mass. Electric and when he brought it closer, the printing jumped into focus—Mr. Thomas W. Moffat.

His blood ran with the chill in the room. Looking at the little girl, Glenn saw in her countenance the dark brow and straight, thin lips of Thomas Moffat, the young man who had been killed on the Lowell Boulevard a year earlier. And the woman who stooped to play with the little girl, in the cold, darkened house, amidst the clutter of dishes and warrants for delinquent payment, was the young widow who had written that letter to the fire department, asking for more time.

Glenn scribbled the notes he was given on a flap torn from the envelope, crammed the paper and work order into his pocket, and hung up the phone. Everything he was seeing told him the story. The crumbs strewn in front of the baby's chair. The chill in the room, with the thermostat set at 59 degrees. The absence of a car in the driveway. What looked like a gradual descent into hard times, Glenn knew, had been brought on by a single catastrophic event.

Thanking the woman, Glenn winked at the little girl who smiled as he stepped to the door. He didn't say a word about the accident. Thomas Moffat was barely alive when they appeared on the scene, and died shortly thereafter. There were no dramatic revelations, no last words, nothing. That Glenn and Gage had been there—and that he was here, now—was a matter of luck, good or bad, he couldn't say.

The door tilted open and the woman looked up from her position on the floor. Glenn nodded, smiling the best he could manage, and then passed outside, closing the door behind him.

It was a freezing cold night, and millions of stars filled the sky. Descending the walk, Glenn took in great lungfuls of the air, realizing in that moment that he would marry Colleen Dixon and that he was lucky to have her; that they would, in all likelihood, produce healthy, athletic children, and live in a house that he would build with his own hands. It felt like someone had pulled back a curtain and he had been allowed a glimpse of the future and made to understand it.

The diesel hummed at the curb, its running lights delineating the glossy bulk of the oil truck. Coming alongside, Glenn further understood that Gage wouldn't be returning to the department. The two friends would never again work together and they wouldn't retire in the same year and embark upon an ocean cruise with their silver-haired wives, as they had once imagined. Glenn

Jay Atkinson

wasn't sure how he knew all this, but he did.

He swung himself up to the cab of the truck. As he shifted into gear, Glenn saw the little girl's diminishing prospects, and how his own good fortune—the very state of his luck—prevented him from doing anything substantial for her, or for anyone who had suffered. He turned on the defrosters and squared himself to the windshield, easing the oil truck down the street. He hadn't been able to save Thomas Moffat, and somehow—in some mysterious, unfair way—that prevented him from comforting his little girl, who had the same dark brow as her father.

Hi-Pine Acres

Katherine gathered the eggs just after the sun came up. Her land was divided by Route 121A, with the farmhouse and several uncultivated acres, now just meadows really, on one side of the blacktop, and a large barn, stable, livestock pens, cowshed, and corrals for the horses and other animals across the road. Katherine Prescott Wilson was a formidable woman with hazel eyes, prominent cheekbones, well-muscled arms, and a rope of silver hair worn in a ponytail falling to the middle of her back. Even that early in the morning, she took pains hurrying across the road as cars and trucks heading for the interstate came over the rise at great speeds.

Now sixty-four, Katherine had lived on Hi-Pine Acres her entire life. It was the family homestead, an irregular parcel of twenty-seven acres located a half mile from Route 111 in Prescott, New Hampshire. Her great-great grandfather, Matthias Houlton Prescott, had purchased the farm from Elliott Cavendish in 1882, for fifteen dollars an acre. Before the Cavendish family, whose ownership predated the Revolutionary War, the Indians had it. In fact, a skirmish between English settlers and the Abenaki had taken place on the land in the 1700s, near the larger of the two ponds on the farm. This oval body of water, occupying a quarter of an acre, was located near the western boundary of the land. Katherine's son, Frank Prescott Wilson, had once dug up a few spear points and the barrel of an old musket from a swampy field nearby. That feat of archaeology had occurred a long time ago, when Frank was a teenager, and the pond was overgrown now, ignored by the horses and livestock, who preferred the narrow, muddy-banked watering hole that was closer to the main road.

Frank was in the barn; she could hear him throwing things around and swearing under his breath. Inside this gloomy structure was a collection of rusty farm implements dating back to the 1930s; a high-seated tractor, old fashioned bicycles, saw horses, a baling machine, and Grampa Prescott's Model T Ford, half covered by a faded green tarp. Frank had the notion that he was going to rehabilitate the old car, and then sell it to an antiques dealer he knew, duplicating the long ago windfall he had enjoyed from the Indian artifacts. He didn't possess an iota of mechanical aptitude however, and had been flailing away at the Model T for two or three years.

Katherine avoided the barn's entrance, going around to the chicken coop. Extending from the rear of the barn was a down sloping, boulder-strewn field, grazed to the quick by the three saddle horses that resided there, dropping away from the corral to a screen of tall pines that lent the farm its name. Beyond the stable, which consisted of an open pavilion with a flat aluminum roof, was a pen containing a half-dozen muddy, orange-tinted sheep. The chicken coop occupied an enclosure next to the pen, where a number of hens strutted about, pecking at the dust.

Katherine exited the warm, acrid-smelling coop with five eggs in her basket. She would make Frank an omelet for breakfast, thinning it with some of the consigned milk, and save a couple eggs for a coffee cake she planned on baking when the day cooled off. While Katherine was throwing down feed for the chickens, a collie dog emerged from the barn to water at the trough and then retreat into the shade. It was very hot, even with the morning sun barely above the trees, and most of the animals were beneath the cover of the pines or by the watering hole.

With the basket in the crook of her arm, Katherine crossed back over Route 121A. The house, which looked empty, was a quiet little clapboard-sided, six-room place, located in a grove of hundred-year-old oak trees; inside the door was a parlor with the usual array of deer antlers, family portraits, and rag rugs seen in that part of the country; the kitchen and pantry located just behind it; and three bedrooms upstairs. A pier-glass hung over the fireplace, along with an old tintype of Grampa Prescott, a stern-visaged man with a flowing mustache. Katherine's wedding photograph also hung on the wall. It had been taken at the county fairgrounds in 1966. Her husband, Tom, had been dead for more than fifteen years, the victim of a traffic accident. Frank was their only child.

It was much cooler inside. The early sun poured in the kitchen windows, but there was a breeze stirring over the meadow and an oak tree shaded the yard. Katherine broke the eggs into a bowl, splashed in the unpasteurized milk, added salt and pepper and turned on the front burner of the stove. While she was thus engaged, a footfall sounded on the walkway, the front door opened, and looking round, Katherine was confronted with her thirty-nine year old son, a big, shambling, unhappy looking fellow, with a disheveled crop of grayish-white hair, plump calves and forearms, and a blocky torso. The gist of his efforts that morning was plain—in the grease-stained cargo shorts, the bits of hay stuck to his t-shirt and in his hair, and the orange mud that edged his boots. He was perspiring and stunk of body odor, rotten hay, and manure.

Frank cast a glance into the frying pan, where the egg-mixture had been transferred, and scowling out the window at two cardinals fluttering around the bird feeder, washed his hands and forearms in the sink. He didn't seem to give a damn about anything. Hay fell from his arms and shoulders onto the clean-swept linoleum, and a trail of clods followed him to the kitchen table. There he sat without a word, taking up the morning paper.

There was something about Frank that wasn't right, though his mother had never been able to put her finger on it. As a boy, Frank had no real friends or interests; he never rode a bicycle, or joined the 4-H Club or the Boy Scouts. He was twenty-one when his father was killed, but carried on afterwards as if nothing significant had occurred. Entering into manhood, Frank showed little aptitude for farming, repairing things, or taking care of the animals. His experience with women amounted to zero. Prematurely middle-aged, he woke early each day, stayed busy doing what amounted to nothing, and rarely left the farm, although he ranged over the acres. As far as Katherine could tell, Frank's biggest misfortune was being homely without any brains. But she loved him as much as any mother loved her son, and looked after his needs.

For her part, Katherine was lean as a lath, with a commanding presence and a determined look about her—a self-assured, can-do sort of person, who accomplished more in half a day than her most industrious neighbor did in two. Although you couldn't call Hi-Pine Acres a working farm—the main fields had been lying fallow for years, the dozen cows belonged to Mr. Hazey in Plaistow, and the horses were kept for a modest fee—Katherine managed to support herself and Frank with a combination of shrewd management and thrift. Fruits and vegetables, including the spinach and a tomato that she had sliced into the eggs, came from the garden she kept behind the house, which produced rhubarb, beets, asparagus, tomatoes, spinach, carrots, and lettuce.

Bordering the fence were two Red Haven peach trees, four Ida Red and three Cortland apple trees, a cherry tree, mulberry tree, and herb garden enclosed by a miniature green house. Each spring, Katherine grew dill, basil, parsley, tarragon, and thyme in little pots on the windowsill, moving them outdoors after the last frost of the season. She also put up preserves, keeping enough to last the winter and selling the rest.

A Yankee by birth and temperament, Katherine bartered with Mr. Hazey—grazing and milking his cows in exchange for propane, firewood, and twenty percent of the milk each year— and boarded eight sheep for a woman over in Durham, keeping half the wool in payment. On Sundays in late summer and fall, Hi-Pine Acres hosted a farmer's market, charging a fee for the potters, jam and jelly peddlers, vegetable growers, doughnut makers, woodworkers, and glass blowers to set up their booths. A clan of gypsies paid Katherine for the right to give pony rides on an ill-tempered Shetland, and the local 4-H club sold apple pies.

Their only cash crops were hay and honey, and since the cultivation of both posed few difficulties, Katherine only had to enlist her son's help in the mowing, raking, and baling of the hay. She managed the beehives and tractor herself, leaving Frank to wield a pitchfork now and then, and to assist her in rolling up the bales and getting them onto the hay wagon. Combined with other miscellaneous income, Katherine had been able to scratch together enough to pay the real estate taxes, electric bills, and the staples they weren't capable of producing on the farm: white flour, cooking oil, pork, oats, and sorghum for feed; gasoline, insecticide, barbed wire fencing, and the like. Of course, the bulk of what they required came from, or returned to, the land itself, including well water, compost, and an old fieldstone septic tank, for as Katherine's late husband was fond of saying, "No use keeping a dog, and barking yourself."

Frank's omelet was ready. Katherine cut four slices from an Irish soda bread she kept under a glass bell on the counter. Putting aside one piece for her own breakfast, she spread the others with salted butter, and laid them on a plate by Frank's elbow, who only rattled his paper and grunted. Katherine slid the omelet onto another plate, took down a bottle of hot sauce from the cabinet, and placed bottle and plate within her son's reach.

"When you're through, can you open the north gate for me?" asked Katherine. "I'm going to run the sheep over before I go to Bill Hazey's place."

Frank nodded without looking up.

Wrapping the extra piece of bread in a napkin, Katherine cleaned the frying pan with a scouring brush and water—using soap would remove the temper from the cast iron—and went out the back door into the sun-dappled yard. Few vegetables were ripe this early in the season, but as she nibbled on the soda bread, Katherine picked a dozen spears of tender young asparagus, another bunch of spinach, and several veined stalks of rhubarb. Setting these aside, she weeded between the rows, twisting the shoots out of the ground, her knees and elbows leaving their impressions in the warm loam. There was a feudal obstinacy to her movements.

After a half hour's work, Katherine left her harvest in an empty flowerpot by the door, and whistling for Tanner, the collie, she passed alongside the house beneath the shade from the oak trees. When she stopped to let a tow truck rattle past, Katherine saw a line of bees coming from the hive, pollinating the lilacs bordering the yard. Joined by the collie, she traveled over the crown of the road, saying "*gee* now, *gee* now," as she came, drawing the attention of the sheep.

Katherine gripped one of the palings, hopping over the fence that separated the gravel apron of the barnyard from the paddock. After running to catch up, Tanner described a graceful arc through the air, clearing the up-thrust pickets and landing beside her. The dog circled partway around the enclosure, and then back the other way, growling in his throat, running at the sheep from various angles and pushing them together. Walking behind with a switch, Katherine exhorted them toward the gate by calling "*gee* now, *gee* there now."

While the dog worked, Katherine hurdled the fence again,

crossed back over Route 121A, and pushed on the wire gate that opened onto a flower-dotted meadow just north of the farmhouse. Unhitching the gate had slipped Frank's mind. She tamped down the gorse and loose strife that had cropped up with the edge of her boot, and then returned to the paddock and opened the barred metal chute.

Inside the enclosure, Tanner was harrying a lone sheep that had eluded him, causing the others to scatter again. At length they were brought together as a unified whole, and after numerous halts and starts, as well as lowing from the cows in the adjoining meadow, with the usual variations of speed peculiar to this small herd, they found themselves going out through the chute. Away they swept from the paddock and trotted over the crest of the road with the dog at their heels. On the other side, Katherine shut the gate after them and returned to the barn.

Beneath one of the shade trees was a rusted container truck. It looked like it hadn't been driven in a while, and was imprinted with *Hi-Pine Acres. Prescott, NH. T. G. Wilson & Family* in white lettering on both sides. An old wooden trailer, also deep in the weeds, was beside the truck, outfitted with a hayrack and nose down on the ground. Katherine pulled out the canvas tabs at the back of the truck, and boots ringing against the steel, she mounted the ramp and threw open the doors. The interior of the truck smelled of moldy hay and livestock; she swept out the tick that littered the floor, walked back to the cowshed, and rolled out a pair of sloshing, ten-gallon milk cans. Manhandling them onto a dolly, she ran them up the ramp, secured them with bungee cords, and then went back to the shed where earlier that morning, after the milking when it was still dark, she had tied up a week-old calf. Leading it by the tether, she pulled the calf up the ramp into the truck, fastened the rope to one of the iron loops welded to the decking, and closed and padlocked the doors.

Climbing into the cab, Mrs. Wilson released the brake and put in the clutch and turned the key; the engine coughed, sputtered, and then started with a rumble as she set out to deliver the larger share of the milk to Mr. Hazey. The truck rode low on its chassis and she turned onto Route 121A, grinding the gears, the high-pitched sound of the calf's bleating coming to her through the slats.

A quarter mile along, just beyond the stand of trees where Abenaki warriors had lain in wait for the settlers, Katherine crossed a bridge over the little stream and arrived at the stop sign marking the intersection with Route 111. A modern, newly-paved road, NH 111 ran from just south of Nashua to Little Boar's Head on the coast, a total of fifty miles, cutting east-west across the rugged, forested belt of Hillsboro and Rockingham counties. Tucked away in a rural corner of Prescott, Mrs. Wilson was never quite prepared for the fast moving, horn honking, relentless vulgarity of the traffic she encountered on that road. She imagined that the calf riding in back was frightened half to death.

Although Katherine passed through lowlands that contained ponds and marshes and brooks, all of which were protected from development, along the higher ground strip malls, pizza restaurants, and gas stations were crowding out the landscape. Near the expanse of Angle Pond, a giant, fenced-in marine dealership had filled its lot with dozens of shrink-wrapped pontoon, paddle, and powerboats of every size and color; stacks of canoes and kayaks, and row upon row of massive trailer homes. It was a breathtaking display of aquatic and recreational mobility, far superior to the lesser dealerships that lay within a half mile.

Huge banks of condominiums, some made of artificial logs and others that were faux chalets, dotted the roadway on both sides. If her late husband was somehow able to visit this particular stretch of Route 111, Mrs. Wilson was quite certain he would not have recognized what had been just two lanes of asphalt a few years earlier. Up and down she went in the slow lane, bouncing on the rusty springs of the old truck, the top of her head nearly striking the webbed canvas of the roof.

Bill Hazey's property was seven miles from the farm, just outside the Old Village in Plaistow. Originally from Virginia, Mr. Hazey was the CEO of a software company over in Portsmouth. He was a vigorous, balding man of forty-six, loving husband to Gretta and proud father of twin eight-year-old girls, Maeghan and Sophie, with something of the country squire about him. Katherine had made Mr. Hazey's acquaintance two years earlier, when he had stopped to wander through her farmer's market. They took up a conversation that led to a tour of the outbuildings and fields, where Mr. Hazey revealed that the summers he'd spent on his grandparents' dairy farm in the Shenandoah Valley were the most cherished periods of his childhood.

There in Mrs. Wilson's pasture at dusk, Bill Hazey suggested that buying and boarding a small herd of Jerseys at Hi-Pine Acres would provide the farm with some needed income while indulging an old passion from his youth. So the two strangers struck a bargain at the paddock gate, and with that handshake, what soon began as an agreeable business arrangement had grown into a sturdy friendship.

They helped each other in various ways. Bill Hazey was

Jay Atkinson

new to the area—his wife had grown up in Newmarket—and as a southerner, he had difficulty "reading the locals," including the computer science grads he hired right out of the University of New Hampshire. He took to consulting with Mrs. Wilson on key personnel decisions, usually in an informal way. And as the business of the farm had narrowed, and her margin grown ever so dear, Katherine, in turn, came to rely more on her partner's horse sense. Bill did her taxes every year, which consisted of an hour at his dining room table with the EZ form and a glass of Zinfandel while Sophie and Maeghan frolicked on the rug. He coaxed her into raising the fees for boarding horses, which hadn't changed in years, and adding a cash payment to the percentage of wool from the sheep. And Mr. Hazey listened with a sympathetic ear when Katherine, halfway through her annual glass of wine, cataloged how much work at Hi-Pine Acres fell on her side of the ledger, and how little on Frank's.

Katherine turned off Route 111 in Plaistow, driving beneath an arch of fir trees and then over the bridge that spanned Bryant Brook. The Hazey residence was a mile beyond the bridge. It was a handsome, four-storied, small-windowed house of red brick, standing in the midst of a well-maintained lawn, its front door reached by a flight of granite steps. The house had been built in 1889 by a former governor of New Hampshire, and the three-stall garage on the east side of the building had once been used as a stable. On the long, sloping front lawn, a sprinkler fanned back and forth, its droplets falling like diamonds in the slanting rays of the sun.

Wearing little sundresses in the heat, the two girls tore around the side of the house chased by a barking dog and, one after another, the three of them leaped through the gauzy curtain of droplets and disappeared out back.

Easing up the driveway, Mrs. Wilson gained perspective on the homestead, where golden-haired Sophie cartwheeled over the lawn, followed by little Maeghan who went gamboling after her sister alongside Lonnie, their short-haired terrier. The huge lawn was enclosed by a stockade fence, inside of which stood a miniature cabin that the twins used as a playhouse.

Katherine set the hand brake and jumped down from the truck. Coming around, she pulled out the metal ramp and unlocked the doors just as the twins and Lonnie scrambled under the boards of the fence, eager to greet their visitor and to pet the knock-kneed calf. Katherine led the animal down the ramp to where the girls stood, hopping from one foot to the other, the excited terrier springing into the air between them.

"Good morning, ladies," said Mrs. Wilson, throwing one of Tanner's milk bones over the fence to divert the Hazey's dog. "I brought you something, but don't tell your father." She handed them each a bag of homemade candy drops made from sugar crystals and honey. "They'll spoil your lunch," she told the girls.

The twins were fraternal: Maeghan was dark-haired, taller than her sister, with a solid, athletic carriage and a fresh-faced, wide-eyed look that suggested a sturdy little tea rose. Lithe, blond-haired Sophie was the delicate one, reticent unless spoken to, permeated by an understated grace that affected every gesture and movement.

"Ooo, a baby cow," said Maeghan, clapping her hands. "I wanna keep it in my room."

Lonnie was back. Yelping, and darting to and fro, the terrier nipped at the calf and then rolled on its back, wriggling in the grass.

"*Stop it*, Lonnie," said Sophie, grabbing the dog by its collar. The terrier backed up, yanking the little girl forward, which caused her to stumble over the edge of the lawn bordering the fence. Just then, Bill Hazey emerged from the bulkhead attached to the rear of the house.

"Fortune favors the brave, Soph," he said, and vaulting

over the palisade that separated his lawn from the driveway, he advanced toward the parti-colored tumult—Mrs. Wilson holding the calf in her arms, Sophie being pulled along in the grass, Maeghan capering about and shrieking—whistled to the terrier and brought him to heel, while smiling at his guest.

"Hello, Mrs. Wilson," he said. "I see you've brought up the milk."

A paternal calmness ensued. Bill told the girls to put Lonnie in the house, adding, "Don't eat that candy before lunch. Your mother will be home soon, and we're going to Strawberry Banke." When the twins giggled and ran off with the dog, Bill Hazey took up the bleating calf, rubbing it behind the ears to soothe it, whereupon he led the animal by the rope into the enclosure.

Pushing a heavy eye-bolt into the lawn with his foot, Bill motioned for his visitor to take down one of the clotheslines that ran from the back of his house. He thereby lengthened the calf's tether, allowing the animal to graze over the backyard.

"There," said Mr. Hazey. He was dressed in a pair of blue trousers with matching canvas belt, a white polo shirt decorated with a mallet-wielding figure on horseback, and a pair of deck shoes without any socks. "That should hold her," he said.

Beneath a wide-brimmed hat, Katherine wore a light gray

sleeveless blouse with black stripes, a piece of rope for a belt, and denim culottes with a set of muddy paw prints on the rear end. (Tanner had leaped on her when she was closing the gate to the sheep's pen.) Her dirty tennis shoes lacked a pair of laces, and strands of long silver hair had come loose from her ponytail.

Laughter floated through the open windows, and Katherine looked that way, shading her eyes now that the sun had risen above the trees. "Those girls of yours are the most beautiful things I've ever seen," she said.

"Try getting them to bed on time," Bill said. He was kneeling beside the calf, inspecting its oversize hooves. "We fight like a bunch of sailors every night."

Bill Hazey's face, below his high-crowned black hair, was tanned very dark from being on his catamaran, the *Gretta B.,* which he tacked out to the Isle of Shoals every weekend. His blue eyes, set off by his trousers, wrinkled up at the edges when he smiled. "I should have you put them to work on the farm," he said.

"Any time," said Mrs. Wilson. "They should learn to ride, at least."

Bill Hazey's lawnmower had a trailer attached to it, and he went behind the looming edifice of his house and then drove it around front. They wheeled the milk cans down the ramp into the trailer, and Bill puttered over to the garage, where a walk-in refrigerator occupied one of the stalls. Later that day, he'd siphon off a few gallons of raw milk for their own use, and the rest he sold to a dairy farmer over in Stratham, who would homogenize and pasteurize it, before reselling the milk under his local brand.

In the garage, Mr. Hazey turned to his visitor with a furrowed brow. "How're things at the farm?" he asked. "Surviving?"

"I guess so," said Katherine. There were no secrets with Bill, and it wasn't her way to be coy. "There's a ton of work, and only so many hours to do it in."

"Katherine—I want to make a suggestion." Mr. Hazey's gaze was steady. "I think you should consider selling off some of the land. Not all of it. But a good-sized piece."

Mrs. Wilson made a small noise in her throat.

Bill unfolded a pair of lawn chairs, placing them in the shade near the entrance to the garage. "Sit down," said the Virginian, his hand one of the chairs. "I know the property's been in your family a long time. But let's face it: you're not going to leave it to Frank. Not really. As soon as you're gone, he's going to sell it."

Seated beside each other, they gazed at the pine forest across the road. Bill had purchased the house because it was a quiet area and the abundance of spruce trees reminded him of the

Shenandoah Valley. After a moment, Bill excused himself and got up from the chair. Opening an interior door, he called into the house for some iced tea. While they were sitting there, Maeghan lumbered in with the sweating pitcher and Sophie delivered two glasses printed with sailboats around the rim. She curtsied before running after her sister into the house.

"I know a developer who's approaching landowners all along one-eleven. What you have across the street is exactly what he's looking for, and he'll pay you quite well." Bill Hazey's southern heritage was never more prominent than when he added: "I'm talking about a fine sum of money."

"You mean the barn, the animals, everything?" asked Katherine. She drank some of the sweet tea, her hand shaking.

"If you sell it, you'll still have eight—or is it ten?—acres behind the house you can farm. Heck, these people will move the barn, the stable, everything, right across the road. You'll have a piece of property you can manage, and enough money to bring on some help. Given your situation, it makes a lot of sense."

"I can hold on another year or two," Katherine said. "I like the work."

Bill's voice was gentle, blending with the rustle of the pines as the breeze came up. "Here's the thing. After what happened in New York"—there was a pause in remembrance of the World Trade Center—"the economy, real estate prices, even my business, we're ripe for a downturn, maybe even a crash. It's inevitable."

"These people are looking to buy *now*," Bill said. "And they'll find what they want somewhere, believe me." He took Katherine by the hand. "You can keep a chunk of Hi-Pine Acres, even set it up so it remains in the family—or you'll end up losing every bit of it."

Upon finishing her tea, Katherine bade Mr. Hazey goodbye and climbed into the empty truck, waving to Sophie and Maeghan as she backed down to the main road. Off she went amidst a rumble from the tailpipe, and the vexing thoughts and reflections of the noon hour. Sell the farm! It was perhaps the very last thing on her mind that morning while gathering eggs, making Frank's breakfast, and tending to the sheep. It was more likely that she would've been preoccupied with the moons of Saturn, or with getting her hair done.

Back on Route 111, Katherine took little notice of the karate studios and lube shops and discount stores crowding the landscape. It was all very sudden, and although she thought of him often, it was the first time in a decade that Katherine yearned to consult with her late husband. Glancing across the cab, she imagined Tom sitting there and what they might have said to one another, given the circumstances. It was a small but fleeting comfort, and as the hay-motes that filled the truck descended through rays of sunlight, just as quickly the feeling passed.

Before they were married, Tom Wilson drove truck for A. Duie Pyle, long-hauling from the Carolinas back and forth to Presque Isle, Maine, and sometimes as far west as Ohio and Illinois. He often traveled two hundred thousand miles a year, and it was therefore a significant irony that he'd never been in an accident until dying in one less than a mile from the farm. Tom had grown up in a three-decker on Tauvernier Street in Carter, Mass., where the only green thing he ever saw was the tomato plant on Mrs. Calabrese's fire escape. But he took to farming straight away, remarking that all cats were gray in the dark, and he'd just as soon bust his ass planting and harvesting a piece of land as driving all over creation.

The year Tom was killed, he and his wife and grown son had twenty-three acres in cultivation: butter & sugar corn, pumpkins, winter squash, and tomatoes, with six additional acres leased to the local 4-H collaborative. Assisted by a group of Cambodian workers from Lowell, who were hired on from Memorial Day to the first frost, the Wilsons also kept thirty-one milk cows, two steers, a rooster, forty-three chickens, five goats, and nineteen sheep. They boarded seven horses alongside two of their own. After state and federal taxes, wages, feed, and all their other expenses were paid, in 1986 they netted just over $18,000, the best year they ever had. Hi-Pine Acres hadn't come anywhere close to that profitability since Tom's accident.

A hell raiser in his youth, Tom Wilson had slowed down by the time he made Katherine Prescott's acquaintance in front of the barn one morning when his truck broke down. She brought out a canvas bag for his overheated radiator, and was taken with his understated manner and easy smile. He was a tall, lumpy-featured man, with not much hair on his head and a great deal covering his arms and his back. Though Tom Wilson was ugly enough by conventional standards, and not at all prone to lengthy conversation, there was something decent and modest about him that Katherine liked from the start. Neither party was just starting out; he had turned thirty-seven the previous month, and she was twenty-eight. When word got around after they started dating that Tom had once gone in for a fair amount of carousing, he replied that hard falls had somewhat cured his love of leaping, and that "drivin' and drinkin' are two men's work."

Katherine turned onto Route 121A and passed the entrance road near what used to be Burkett's Mill. Here on the night of January 21, 1987, in the midst of a snow storm, her husband had been returning from the veterinarian where he'd dropped off a sick calf. Tom's pickup had slid off the road, crossed the running stream, and piled into an oak tree. He was dead at the scene. In fact, he'd been dead nearly as long as he and Katherine had been married.

Even when her husband was alive, developers were snooping around, looking to buy up land. One outfit, a company from Rhode Island that built drug stores, offered the Wilsons $45,000 for a six-acre parcel. It was two days after New Year's and Tom was sitting in a chair by the kitchen stove with the developer's letter in his hand. Outside, sunlight fell on their empty trees, glistening on the stubble of snow-dusted corn stalks beyond them. The money offered by the developer had sent a bolt of excitement through the household, particularly in January when most of Hi-Pine Acres lay dormant and their income, never abundant, was winnowed by the season.

But like most farmers, they put their faith in the spring, and though neither of them ever took the notion seriously, Tom put it to rest when he set the letter aside. "A man doesn't deserve a good horse that's always looking to sell it," he said.

Things were different now. In his garage, Bill Hazey had asked Katherine if he could give her phone number to the developer's agent, and after gazing into the trees across the road, she acquiesced. It was a fair bet that the agent would have trouble reaching her, as Katherine was outdoors from before sunrise to well after dark. She rarely answered the telephone, and had never bothered with an answering machine. She preferred to do business in person because she believed that character was revealed in trifles, and that you could learn more from a man's face than his prospectus.

But two days after her conversation with Mr. Hazey, Katherine was returning to the house after running errands when Frank met her at the door. A man had stopped by to see her, Frank said. He glanced down at the business card the fellow had left—Mr. John Jorrocks, of Northpointe Financial.

Katherine instructed her son to leave Mr. Jorrock's card by the telephone. When her duties allowed a free minute, she would call him. But she was a busy woman and it was that Friday, often considered the unluckiest day of the week, when Molly the exercise girl walked over in her jodhpurs and tall boots to say they had a visitor. Katherine was knee deep in the watering hole, trying to extricate a young calf that was in distress. The calf had become tangled in a portion of the wire fence that crossed the slough, and its pathetic bleating had summoned Katherine from the barn.

"Mrs. Wilson, there's somebody looking for you," said Molly, staying back to keep her boots dry. She was a blue-eyed, flaxen-haired teenager who had grown up on a neighboring farm and was hired to ride the horses. In answer to Katherine's puzzled look, Molly said, "Some kind of business guy, wearing a suit."

Pollen from neighboring trees and a virulent form of algae had combined to turn the pond a brilliant shade of green. While several of the cows waded past, Katherine stood in the swirling bog to the top of her Wellingtons, her arms thrust into the water where she groped around in the muck. "Whoever it is, I can't talk right now," she said. "Tell him to come back later."

Before Molly could answer, the bushes rustled behind her and a large, perspiring, flat-footed gentleman emerged into the clearing. "Good morning, Mrs. Wilson," he said. "I have a matter of some importance I'd like to discuss with you."

Katherine remained bent over, picking at the fouled wire with the calf mewling beside her. "I'm a little preoccupied right now," she said.

"Well, then, perhaps I can be of some assistance."

Hi-Pine Acres

Katherine stared with astonishment as the man came looming along, buttoned into a light-colored tropical suit, with a white oxford shirt, suspenders, and well-polished shoes; his short, fat neck was adorned with a green-on-black striped tie, secured by a gold Rotary Club pin. Handing his briefcase to Molly, without hesitation the gentleman waded straight into the pond, the bright green furze roiling ahead of him, which sent several cows moving away at an increased pace. The man's trousers were sopping to the knees, and his wingtips made a sucking noise against the humus at the bottom of the pond. Still, he managed to keep his nerve; and advancing with a smile as he pushed up his sleeves, he joined Mrs. Wilson at the fence, his bristly red face coming near to hers as he plunged his arms into the water.

"Ah," the man said, feeling around with his stubby hands. "Fix this in a jiffy."

Gripping the lower edge of the fence, which was a cable running from a post by the road to the other side of the slough, the gentleman raised the span a few inches off the bottom. This allowed Katherine to find the aperture where the calf's hoof had shot through and lift it clear. Bawling and baying, the calf struggled away through the chest-deep slime in search of its mother.

Katherine and her visitor waded onto the embankment.

His suit was dyed the color of pea soup to the knees and up to the elbows of his jacket, which had slipped down in the effort. His round, sweating face, peppered with the stubble of his whiskers, had already been inflamed by what had become an infernal July day. Now it was positively crimson, and the gentleman, who looked to be in his mid-fifties, rested his bulk against the fence bordering Route 121A.

"I have to start—*wheeze*—getting to the gym," he said. "Sorry—no manners. Let me—*puff*—introduce myself." He extended his hand, dripping with the slime of the pond. "John P. Jorrocks, field director for Northpointe Financial. You must be Mrs. Wilson." He pumped Katherine's hand up and down. "And I'm guessing this young sportswoman is your lovely granddaughter," he said.

Katherine and the teenager laughed, and the elder woman explained who Molly was. "My apologies, Miss," said Jorrocks, with a comic little bow. "There is nothing people dislike so much as being misnamed."

"That's okay—I like working here," said Molly, and it was Mr. Jorrocks' and Mrs. Wilson's turn to laugh. With that, the teenager said, "I better go. Harkaway was looking a little sluggish this morning."

Katherine and Mr. Jorrocks followed the girl through the trees to the rail fence surrounding the pasture. "Well, Mr. Jorrocks, thank you, but there was no need to ruin your lovely suit," she said. "I'm very busy, so..."

They both knew the reason for Mr. Jorrocks' appearance on the farm, and he wasted no time getting to the point. Resting his briefcase on the fence, he removed a dossier containing Northpointe's proposal for Hi-Pine Acres. "Mrs. Wilson," he said, "what I've done is provide you with an exceptional level of compensation for a land transfer that Northpointe might just as easily find someplace else."

Katherine recalled something that her late husband was fond of saying. "When does someone have enough money, Mr. Jorrocks?" she asked, and her visitor shook his head. "When he's gotten a little more than he already has," said Katherine.

"I think you'll find it satisfactory," said Jorrocks, snapping up his case while indicating the folder in Katherine's hand. "I discussed it with your son the other day, and he was very impressed."

Mrs. Wilson hitched up her dungarees and with the folder tucked under her arm, hopped over the railing and walked away.

"I'll be in touch," she said.

That evening, after a long day of chores and the sort of minor emergencies that regularly visited the farm, Katherine sat at the kitchen table, drinking a cup of tea. Spread across the table top was the contents of Mr. Jorrocks' folder: a large aerial photograph of the farm with the nineteen-acre parcel outlined in red; a proposed easement for an access road crossing the remaining eight acres; and a development timeline, including the removal of the barn, stables, and outbuildings across Route 121A onto the "new agricultural complex" in the cornfield.

Beneath the photographs were appraisal documents, assessing the value of the land for various activities: residential, agricultural, and commercial, along with tax valuations, and a copy of the town's zoning ordinance, noting the property's coveted status as a "mixed zone," freeing it for the sort of development Northpointe was interested in.

Above the sink, a wall clock ticked on past eight PM. Katherine got up from her chair with some difficulty and went over to rinse out her teacup. Outside, the moon had risen above the wall of fruit trees that hemmed in the garden. It was round and golden in the light of the departed sun. Across the fields, she could hear Tanner barking at a fox or coyote that had wandered too near the hen house. The ticking of the clock resumed its preeminence, and the moon climbed higher above the trees. There was a mysterious regal figure etched in profile on its surface, like the coin of the realm.

Northpointe's offer appeared reasonable, and according to the research Katherine had done, their offer of remuneration was a fair one. Returning to her chair, she separated out the two most important documents, stacking the rest to one side. The first was an artist's rendering of the proposed site, with a map printed on the back. The development was planned as a quartet of multi-unit residential buildings, set back from Route 121A near the western edge of the land. The "cluster housing" would comprise eighty-eight units of "upscale assisted living," with space provided for an additional cluster, if necessary, as well as five acres marked off for "potential commercial development," whatever that meant.

The drawing indicated that most of the trees would be razed, and that the complex would include a walking trail, an artificial pond with a fountain, a members' clubhouse, and a groundskeeper's shed. A driveway led to the cul-de-sac in front of the buildings, and the fences and landscaping would be replaced and improved. Sight lines from the farm house would provide a view of the lawn, with the housing set five hundred yards back from Route 121A.

Katherine picked up the other document. It was a cover letter, printed on expensive paper embossed with Northpointe Financial's insignia of a ram's head. Mr. Jorrocks, who was vice president of development, had signed the letter. Amid the boilerplate language, along with what Katherine detected was a small amount of condescension, was the eye-catching phrase "in consideration of said land transfer and irrevocable sale, the sum of $328,000, delivered in a single payment upon closing."

Now Katherine held the parchment in her lap while gazing out the window at the ascendant moon. Gradually the noise of the clock was overtaken by creaking sounds overhead, then footfalls on the stairs and along the hallway toward the kitchen door. When it opened, Frank stood in the glare of light, dressed in an old t-shirt and sweatpants, bare-footed, with his hair mashed flat atop his head and his small eyes red-rimmed and weary.

"Are you gonna sell it?" he asked.

Katherine put the letter on the table. "I don't see what choice I have," she said.

Although they had lived together for many years, Katherine felt a pang of embarrassment at such intrusions. Glancing down, she couldn't help noticing Frank's thick, discolored toe nails and lopsided ankles.

"If you sell, Jorrocks says there'll be something in it for me," Frank said.

"We won't have the farm, anymore—not the whole thing, anyway. But I'll be able to pay our bills, and you'll have a good stake when I'm gone."

Frank shook his head. "Jorrocks told me that if you sign the papers, he'd buy me a new truck," he said. "An F150 with a cap."

Mother and son looked at each other like two strangers. The clock seemed to grow louder, and then Katherine said, "When I sign those papers, Frank, it's going to mean a lot more than just a new truck."

Frank wore the look of a cow standing in the bog until, scratching at his hindquarters, he went back through the flimsy door and lumbered down the hall.

Over the next few weeks, Katherine arranged to have her own appraisal done, and afterward surveyors came in, establishing the property lines and markers. Bill Hazey recommended an attorney to conduct the title search, after which he and Katherine marveled at the unwavering lineage this fellow's research uncovered—just two owners had possessed the land since the provincial governor of New Hampshire, Benning Wentworth, had declared the Crown's presumptive sovereignty over it. Hiram Anaximander Cavendish had purchased the original forty-five acres from the land grant commission in 1739, at three pounds sterling apiece. Katherine's great-great grandfather bought the existing twenty-seven acres from the Cavendish family one hundred and forty three years later. The original deed, with Matthias Houlton Prescott's signature on it, was discovered in a box at the town clerk's office.

In the waning days of August, with the Red Haven peaches coming into season and the hayfields mowed to stubble, Katherine was busier than ever. Letters had gone back and forth between Mrs. Wilson's attorney and Northpointe Financial, the price agreed upon, and everything seemed in good order. Then, on a brilliant morning that presaged autumn, Gretta Hazey brought the twins, Maeghan and Sophie, to the farm for their riding lesson. Molly was in the stable brushing the horses, and Mrs. Wilson came out to help her with the saddles.

For the day's exercise, Molly was dressed in a cutaway coat, breeches with a padded leather seat, mahogany-colored top boots, and a dun-colored riding helmet. The twins wore blue jeans, rag wool sweaters, and their bicycle helmets. In the musky darkness of the stable, Katherine slipped on the bridles for the two most docile animals in her care—a tawny-coated mare named Challenger, and Cockbird, a nine-year old bay—and after tightening their girths, Molly led the horses into the sunlit yard.

When the horses appeared, Sophie and Maeghan hopped up and down, shivering with excitement. Beside them, Gretta was the picture of calm—a green-eyed woman of forty, with auburn hair and radiant white teeth, which she showed often in conversation. Gretta smiled now, first at Molly and the horses and then in conspiratorial glee with Katherine, this morning in a broad-brimmed hat, flannel shirt, and canvas pants below which she sported a pair of work boots.

"I heard it might be a red-letter day around here," said Gretta, walking over the lumpy pasture to touch Mrs. Wilson's hand.

Katherine understood that Bill Hazey shared everything with his wife, just as she had done with her late husband, and not being shy or private by nature, the silver-haired widow looked straight at her visitor, and said, "If Tom was here, he'd be blown over by the news."

"I guess there's a right time for everything," said Gretta, patting her hand.

Earlier that morning, Katherine and Molly had created a

makeshift riding circle in the pasture using saw horses and trash barrels. Now, atop their mounts, the girls were tit-tup-ing around the perimeter while Molly stood in the center, encouraging them and offering a few words of advice. "Elbows higher, Sophie. Maeghan, tall in the saddle. Straight back. That-a-girl."

Earlier, Katherine had spent an hour leveling the circle, and now, retrieving a wheelbarrow from where it leaned against the stable, she picked up the rake and rolled over to the fence with Gretta alongside. "I can't imagine what it'd be like without all this work to do," Katherine said, filling in a hole that Tanner had dug under the fence.

"It's going to free you up to do other things," said Gretta. "To think about the future."

"To be honest, I'd rather be on the farm than anywhere else," Katherine said.

Inside the makeshift circle, the horses were cantering now, the twins raised in their stirrups, their faces serious, riding faster than a trot for the first time.

"That's beautiful, girls," Gretta said. "You're doing awesome."

While she and Katherine watched from the fence, a shiny black Town Car pulled up near the barn and Mr. Jorrocks got out.

This time, he'd dressed more appropriately—new duck boots, khaki pants, and a V-necked pullover with a polo shirt underneath. Between his first visit and this one, he and Katherine had maintained an intermittent and mostly brief and harmonious correspondence by telephone regarding the appropriate details, including a possible date of September eleventh for the closing. Much of their preliminary business being concluded, Mr. Jorrocks had delivered himself to Hi-Pine Acres to procure Mrs. Wilson's signature on the Purchase & Sale agreement—allowing, of course, for the signatory's review of the terms contained therein.

"The young equestrians have it right," said Jorrocks, coming toward them with his folder and pen already in hand. "Sally forth—without trepidation." He drew himself up at the fence. "I hope I'm not interrupting, Mrs. Wilson, but after pulling it all together, I wanted to give you the opportunity of signing right away."

Finished with the lesson, the girls ran over to their mother and started talking in high-pitched voices. Inside the circle, Molly walked Cockbird and Challenger till their lather came down, whereupon she led them to the stable for their oats and some water. With her arms around the girls' shoulders, Gretta took Maeghan and Sophie over to visit the sheep while Katherine pushed the wheelbarrow toward the stable.

"If you want to leave that on the front seat of my truck, Mr. Jorrocks, I'll look at it as soon as I have a few minutes," Mrs. Wilson said.

Jorrocks wiped his brow with a handkerchief. "I was hoping to go over it with you," he said. "The potential closing date is just two weeks from Friday."

Round bales of hay, each as tall as a man, were piled high on the trailer, which had been resurrected from its location beside the barn. Katherine laid the wheelbarrow against the whorls of hay, maneuvering around Mr. Jorrocks when she heard a ruckus coming from the stable. "There's only so many hours in a day," she said. "I'll go over them when I'm finished with everything I have to do."

Inside the stable, Molly had succeeded in getting Cockbird into her loose-box but Challenger was neighing and stamping her hooves as the girl tried to coax her in. In the next stall, Harkaway, who hadn't been exercised yet, tossed his head and snorted in reply. The two horses, which had been on cordial terms for years, were on the verge of taking umbrage with each other, while Cockbird looked on mildly, chewing her oats.

"Do you want me to take Harkaway out?" asked Katherine.

"Yes, thanks, Mrs. Wilson," Molly said. She was stroking Challenger's neck and whispering to her. "I don't know what's got into these two."

"Harkaway must be jealous," said Mrs. Wilson. "He missed all the fun."

The horse was saddled in anticipation of his exercise period, and Mrs. Wilson caught him by the bridle and went out to the pasture with Mr. Jorrocks tramping along behind them. Harkaway was a jet-black steed with a shiny, well sculpted neck, clean flat legs, and immense loins and hocks; he stood fifteen hands, though the length of his tail made him look smaller. Riding him for thirty minutes would be more time-efficient than walking him, which would take an hour to bring up his lather, and Mrs. Wilson felt her own urge to run.

Coming around, she put her foot in the stirrup and swung herself onto the horse. Although she hadn't ridden in quite some time, Katherine Wilson had spent many hours on horseback in her youth, exploring every inch of the farm and a great deal of the countryside beyond. When Tom was alive, they had kept two horses of their own, riding on the weekends for pleasure, and over the years she had owned a few other horses. Harkaway was eight years old, with a thruster's spirit and temperament—overall, a very impressive animal.

"Mrs. Wilson, just a few minutes of your time," said Jorrocks, holding out the folder.

From the saddle, Katherine looked down on Mr. Jorrocks' head. "Harkaway needs his exercise now. The papers will have to wait."

Chucking the reins, Katherine started the horse off at a walk, with Jorrocks hurrying alongside. "How long will it take?" he asked. "Because I'd be willing to postpone my next appointment."

"Really, Mr. Jorrocks, I don't see what differ—"

But Jorrocks wheedled and bullied, always presuming on Mrs. Wilson's need of the money, and though never saying it, hinting that Northpointe Financial was ready to take its investment elsewhere. "S'pose then," he said, "that I hadn't (*wheeze*) come along, and we hadn't (*puff*) freed that calf together, and I had visited some other property owner. I wouldn't have this promissory note in my hand for (*puff-wheeze*) three hundred and twenty-eight thousand dollars."

"If it wasn't you, Mr. Jorrocks, I'm sure someone else would be standing there with papers in his hand," Mrs. Wilson said, nudging the horse into a canter. Harkaway soon left Jorrocks behind, and if Katherine had glanced back, she would've seen the developer's agent losing his breakfast over the pasture fence.

Twice she circled the enclosure, and feeling the horse's confinement in so limited a space, she kicked him into a trot, throwing clods along the straightaway. The pasture sloped downward, the tussocks of grass becoming scarce until the horse's hooves met a stretch of hard-packed dirt approaching the fence. On a sudden impulse, Katherine struck the horse into a full gallop, cramming him at the fence. Left and right, the forest beyond the pasture was reduced to a blurry continuum. Grabbing fistfuls of Harkaway's mane and leaning down upon his neck, Katherine rode with the stirrups pushed back as horse and rider arrived at the obstacle.

Collecting himself, Harkaway sprang into the air. Katherine felt his muscles roll in a wave from his chest to his withers, and down his back to his loins. They cleared the fence in a lovely arc, and Harkaway galloped along the path that followed the original line of the Cavendish property. Here the remains of a barn from the 1800s consisted of a fieldstone outline and a few timbers, with the empty shaft of a well beside it. Beside an unruly hedgerow, the path curved off through the pines, narrowing to just six feet in width.

Harkaway slowed, and Katherine used the reins to pull him into a trot. Primroses littered the hedge, and in the brightening ether that ranged above them, insects droned past in various directions. This rarely visited precinct of the land, to Katherine's knowledge, hadn't been farmed since the original Cavendish homestead, built in 1743, had stood beside the old barn. At one time the post road had wandered through here, but now it was all trees, wild grasses, and scrub.

A deep triangular dell of some three acres, abounding in purple loosestrife, brambles, and marsh, this parcel had contained the original settlement but had become obsolete with the widening of the upper stream, which provided sufficient water for the animals. The appearance of Route 121A, crossing the land at its highest point, shifted the business of the farm eastward, leaving the ruins of the old Cavendish place forgotten.

It was here that Tanner found them, and the collie trotted alongside with his nose to the ground, marking scent. Harkaway was winded from his gallop, which was beyond the exertion that Molly usually provided, and Katherine dismounted to walk ahead, leading the horse by the reins.

Odd-shaped on all the surveyor's maps, this section of the farm angled toward the intersection of the old post road and a stone wall demarcating the original "Kingston grant," from which Prescott had been created. Hidden there was a small body of water, the so-called "lower pond," fringed with tall weeds and about ten feet deep. The only access was a place along the embankment where deer, foxes, and other wild animals had trampled the undergrowth, and as Harkaway's lather came down, Katherine led him over to drink.

Cicadas whirred among the reeds, and occasionally a bull frog erupted from the lily pads, otherwise an ancient silence reigned over the pond. Off to the left, a great blue heron, indistinguishable among the bulrushes, stepped out from the embankment, spread its massive wings in a gesture of imprecation or warning, and then flapped away, leaving a glyph of droplets across the pond.

With the sudden departure of the great bird, Harkaway refused to drink. Tanner crossed over the bank and lapped up a huge draught, but the horse wouldn't budge. It was a forsaken place. Not long after the change in boundary lines between Massachusetts and New Hampshire in 1739, an ambush had occurred here, when Abenaki warriors incited by the French had attacked a small group of homesteaders. Six people were killed. According to local lore, this group included relatives of Hiram Cavendish, the man who would later purchase the land from Governor Wentworth and establish a farm. When Frank was a teenager, he helped to prove this legend by the artifacts he dug up. The arrowheads and musket bore were sold to an antiques dealer in Pembroke, with the condition that neither party would reveal where they originated. The last thing they needed at the farm was a bunch of scavengers.

Leaving Harkaway to graze, Katherine took off her hat and knelt on the embankment, cupping some water to splash her neck and picking a few green fronds from the shallows. She rinsed the dirt from their roots and wound them inside the crown of the hat, returning it to her head. Retrieving Tanner from his expeditions with a low whistle, she caught up the reins again, came astride Harkaway with a nimble movement and boosted herself into the saddle.

Back when young Frank had rented a metal detector and found parts of an eighteenth century musket, arrowheads, spear points, and a few small bones from a woman's hand, he also discovered an old belt buckle at another location on the property. After the antique dealer's itemized list noted that the brass buckle was from the late 19th century and could not possibly have belonged to one of the homesteaders, Katherine's late husband found the belt buckle in the wastebasket where Frank had discarded it.

Tom Wilson removed the buckle, cleaned it with a can of Brasso, and attached it to a worn leather belt from his closet. When his wife noticed it one day, he said, "The person who wore this was one of your people. And so am I." Katherine made sure her husband was wearing the belt on the day he was buried.

All her ruminations led Katherine to the uncomfortable fact that the property must be sold—at least, the main part of it. But she knew after visiting the pond that she could never bring herself to countersign the original deed. Hard times lay ahead, and she was certain to a penny that Frank would reverse her decision just as soon as he was able. Still, the fact remained that, right or wrong, some of her people had died fighting for this land. Chucking the reins against the horse's withers, she trotted toward the stable knowing that her own bones would be scattered here someday. That was all she really wanted.

Java Man

The Hornets' guard brought the ball up court, glancing left-right and calling out a string of numbers. But with 17 seconds left in the game and the scoreboard showing

>| *Home:* | *Carter Hornets 98* |
>| *Away:* | *Shawsheen 73* |

everyone in the gym knew where the ball was going. Loping along the sideline was the Hornets center, Pete Lincoln, a deft, agile player with quick hands and feet. Pulling up for his beautiful, arcing jumper, and knifing inside for layups, Pete had already scored 28 points, snagged nine rebounds, and blocked seven shots, willing his team to the verge of a school record. The Carter High Hornets had never scored 100 points in a game.

My best friend Jeff Murdock and I were sitting in the balcony, poised above the basket where Carter had taken the ball out. I felt like God up there, looking down on the Hornets in their gold satin shorts and white singlets; the vaunted Shawsheen five in their maroon away uniforms; the team benches crowded along the sideline to our left, and the bleachers filled to capacity for the last game of the season. Throughout the fourth quarter, the stands had been roiling with pompoms and blaring with klaxons, but had grown quiet.

Thirteen seconds, twelve—the guard crossed over to the right, picking up his dribble. Meanwhile, Pete glided along the baseline, six-four and loose-limbed, with the same mild expression he wore during the games he played against Murdock and me.

In addition to being Carter High's star player, Pete Lincoln was the coach of our C.Y.O. basketball team. We played on a dank court in the church basement, wearing threadbare St. Charles Borromeo wife beaters, our gym shorts, and black hi-tops. Murdock was three inches taller than me, a real basketball nut, but Pete treated everyone the same, teaching us how to set a pick and play zone defense. We were the envy of the other sixth grade

Jay Atkinson

teams.

Now, as we looked on, the beeswaxed floor shone under the lights, dark and smooth except for the cattle trail of scuff marks under each basket. Everyone but Pete Lincoln and the Hornet's guard was frozen in tableau, even the Shawsheen coach, standing with an arm outstretched, his mouth in a gaping O. A zeppelin of rosin dust hovered between the benches, and the referee, small and trim in his striped jersey and black trousers, had one eye on his watch, the other on the ball handler, and his whistle in his mouth.

Five seconds, four...

Cutting inside, Pete was already rising from the floor when the ball arrived. Shawsheen's center, two inches taller than Pete Lincoln, jumped at the same instant, thrusting his hands up-ward like a diver. But Pete had already let it go—a soft, parabolic lob that rose in the air, dropping straight through the basket as the earsplitting *dit-dit-dit* of the buzzer tore through the gym.

Jeff Murdock and I scrambled downstairs and dashed onto the court, which was teeming with cheerleaders, parents, high school kids, and the ref, who looked like a man escaping from a fire. Grabbing at Murdock's belt, I swung along behind him, rolling with the surge of people. Suddenly, Pete Lincoln appeared, swooping down to embrace Jeff and me. But at the last instant, we were shoved aside—"Get the fuck outta here"—as one of Pete's teammates grabbed him and pivoted for the exit.

It was Kenny Dussault. He'd fouled out in the third quarter, after breaking the Shawsheen captain's nose. Dussault was a burly, black-eyed, wild-haired reserve, six feet tall and weighing about two hundred pounds. He couldn't shoot, pass, or dribble, but when he ran the court, opposing players got out of his way. Kenny's teammates called him Java, because he resembled a prehistoric man.

With his bony forehead, protruding brow, and large rounded jaw, Java Man was an intermediary species, arriving between apes and humans. When I walked into my Carter High biology class three years later, I noticed a poster of Java Man, or *Pithecanthropus erectus*, hanging on the wall. Some wag had drawn a 7 on his chest, which was Dussault's uniform number.

The Carter gym occupied the upper half of the building, with stairs leading down to the locker rooms and out to the street. When the horn sounded, the opposing team sprinted off the court and through the nearest exit. Now, stumbling along, we were rushed downstairs with everyone else, buzzing over Pete's shot and beating Shawsheen, who won the league title every year. Java

Jay Atkinson

and Pete Lincoln were below us, shoving their way toward the locker room. As they descended, Shawsheen's coach, apparently having left something in the gym, popped out of the visitor's room and began struggling against the tide. He bumped into Java, who thrust out his arm, sending the coach, who was a pretty large man, flat on his back against the metal landing. But Java charged past him into the locker room, where he was greeted by more laughter and shouting.

Murdock finished the C.Y.O season, but I sprained my ankle jumping off our garage roof, and then school ended. Pete Lincoln graduated from Carter High and left for Notre Dame that fall. He played basketball there, and married a girl from Indiana. I never saw him again.

*

In ninth grade, I stopped growing and took up soccer. But Murdock was a star on the basketball team, and eventually broke most of Pete Lincoln's records. High school came and went. Murdock attended junior college for a while, took the Civil Service exam, and got on the Lawrence fire department during my freshman year at St. Trinian's in Maine. Occasionally, Murdock rode up on his motorcycle, just to eyeball the coeds. At St. Trinian's, I made the soccer team, playing in the midfield. Even at such a tiny school, the competition was stiff, but after my first season I'd improved enough to become a pretty good player in the summer league back home.

By sophomore year, I was dating a smart, long-limbed blonde named Madison Gray, who I met in Economics class. Maddi was an all-state high jumper from Shawsheen, Mass., and placed regularly for St. Trinian's. Since Maddi lived one town away, our relationship naturally carried over to the summer. But when she and I went kayaking on the Merrimack, or biking through Groveland and Boxford, I struggled to keep up. Maddi Gray blew into my life on a zephyr, glowing like Venus on the half shell. I knew I was in trouble.

That summer, I worked a shit job at the Coca-Cola bottling plant, and Maddi taught sailing to little kids. On Monday and Wednesday evenings, Maddi ran intervals on the Carter High track while I played in the midfield for the Pepperell Bismols. With my leggy girlfriend zipping around the oval, I scored a mess of goals and we made the finals against a team called the Hellenic Spirits. They had a long-haired striker named Kostas who did a back flip every time he scored a goal. He'd beaten us with a header in the semis the year before.

Five minutes into the game, Kostas scored on a penalty

kick and performed his signature flip. We hated his guts. But late in the second half, we tied the score, and with a minute left, Turf Walton snaked a pass between defenders into space on their right flank. Running onto the ball, I stabbed a low hard shot just inside the post. As I wheeled around, there was Kostas, head down, his hands tightened into fists. Running over, I did the kind of somersault you learned in first grade, and as I came to my feet, I spotted Maddi on the track, shaking her head and laughing. Turf came over and mussed my hair and the whistle blew. We were the champs.

I threw my cleats into Maddi's VW and we headed to the Rally Club, a rickety beer joint perched on a gravel lot on the east side of town. The plywood door lacked sashes and sill, opening into a smoky, rattling joint that looked like an old boxcar. The bar stood to the right, stocked with Calvert whiskey, Crystal Palace gin, and other bottom-shelf brands. Wooden booths ran along the left-hand wall, with a few tables occupying the space between the booths and the bar.

Turf Walton brought in our trophies while Maddi and I perused the jukebox, which was filled with great old records by Petula Clark, Smoky Robinson and the Miracles, and the Yardbirds. From the kitchen, a skinny cook handed pork cutlets in little greasy paper boats out through a window. But we ordered the specialty of the house, chicken BBQ, which consisted of boiled chicken served on a hamburger bun with a dab of industrial mayo and a ragged piece of lettuce. Any customer who didn't live within five miles of the Rally Club, expecting a hunk of barbecued chicken, was surprised to receive a soup sandwich.

With Johnny Cash singing "Ring of Fire" from the jukebox, Turf heaved the box of trophies onto the table. My best friend on the team, Walton was a square-built, bandy-legged defender, originally from Pepperell, Mass., with a head of wavy close-cropped hair that resembled Astroturf. Studying for a degree in criminal justice, Turf had an unsentimental way of looking at things, which involved a perfunctory dismissal of anything that didn't interest him, and his interests were limited—soccer, eating, and becoming a cop. But he was a scrappy little player, and a terse master of ceremonies at all official team functions.

"Hey, Fillion, shut up," Turf said, directing his ire at our congenial left wing. "It was good to beat those fuckin' Greeks, thanks to—"

From outside came the threatening roar of motorcycles. It sounded like a pride of lions, and Maddi wriggled in, squeezing my arm. The bikes, perhaps four or five of them, bleated in several chest-pounding registers, but there was a growling *fup-fup-FUP-*

FUP that was darker and louder than all the rest.

Suddenly, a large Harley Davidson barged through the front door. Astride it, a shaggy, bearded fellow in a leather vest was shouting in a voice that couldn't be heard over the rumbling motorcycle. Pawing the floor, the biker emerged from the gloaming of the parking lot until the entire 1,000-cc Sportster was inside the club. Smoke poured from the exhaust, and as the rider goosed the throttle, the walls shook, and a bottle of vodka plummeted from a shelf above the bar. Waving his arms, the bartender contorted his parboiled face, telling the biker to get out. But he just laughed.

Although I hadn't seen Kenny Dussault in eight years, I knew him right away. He'd shed the rawboned look of youth, and now, in his late twenties, had taken on the bulk of someone who dug ditches for a living. Occasionally, Java's name would come up—he'd done three months at the Farm for receiving stolen property; then a year in Middleton for assaulting a guy with a crowbar; and another six months for intimidating a witness.

Walking the Harley up to our table, Java leered at Fillion's girlfriend and then at Maddi. His hair and beard were unkempt, and when I stood up, he trained his little pig eyes on me. But there wasn't a glimmer of recognition and Java pushed on, shouting the sallow-faced cook back into the kitchen, and rolling out the back door into the night. Soon the other bikers circled around and they zoomed off.

The rocker on the back of Java's vest, spelling out MASSACHUSETTS in block letters, meant he was a Hell's Angels prospect. "The man has ambition," Turf said. "He's climbing to the very bottom."

In May 1983, I graduated from St. Trinian's with a psychology degree. My diploma stated that I was entitled to "All the Rights and Privileges Thereunto Appertaining," of which there were none, apparently. So I spent a lot of time evaluating my decision to study psychology in the first place. That spring, Maddi and I broke up when she met a Swedish exchange student who was a pole-vaulter. With his blonde hair and form-fitting tracksuit, Lars was always whizzing around campus, leaping over shrubs and vaulting fences, and at the end of the term he and Maddi bounded away like jackrabbits.

I owed nine grand in federal student loans, and the economy was a shambles. Murdock was assigned to Engine 7, and Turf graduated from college and entered the Massachusetts State Police Academy, both settling into their careers. I worked as a substitute teacher, newspaper reporter, and employment counselor. Eventually I cycled through all the occupations available to a person with a college education and no discernible skills.

An old roommate offered me a job selling timeshares and I moved to Fort Lauderdale. I met a cocktail waitress named Ginger and we got married. To say it was a mistake of youth is an insult to young people everywhere. The marriage lasted a year, and the less said about that, the better.

By the time I came back, the Rally Club had been demolished to make way for another CVS. Now in our thirties, Murdock and I would drink at a place called Maxwell's, where we occasionally ran into Java. When I was in Florida, he'd served eighteen months at Concord MCI for dealing coke. Java hung around the bar, smiling and laughing, but with a definite air of menace about him. I pretended I didn't see him, but Murdock usually bought him a beer. Turf said that Java was a strong arm for some organized crime guys in Boston, while maintaining his status with the Angels. Except for Murdock, hardly anyone talked to him. It was like getting into a cab and finding Stalin behind the wheel. You just paid your fare and got the hell out, with as little interaction as possible.

That fall, Maxwell's burned to the ground. A local character named Doug Tbilisi owned the club and there was ample suspicion about the fire. Originally an old barn, Maxwell's stood amidst a clump of oaks on a rise overlooking Carter Pond. The fire was so big, Lawrence sent Engine 7 on mutual aid. Murdock said it was fully involved when they rolled up. They helped Carter firefighters throw water on the blaze until mid-morning, trying to keep the woods from catching fire.

Doug Tbilisi was the kind of guy who'd smile at you while rifling through your wallet, stealing your jewelry, and groping your wife. Reeking of aftershave, deodorant, and mouthwash, Tbilisi, who was in his mid-forties, resembled a Baltic strongman who'd fallen on hard times. Over the years, he'd pursued a number of vocations, few of them honorable, and got into the restaurant business when his third wife, who owned a Mercedes dealership, fell off his sailboat and drowned. After that, I certainly wouldn't go swimming with Doug Tbilisi.

The case took a turn when Tbilisi bought a rundown bodega in Lawrence and turned it into a sports bar called Overtime. By the early nineties, Lawrence was a grand old mill city in steep decline, and sports bars were all the rage. A raft of TVs blasted Australian Rules football, synchronized swimming, and other dubious spectacles while buxom waitresses served drinks to morose looking guys who hadn't touched a football in years.

Late one night, Murdock and I were in Overtime watching some rednecks hunt for alligators on TV. The place was nearly empty, with a mailman nursing his drink and a waitress in a skintight referee's jersey. The plate glass window, etched with the name of the bar, was like a black slate in the darkness. By chance, I happened to notice a vague shape going along the sidewalk past the bar. Moments later, the figure reappeared and threw a large object through the window.

There was a crash, and the object bounced away, under a table. Shards of glass rained down on the carpet. The waitress in the referee jersey began running around, blowing her silver whistle. "What the fuck was that?" she said.

The noise drew Tbilisi from his office, with the exclamatory stub of a cigar jammed in his mouth. "Who broke the window?" he asked.

"Somebody—a guy outside—he threw something," said the waitress.

"Who?" asked Tbilisi, his eyes shifting around like she'd mentioned the IRS.

Murdock and I, the referee, bartender, postman, and Tbilisi stood regarding the dark, empty street through the hole in the window. Just then a large triangle of broken glass, pulled downward by its own weight, smashed to the floor. Puffing on his cigar, Tbilisi crawled beneath the table and retrieved something wrapped in paper—an old brick. The paper drifted to the floor and as I reached down, Tbilisi snatched it away, tearing off a corner.

My piece of the note read, "...*the fuckn money. Java.*"

"Everybody *out*," said Tbilisi, balling up the paper.

Up and down South Broadway there wasn't a car, pedestrian, or prostitute in sight. I told Murdock what was scribbled on the paper, and he laughed. "He should've just called," Jeff said.

*

A week later, the state fire marshal opened an investigation into the fire at Maxwell's. Tbilisi had given Java $500 with a promise of five hundred more if he received a settlement from his insurance company. Then he reneged on the second payment. If Tbilisi wasn't so cheap and Java wasn't so stupid, they would've gotten away with it.

Java got two and a half years at Concord MCI for arson, while Tbilisi received nine months at the Farm on a conspiracy charge. He served six, obtained early release, and within the next year, sold Overtime and built a nightclub called Bottomley's on the site of the old Maxwell's.

I had nothing against Tbilisi that free booze couldn't fix,

and attended the opening. Bottomley's was a replica of an old town hall, with four white pillars out front. A gallery ran around the upper level, where patrons could look down on the dance floor. Tbilisi had even hired the Fabulous Thunderbirds to play that night, and they were banging out their opening number when I walked in.

Now in real estate, I came to mingle with some of the wealthy people in town. But while I was working the room, confronted mostly by other real estate brokers, I couldn't help noticing that Doug Tbilisi, convicted felon, was drinking champagne with the mayor, while Java spent most of every day, including Christmas, in his tiny cell, shitting into a steel basin while another dude watched. It almost made you choke on your bacon-wrapped scallop, if you thought about it too much.

*

A year later, Jeff married a bartender named Sharon Campesi who worked at the 99 Restaurant. Under her steadying influence, Murdock got a dog from the shelter and moved into a little bungalow on Carter Pond. Sharon's family owned half the shoreline, which was thickly wooded and included a narrow beach. That fall, Turf made detective in the state police, and I heard from a college pal that Maddi Gray had married a thoracic surgeon and moved to Aspen. Tired of chasing nickels, I snagged a job in commercial real estate in Boston. The Winthrop Company was established in 1697, after their surveyor, John Butcher, laid out, bounded, and measured the twelve divisions of land that comprised Dorchester. The original map, on a yellowed parchment in Butcher's own hand, was kept under glass in the company headquarters on Hereford Street. Outside, iron rings pierced the foundation, where company employees had once tied up their mounts. Since then, the horseshit had not abated.

One afternoon, I was showing a client an eighteen-story glass tower that housed, among its thirty or forty lessees, WROX, a semi-popular FM radio station. So far, my contribution to the Winthrop Company had been selling a rundown garage in Somerville that had been the headquarters for Howie Winter, the old gangster. We were on the seventh floor, examining the WROX offices along with the manager, when I caught sight of a petite, black-haired woman in a mini skirt. She flitted from one room to another, like a sleek little bird.

My client followed the manager into his office. Hanging back, I opened another door, and there was the rock n' roll chick, eating a hamburger and fries from a paper bag.

"That stuff'll kill you," I said.

The woman raised a mug with *My Job Sucks* printed on it. "You just wash it down with coffee," she said.

Husky-voiced Judy T. was a deejay at WROX 91.9, an indie rock station that catered to the beard and sandals crowd. With her heart-shaped face, spiky black hair, and Cleopatra makeup, she wasn't my type, since I usually dated athletic blondes, like the vegan hat check girl at Maxwell's. But there was a definite charge in our first meeting, like that buzz of electricity when they pass a wand over you at the airport. Peering through gray-green eyes, Judy T. made a quick appraisal of my oxford shirt and khaki pants.

"It's across the hall," she said.

"What is?"

"Are you here to fix the copier?"

I shook my head. "I'm selling the building to that old guy."

"Tell him I'm available," said Judy T., lighting a cigarette.

Throughout my life, certain women have shown up like an approaching storm, disrupting my barometric pressure. Madison Gray was a soft summer rain, the kind that lengthens a pleasant afternoon, lulling the senses with its patter. Such a rainfall ends before you want it to, puddling the street and revealing an unwelcome sun. My marriage was a vicious little coastal storm that brewed up in the Gulf of Mexico, turning the sky black. It barreled across the strand and flattened a couple of grubby beach towns, then moved out to sea, as brief as it was objectionable.

Judy Tornado, as I called her, was a dark funnel cloud that wheeled all over the landscape, with a caravan of thrill seekers forever giving chase. When I met her, Judy T. was living with a Brazilian guy who owned an electronics store; their favorite activity was throwing dishes at each other and swearing. Never one to make plans, she'd show up unannounced at my office, like the prairie twisters she was named for. Sometimes I'd call the station when she was working, altering my voice to get on the air. As soon as I'd requested a song by Pat Boone or Trini Lopez, she'd slam in a commercial and pick up the phone: "Very funny."

"I like to think so."

Judy T. worked 7 PM to midnight. Alone in the building, she'd call me when a song was playing, her voice hushed like a child's. She had none of Madison Gray's inner strength or confidence, but for a man in his late thirties, with a failed relationship or two behind him, life is an extension of high school. He's all for going, all for taking risks, all for making hay while the sun shines. So, despite my skepticism, having a definite attraction to Judy T., and not disinclined to seeing her more often, I began to ignore the crockery-throwing Brazilian, and would arrive at the lonely tower at the stroke of midnight, seeking, if not to rescue its sole occupant, to buy her a few vodkas.

One Sunday, Judy T. drove up to Carter, avoiding the scrutiny of her jealous ex-boyfriends, who I found out also included the singer for a band called "The Question?" (Answer: "Fuck off"), a car salesman, and a professional dog walker. Evidently, Judy T. was an ace at starting relationships, but not very good at ending them. But that night all I wanted was a cold beer, after which we planned to have dinner with Jeff and Sharon.

At Bottomley's, Judy T. and I walked beneath the oak trees, their shade giving way to the early darkness. Inside, the faux gas lamps were turned down low, and the gallery was thronged with shadows. A few parties were scattered across the dining room, and the bar was nearly vacant, just an absentee drinker, his place marked by a canvas jacket thrown over one of the stools.

Holding up two fingers, I pointed at the Bass Ale sign and the bartender nodded. Then I left Judy T. by the jukebox and proceeded to the men's room. Feeling pretty good about myself, I strolled back down the hall, whistling the old Bob Marley tune that was playing. Rounding the corner, I noticed Judy T. backed up against the jukebox, her chin thrust downward into her leather jacket, like a turtle retreating into its shell. A large, disheveled figure loomed over her, the heel of each hand resting on the jukebox to either side.

It felt like someone had punctured my lungs with a knitting needle. Suddenly I realized that the greasy jacket draped over the barstool was Java's, and that he'd probably been off snorting coke as we arrived. Apparently, he and Doug Tbilisi had buried the hatchet, at least to the point where he could drink in Tbilisi's joint. In ratty jeans and a pair of hobnail boots, Java leaned over my date, speaking softly.

Nobody had seen Java in six months. He was down in Mexico, they said, or riding with the Angels in Florida. Recently, Turf said Java's name had surfaced during a murder investigation. A bookie that owed money to the wrong people was rumored to have been buried in an Everett landfill.

Java's hair fell to his shoulders, obscuring his face. But there was no mistaking the cannonball shoulders and bulky torso, the dingy clothes, and a large, unkempt beard that would've made a Viking jealous. By this time, Java was past forty, and weighed about two hundred-fifty pounds.

When my footfalls sounded on the parquet, Judy T. gave me a look that said, *who the fuck is this?* My legs went numb as I closed on them, trying to think of something to say.

"Hey, Kenny," I said. "How ya doin'?"

Java swiveled toward me, though he was still looking at Judy T. "That's my boyfriend," she said, in a tiny voice.

I hadn't been this close to Java since the Rally Club, fifteen years earlier. At the sound of the word *boyfriend*, he turned from the jukebox. He was a jowly man, and despite the undergrowth of beard, which crept up from his neck, I could see his rotten teeth. Judy T. cowered against the jukebox, while Bob Marley kept insisting that everything was gonna be all right.

Java shot me a baleful look, his red-rimmed eyes as empty as the moon. I couldn't think of anything else to say, and Java never talked much, anyway. Outwardly, he was calm, though there was always something untethered about him. I just stood there, hoping he'd remember that I was Murdock's buddy. Java liked Murdock.

He studied me for a moment, his pupils like two black dots, and then ambled back to his drink. Judy T. came over and took my hand. It felt like that encounter at the basketball game, so many years before. Only this time I had stood my ground—a little.

Soon, Judy T. was spinning westward, headed for a gig in Iowa. We had a short conversation about going there together.

Over the previous months, Judy T. and I had argued everywhere except the bedroom, which crackled like an electromagnetic field whenever we entered. But I couldn't see myself living in a cornfield, and I doubt she really wanted me to go.

*

I'd quit playing over-the-hill soccer, focusing on the popular sport of making money. For every deal, several went nowhere, and as a result, I drove a leased sedan, and floated a large note on a condo in a middling section of town. I dated a succession of waitresses and bank tellers, ate out five nights a week, and started drinking gin and tonic. After seven years of marriage, Jeff and Sharon divorced, mainly because he wanted to have kids and she didn't. Murdock and his dog Bruno moved into the attic bedroom in the old fire station that housed Engine 7. Sharon came by twice a week to take Bruno for a walk. Murdock said that Sharon was the ex-wife he'd always dreamed about.

Murdock usually worked New Year's Eve, giving one of the younger guys the night off. I'd buy a pizza, and we'd watch the Three Stooges Marathon on a little TV he had up there, with Bruno sleeping on the rug at my feet. At midnight, Jeff and I watched the ball drop in Times Square and then I'd go home. Descending from the attic with Engine 7 gleaming in the light from the street,

I'd have the strangest feeling, like I was a ghost passing through a different life, something I'd grasped at and missed.

On my fortieth birthday, I met Turf Walton for dinner at the 99. He was a captain in the Special Investigations Unit, maybe half a dozen years from retirement. The subject of Java was raised, and Turf said they'd gone over a particular landfill in Everett with cadaver-sniffing dogs, but never found that dead bookie. It was now a seven-year-old case, as cold as that bookie, and represented the nadir of Java's career. More recently, he'd broken into a butcher shop after midnight, grabbing a few bucks from the register and absconding with three hundred pounds of meat. He loaded the T-bones into his car, and spent the night trying to sell them, lowering his price to a dollar apiece as the steaks thawed out. Lawrence police found him sleeping in his car the next morning. When they saw all the blood on the floor, they drew their guns, fearing the worst. Java woke up and said, "Anybody want a steak?"

Kenny Dussault went back to the Farm, and Carter returned to normal. That spring, I was trying to pull off the biggest deal I'd ever attempted. At length, I convinced the federal government to buy a parcel of land near Logan Airport, and then lease it to the Mass. Redevelopment Authority for a dollar a year. Also, the feds agreed to build a transportation hub for the city, which would eventually comprise a great number of plot plans and architectural drawings, but ended up being a vast parking lot choked with weeds.

With my share of the filthy lucre, I bought a little place on Carter Pond. From my deck, I'd gaze across at a shuttered cottage, now obscured by hedges and tall grass, where Jeff and Sharon Murdock had been happy for six years and nine months of their seven years together.

One July afternoon, with a light wind rustling the trees, I was talking on my cellphone to the CEO of a bank in Madrid, when I heard my landline ringing inside the house. Señor Uribe said they wanted to locate the bank's North American headquarters in Boston, so I let the other phone go unanswered, echoing over the glassy pond until it finally stopped ringing.

A minute later, the house phone started up again. I offered my services to the bank, Señor Uribe accepted, and we hung up. But the other phone went silent just as I opened the screen door. I poured some Beefeater's into a glass and splashed tonic water over it. Land one good deal, and suddenly you're a rainmaker.

Carter Pond glowed with a queer phosphorescence from the absorbed light of the day. The ripe smell of the pond brought on daydreams of old Spanish money, and no sooner had I regained

Jay Atkinson

my chair than the landline rang again. Too happy to get annoyed, I drank some of the cold, bittersweet gin and jerked open the slider.

"Hey," said Turf, when I picked up the phone. "Jeff was in a motorcycle accident."

My lips moved, but nothing came out. "On route ninety-seven," Turf said. "He's dead."

It appeared that neither speed nor alcohol was a factor, and that an oncoming car, or an animal darting from the woods, had forced Murdock off the road and into a tree, killing him instantly. There wasn't even a scratch on his Harley.

"Sorry, man," Turf said. "I'll call you later."

Slinging the receiver, I was back on the deck before I noticed the gin in my hand. I drained the glass, but it tasted like kerosene. Just like that, Murdock was gone.

*

At Racicot's Funeral Home, the line for Murdock's wake stretched for a block, extending into a residential neighborhood. It was hot as a blast furnace, with hundreds of mourners in a long, shuffling row, perspiring in their black suits and dresses. I joined the queue after going into Boston for a meeting, adopting that peculiar habit of not being inconvenienced by someone else's death, even a close friend like Jeff.

In the line were roofers in their work clothes, professional women in smartly-cut suits, dental hygienists, hulking dudes in leather vests, and a small army of hair dressers, waitresses, bartenders, plumbers, and bookies, each of them silently testifying to Murdock's easy-going nature and the quality of the short life he had lived.

When I approached the white-pillared mansion, I saw Turf among a group of state troopers. Raising his eyes, he broke off, coming toward me in his shiny boots and stiff-brimmed hat. Our handshake turned into a hug, and it occurred to me that the last time I'd embraced him was on the soccer field twenty-three years earlier.

"It's bad," said Turf.

At that moment, Sharon Murdock exited Racicot's, wearing a black dress and the wisp of a veil, her face streaked with mascara. She hurried toward her car, with one of Racicot's flunkies trailing behind. The man wore a discomfited expression, caught as he was between the obsequiousness of a funeral director, and a pique related to whatever had occurred inside.

"It's reality, Ms. Murdock," said the undertaker.

"It's bullshit," said Sharon, who slammed herself into a little sports car, jerked it backwards, and sped away. A Lawrence firefighter came over. Apparently, when Sharon reached the coffin, she said, "Jeff, are you fuckin' kidding me with this?"

"My sentiments, exactly," Turf said.

*

Murdock was buried at St. Charles Borromeo Church. St. Chuck's, as we called it, was a massive cathedral with stained glass windows. Turf and I sat in the back, sweating in our jackets and ties. It was hot as hell that week. When the coffin was rolled down the aisle, a dirigible of incense floated along behind; and I was reminded of Carter High's one-hundred point game, young Murdock and I running through the cloud of rosin dust onto the court.

The cardinal, the pastor, and a deacon said the Mass; the first twenty pews were a solid blue wall of firefighters; and a bagpiper marched in to the skirl of "Amazing Grace," followed by the deputy chief, carrying Murdock's helmet emblazoned with #7. After communion, six firefighters hauled Murdock down the granite stairs, then placed his coffin on the bed of Engine 7, parked at the curb.

Two limousines were behind the fire truck, buffed to a glossy sheen and occupied by family members and colleagues. Engine 7, radiant in the sun, had been polished so diligently that the entire scene—from the trio of clergymen, resplendent in their vestments, to the floral arrangements lining the sidewalk—was reflected along its length, the figures and shapes miniaturized in the shiny chrome fittings of the truck.

Turf and I stood at the top of the stairs. As the bagpiper segued into "The Wild Colonial Boy", the lights on the fire truck began to revolve. Then the funeral cortege, all of a piece, inched out from the curb, with thirty or forty cars parked down that side of the street, each topped with a small flag marked "funeral."

The bagpiping stirred in my chest, but it felt like something was missing—something that hadn't been communicated through the bishop's sermon.

From beside St. Chuck's came a guttural sound, erupting in a roar that drowned out the bagpiper. Just ahead of Engine 7, which was creeping along South Broadway, a black Harley Davidson, coughing and snarling like a beast, pulled out from the alleyway, establishing itself in front of the cortege. Atop the motorcycle, revving its engine, was a black-eyed, bushy-whiskered man, riding bare-chested in a leather vest with MASSACHUSETTS rockered along the bottom. With his Nazi helmet and straggly gray hair, he resembled some accursed Rider of the Apocalypse, a defiant emissary from the lower regions of hell.

Jay Atkinson

"Apparently, Java's out of the can," Turf said.

Now in his mid-fifties, large-limbed, and broad across the chest, Java led the odd-looking cavalcade down South Broadway. His face was ridged and buffeted like an old coin, his sunglasses reflecting the mourners that fanned over the sidewalk. Past the bodegas and check cashing places, Java continued on, keeping a thirty-foot interval between his bike and Engine 7. Two cops stood at every intersection, preventing motorists from cutting into the procession, but nobody made an effort to stop Java, or direct him to the curb. It was like *fuck you* to the whole rotten deal, and knowing Murdock the way I did, seemed exactly right.

*

It starts as a trickle: a close friend killed in an accident; a co-worker struck down by cancer; you lose your grandparents; an uncle; a favorite teacher dies. Then it becomes a deluge. Your parents are gone; another childhood friend; even people younger than you; and soon you've entered a fast moving current of wakes and funerals and boozy dinners, saying goodbye to your auto mechanic, a neighbor's son, your accountant, and a workout fanatic from the gym, until it seems like you've buried a third of the people you know. At least, you've said good-bye to a lot of folks you knew twenty years ago, replacing them with a new gym buddy, accountant, neighbor, and mechanic. You wake up one day and you have a crippling mortgage, a dozen extra pounds, and a pair of cheaters from CVS so you can read a newspaper, if you can find one.

I hadn't started power-walking around the local mall, but I could see it on the horizon. Turf retired, and moved to Virginia. He planned to hike the Appalachian Trail with his son and take up fly-fishing. That September, I sold the land for Banco España's tower, closed up my place on Carter Pond, and leased an apartment in Boston's Seaport District. At night I'd pour myself some bourbon, gazing out toward Peddock's Island, where Italian prisoners were held during WWII. When Italy surrendered, the POWs were allowed trips into Boston. Many of them stayed, raising children, starting businesses. They got respectable.

Occasionally, I'd get together with Fillion. Once we attended Carter High's annual football game vs. Shawsheen. It was Thanksgiving, with the assembled fans in a convivial mood, and the Hornets losing 17-12 in the fourth quarter. Bundled in our down jackets, we passed around a flask, the bourbon enlivening our spirits. Carter recovered a fumble, and as the crowd erupted, I glanced down at the field. The bulwark of the stadium dropped twenty feet to the grass below, with the only entrance beside the grandstand, where two cops kept people from getting onto the field. Besides the players and coaches, the only person down there was the mayor, Tommy Burress. He stood at the twenty-yard line, talking to the referee. Burress was a slender, middle-sized fellow, in a gray topcoat and herringbone scarf. Occasionally, I'd notice him shaking hands with a player, or laughing with one of the cops.

Beside the mayor was a shabby-looking man in a dirty raincoat, shouting garbled instructions to the Carter offense. How Java got onto the field was anybody's guess. I reached for the flask and took a snort, laughing at the idea of Tommy Burress chatting with a suspected murderer. Perhaps in the time I'd been absent, Java had become respectable—his tenure as a local institution had somehow eclipsed his notoriety. It was like finding out that he'd become an astronaut. "If only Murdock could see this," I said.

"I'm seeing it, and I still can't believe it," said Fillion, handing back the flask.

When I visited Carter Pond, I'd stare across at Jeff's bungalow, which Sharon had long since moved away from, but never sold. Half hidden by the rhododendrons, Murdock's small, solitary house was a reminder that things hadn't worked out. My success had come too late, and the idea of being neighbors on the pond and raising our families together would never come to pass.

That spring, I became reacquainted with an old college

friend named Marjorie Malkin. A former varsity swimmer, Marjorie was a lanky, dark-haired orthodontist with two teenage daughters. We had lunch, and began dating. Still competing at the master's level, Marjorie bought a house on Sebago Lake, just a few miles from St. Trinian's pool. She had an appealing, girlish quality, and we'd sit in her kitchen laughing at our youthful antics, trying not to wake up her girls. We grew close, and Marjorie asked if I'd like to move in with her. She had plans to remodel her kitchen, and needed a cutthroat negotiator to deal with those Maine sharpies.

A month later, I sold my place on Carter Pond. Pulling a trailer with my belongings, I dropped off the keys to the buyer's attorney. It was Sunday morning, and I passed by St. Chuck's as the bells started ringing. At the top of the hill, some kind of ruckus was causing the traffic to back up. Motorists were craning their necks, wondering what all the fuss was about.

An old, rusted Buick was sprawled across the intersection, the driver's side door thrust open. The car was unoccupied, and a chorus of horns erupted from the vehicles log-jammed around it. The other drivers were trying to ignore the stout, gray-haired man, stumping along on a bad leg, who'd emerged from the Buick and was demanding money from horrified churchgoers.

It was Java. His car had run out of gas, and with the sole flapping on his boot, he stumbled from one car to the next, lurching past my fender. Briefly, Java's wild, frightened gaze met mine, and then he disappeared into the welter of gleaming fenders, shifting vehicles, and well-dressed pedestrians. The light turned green, and I made a careful maneuver around the Buick, dragging the trailer uphill toward the interstate.

It struck me that, all along, Kenny Dussault had been a kind of performer, and finally, he was putting on a show that nobody wanted to see. The trickle of untimely departures had turned into a raging torrent, and it seemed clear that Java was soon going to join what was commonly known as the "vast majority."

Ellie's Diamonds

Rugby practice ended for the year when Jeff Rivas tackled McNulty along the sideline, both of them crashing through the flimsy hurricane fence that bordered the field. Coach Van Valkenburg blew his whistle in the gloom, calling out "Let's go have a drink, boys," and the rest of the players, many of whom were on the other side of the park, gathered up their kit bags and were walking toward the cars. Thom McNulty was busy untangling himself from the plastic mesh of the fence and Rivas, steam rising from his jersey, reached down and offered him a hand.

"Congratulations, Thom," said Rivas, pulling the other man to his feet. "I just heard about you and Simone."

McNulty didn't answer; he had failed to keep the ball in the field of play, and now his shoulder hurt. Only a couple of guys knew that McNulty's girlfriend, Simone Allenby, was pregnant and that he was going to marry her—probably on Christmas Eve, which was less than six weeks away. He wasn't a close friend of Jeff Rivas, but liked him well enough; Jeff was a quiet, hard-working fellow, a medical student from a well-known Manchester family, and very solid at fullback for the club. Rivas had a twin brother, Jonathan, who had also played for a couple years—he was very fast—but had dropped off the previous fall. Jeff's tackle had been a hard one and McNulty got up rubbing his left shoulder, which was burning under the cap.

Beyond them, the New Hampshire Juvenile Detention Center, where the Manchester Rugby Club held its twice-weekly practices, was illuminated by massive klieg lights. The six-story, pebbledash main building, built in the 1880s, loomed up amidst the purplish shadows of a November twilight. Separated from the rugby pitch by a withered cornfield, the JDC was demarcated by twelve-foot fences and girdled on three sides by the cold black ribbon of the Merrimack River. The rugby club had access to the JDC athletic fields because the team's starting eight-man, Dan O'Riordan, taught phys. ed. there. Additionally, a rugby player or two considered themselves "alumni" of the facility, which housed approximately three hundred boys who had been convicted of various crimes in New Hampshire.

McNulty and Jeff Rivas picked up the traffic cones on the far side of the pitch along with a stray tackling dummy, carrying them to the parking lot. Their cars were beside each other and they stood in the feeble light from McNulty's trunk, changing out of their soiled jerseys and cleats. The other players were departing the gravel lot with toots of their horns or stiff-handed waves, heading for a few pints at the Irish Rover. At eight PM on the dot, Coach Van Valkenburg sped off in his little sports car like the devil was after him.

In stocking feet, Jeff Rivas was a mid-sized, trimly built fellow, with short dark hair, a smooth brow, and an aquiline nose. He drove a Jeep, and with the tailgate folded down, he made a bench to sit on and waved McNulty over.

"I need to get Simone a ring," said McNulty, stripping off his socks and jersey and toweling himself down. "I bought a setting, but the stones are fucking ridiculous."

Rivas had a six-pack of beer in the Jeep and handed McNulty one of the cans. "Call the house and talk to Ellie," he said, popping open a beer. "She just got a shipment in."

Ellie was Jeff's mother, Ellie Rivas, formerly Ellie El-Khoury, a brisk, dark-haired woman who had emigrated to the U.S. from her native Lebanon as a young girl. Michael Rivas, Jeff's father, who was known as "Big Mike"—though rarely called that to his face—was a successful real estate developer and political insider. He had turned the moribund local airport into a major transportation hub, acquiring the Republican governor, New Hampshire's senators, and a handful of congressmen as supporters and friends along the way. Mike Rivas also built Manchester's minor league baseball stadium, two hotels, and a vast new shopping mall on South Willow Street, which was under construction. Now that her children were grown, Ellie worked as a part-time diamond merchant, a business her grandfather had started in Lebanon.

Ten years earlier, when Thom McNulty was a senior at Manchester West High School and Jeff and Jonathan Rivas were sophomores, they had played varsity football and hockey together. Two years is a big gap at that age, and McNulty and the twins ran with different crowds. But Ellie Rivas hosted frequent dinners for her sons' teammates, and McNulty had been to their home several times. Even back then, Jeff' and Jonathan's mother insisted that the other boys call her Ellie.

"Ellie would love to see you," Jeff said. "She's making

appointments for Tuesday and Thursday afternoons. My dad's been under the weather, and that's all she has time for right now."

"She sees people at the house?" asked Thom, setting his beer on the ground. Shivering in the cold, he pulled on a hoodie with *Manchester Rugby* printed across the front.

Rivas nodded. "She's got some nice stones right now. And Ellie'll give you a deal 'cause she knows you."

"Sounds good," McNulty said.

Jeff threw the empty beer cans and his boots into the Jeep and slammed the tailgate. "Ellie's got a small clientele," he said. "It's more of a hobby than anything."

"Doesn't she worry about getting ripped off?" asked Thom.

Rivas laughed. "My father's home a lot," he said. "That's all the protection she needs."

Jeff Rivas was a surgical resident at Catholic Medical Center, after graduating summa cum laude from Dartmouth College and enrolling in medical school there. His father ate lunch once a month in the governor's mansion, and played golf with Senator Radcliffe at Winged Foot and places like that. Well versed in the building trades, Big Mike knew the other kind of heavy hitters too, guys from East Boston and New York who wore loud sport jackets and lots of gold jewelry. No doubt Ellie sold them diamonds for their wives, girlfriends, and pinkie fingers.

"Meet you at the Rover?" asked McNulty, stepping into his car. "I'm buying."

Rivas shook his head. "I'm going to my parents," he said. "Then over to the hospital for my shift."

Swinging his door shut, McNulty snapped the seatbelt into place—wincing as it crossed his bum shoulder—and steered his fifteen-year-old MG over the gravel. He passed along the semi-circular drive, the JDC buildings rising above the little car, and then straightened the wheel and went zooming down the access road.

Simone's pregnancy and his impending marriage soon overtook the surge of endorphins that brightened his mood after rugby practice. That, and his left shoulder was beginning to hurt like hell. At one hundred seventy-five pounds, the club's starting outside center was thick across the chest and sturdy on his feet, of average height, with light brown hair and blue eyes. As best he could in such a tight space, McNulty rotated his arm in its socket and flexed his fingers. He hadn't broken any bones, or torn anything as far as he could tell, but something wasn't right—in both the specific and general sense. He loved Simone and had planned on marrying her someday. Just not so soon.

Past the large Colonials with their massive oak trees and brownish lawns, McNulty flew along a darkened stretch of River Road toward the city. The greatest thing about "Manch Vegas," a former industrial city of one hundred thousand people straddling the Merrimack River, was that you could live a mile from downtown and be in the middle of the woods. There was plenty to do in the city—a dozen good bars, restaurants, art galleries, and minor league hockey and baseball franchises, all surrounded by gigantic old mill buildings. Ten minutes from downtown you could fish in the river, or go mountain biking or cross country skiing over the hilly local terrain. McNulty had attended the University of New Hampshire over in Durham, earning a business degree, but he'd never really wanted to live anywhere else.

The streetlights grew brighter as River Road flowed into Elm Street, the main downtown thoroughfare. After Marion's Superette, the Citgo, and David Daniel's Tavern, Thom passed his office, Pro-Max Realty, a storefront that had been a dentist's office when he and his sister Pegeen and their mother had an apartment on Manchester's west side. Pegeen, two years older, was married and living in Scottsdale, Arizona, now. Thom's mother, Rosalyn, had just moved into an elderly housing complex in Londonderry after turning seventy. He didn't know where his father was. McNulty hadn't seen him in ten years.

Thomas McNulty was a "junior," but had dropped that from his name when he first registered at UNH and hadn't used it since. He was too small for college football, so he'd taken up rugby at UNH and found that the game suited him and continued playing after college. A dozen games in the fall, and half of that in the spring, with a full schedule of club social events spread across the calendar—golf scrambles, pond hockey games, team outings to the Red Sox and Bruins, as well as bachelor parties, weddings, and the Christmas Cotillion, held at the Irish Rover on December 23rd.

Business connections were easy to come by among members of the club, and Thom had made a soft landing at Pro-Max a year earlier, when he quit his job selling boats over in Portsmouth. Pro-Max was owned by Bill Hodges, a rugby club "old boy" in his late forties who sported a walrus mustache and drank bourbon from a tooled silver flask. Hodgie was divorced and his kids were grown; he was a fixture along the sidelines and at the bar in the Irish Rover, where late in the evening he would sing ballads of romance and rebellion, harmonizing, after a fashion, with Coach Van Valkenburg and whichever hard luck Romeos cared to join him.

The Rover was located on Kosciusko Street, in what had once been a cobbler's shop. It was a small, cedar-shingled cottage, nestled between a pair of office buildings. Inside, the pub was twice as long as it was wide, with tin ceilings, the wooden floor dented with cleat marks, and a U-shaped bar with a half-wall running down the middle. Contained therein was a portal offering a view from one side of the bar to the other, where the cobbler would hand the repaired pumps and brogans back to his clientele.

Lucky finding a parking spot, Thom McNulty came through the pub door and greeted the bouncer, Dickie Tardugno, the former Manchester Rugby Club stalwart who had also played football at Holy Cross, way back in the 1960s. There was no mistaking Dickie—his tattered denim jacket, steel-toe boots, and most of all, his half-friendly, half-menacing air proclaimed who he was.

"McNulty, you are the world's biggest pussy," said Dickie, grabbing Thom by his bad shoulder as he greeted him, causing the smaller man to blanch.

"*Oww*, thanks for that," McNulty said, gasping as he made his way to the bar. Tardugno's hands were as large as baseball mitts.

The Rover smelled of spilled Guinness and sweat. Some of the younger guys, including Maloney, who was a Manchester fire fighter, still wearing their jerseys and cleats, were leaning over the jukebox and debating the song list—an old Johnny Cash tune, recorded live at Folsom Prison, was playing at the moment. Coach Van Valkenburg was seated beside the team's eight-man, Dan O'Riordan, who stood with his beer cradled against his chest, nodding at something the coach had said. A couple of waitresses in halter-tops were high-handing trays of beer among the dozen or so tables along the perimeter. At that moment, Van Valkenburg paused to take a phone call, and McNulty signaled to Jack, the bartender, that he wanted a pint of Guinness.

"Old Red is begging off the match this weekend," said O'Riordan as Thom came up, referring to their game in Connecticut on Saturday. "Coach is trying to fix it."

McNulty grabbed some peanuts from a bowl at O'Riordan's elbow. "Why are they doing that?" he asked.

"Because they are a bunch of cowards, I guess," said O'Riordan.

O'Riordan was six feet, five inches tall, with a head of curly blond hair and a loud and boisterous laugh—a happy-go-lucky, outgoing, cheerful sort of fellow, thirty-four years old, who would tell you a joke and buy you a beer long before you could get your hands out of your pockets.

"It doesn't matter to me, either way," said O'Riordan. "I can start drinking three hours earlier if we don't play."

Van Valkenburg held up his hand, trying to get everyone to shut up so he could hear what Old Red's match secretary was saying. Jerry Van Valkenburg was a stocky, pop-eyed South African with a large mustache and a round, close-cropped head. His face grew crimson as he listened to the reason that Connecticut Old Red were not going to visit Manchester on Saturday morning. Finally, the old prop forward couldn't restrain himself any longer.

"Listen, mate, that's a scheduled league match, and if you don't live up to your commitment, you can bloody well be sure I'll file a disciplinary complaint with NERFU on Monday morning. Your sorry excuse for a rugby club will be relegated to the second division by the disciplinary committee, and put on probation with the bloody referee's society. Not to mention that I'll come down there myself and stick my foot so far up your arse you'll have to open your mouth so I can change my boots, you bloody wanker."

There was another soliloquy delivered by the opposing match secretary, and then Van Valkenburg finished the conversation by saying, "You bloody well better call me back, and with a bloody solution, or I'll break a pint glass over your knobby little head, you bloody wanker."

Van Valkenburg slammed the phone onto the bar top. "In all my years in bloody rugby, I've never heard a club begging off a league match on a Thursday before the Saturday," he said. "One of their three-quarters is getting married Saturday—during the *rugby season*. What sort of nonsense is that? Bloody hell."

Jack the bartender sidled up and put McNulty's pint on the bar. As Thom hoisted it, O'Riordan winked at him, draining half his Guinness in the same gesture. "The nerve of those guys," O'Riordan said.

Before Van Valkenburg could draw another breath, his cell phone played a few bars of "That's The Way (I Like It)" and he picked it up. Listening with a crease in his brow, the coach said, "Not bloody likely, mate, but I'll ring you back."

The young guys standing by the jukebox had migrated over to the coach, and word was spreading through the Rover that the final match of the season was in jeopardy. Rugby players of various sizes and levels of ability, who comprised just over half the patrons queuing up at the bar, converged on Van Valkenburg.

"They won't come to us," the coach said. "These idiots are saying we can drive down there, and they'll play us in a social match on Sunday. They'll forfeit the league match."

As a deliberative body, a rugby club left a considerable amount to be desired. Voices rose and fell on the tide of opinion, and even Dickie Tardugno, who hadn't played so much as an Old Boys' fixture in years, walked over to say that a rugby match was a rugby match, "social" or not, and that the club should go to them, if only to show those "Nutmeg State assholes" how it was done.

Tardugno's grizzled face hovered over the bar as he leaned on McNulty's bad shoulder, and said, "For the pride of the game, gentlemen, for the reputation of the club, and for the pure joy of knocking their dicks in the dirt."

The pressure on McNulty's shoulder sent a bolt of lightning down into his chest. He'd already ruled himself out of the match and was glad the season was over, though it was a desultory one, with their record at 5-6. McNulty pictured the interior of his body as a cool, dark place but right now, the cap of his shoulder was filled with white-hot light that went stabbing around with every movement he made.

McNulty finished his pint amidst the clamor of the bar and took a few steps to his left, melting into the hurly-burly of rugby players crowding around for one of Jack's pours. It was a homage to the "Rolla fade." Dave Rolla was a guy from Chicago who had played for Manchester for several years. After practices and matches, it could be difficult to extricate oneself from the tribal bonds of the club once the liquor began to flow. Goodbyes turned into bear hugs, and even more heartfelt farewells and several more drinks, until a player's attempted exit became a dizzying circuit around the Rover that terminated where it began, in a further hail of back pats and tender profanities and another round of foam-topped Guinness.

A strong, wiry fellow, Rolla once told McNulty that, when he determined it was time to leave, he opted out of conversations, flowing along the shipping lanes of the Rover toward whichever means of egress presented itself. One night, Rolla dropped down through the trap door at the end of the bar, crawled over the kegs of Guinness that filled the dank cellar, and climbed out of a window. He was the master.

Somewhere, a couple of years back, Rolla had faded out of the Irish Rover for good, taking Zelda, a pretty, raven-haired barmaid, along with him. They lived in Wilton now, with a dog named Scrum and two dark-haired little girls. McNulty's girlfriend, Simone, had also worked behind the bar at the Rover; she was a sultry, green-eyed beauty from the West Island of Montreal, classically trained in ballet, with an erect carriage and a smooth, graceful way about her. She wore her shiny blond hair just below her shoulders and talked in a melodious, French-accented English that made the hair stand up on Thom McNulty's arms the night they met. They'd been dating for six months, and Simone's pregnancy had been accidental.

McNulty was about to exit the bar, his hands thrust into the kangaroo pouch of his sweatshirt. "Summer Wind" was playing on the jukebox—it was O'Riordan's choice, who loved Sinatra and Johnny Mercer, all the old stuff—and the noise level had risen since he had first come in. Coeds were piling into the bar from St. Anselm's and the rugby players waded into this sweet-smelling herd armed only with their wits, a weapon that varied in its size and accuracy, depending on the player.

Just as he stepped out the door, McNulty felt a gigantic paw clamp down on his shoulder. "*Fuck*, Dickie," he said, wriggling away. "Why do you keep doing that?"

The old second row fixed his gaze on McNulty, the fiery dots of his eyes lost in their deep sockets. "Take care of Simone," he said. "I like her."

McNulty stared back. "So do I, Dickie," he said. "Don't worry."

"Simone's a good girl," said Tardugno. Hands on his hips,

he rocked back and sighted on the moon, a white disc riding over the Manchester skyline. "What you do out of rugby depends on what you did *in* rugby. You need the same sort of courage—to always go forward. Know what I mean?"

"Yeah, Dickie," said Thom. "I do."

Thom made way for a passel of St. Anselm's girls and went along the sidewalk, his sneakers quiet on the pavement. Stars were glittering above New Hampshire Bank, and the wind had come up.

Starting the MG, Thom shifted into gear, the cobblestones making a racket beneath his tires. Traffic was light going south on Elm Street, through the collection of ten- and fifteen-story buildings that marked the downtown. McNulty drove past an old mill building that housed a discount furniture store. A few miles beyond that, near the vast acreage where Rivas Development Corporation was building the largest mall in the state, McNulty pulled up beside an abandoned two-family house and set the hand brake on the MG.

In the eleven months he'd been working at Pro-Max Realty, Thom had eschewed the residential listings that the other brokers depended on. After giving Hodgie a percentage of whatever he brought in, his end was usually a couple grand on the sale of a single family house. As the recession worsened and home pric-es in New Hampshire continued to falter, McNulty decided this aspect of the business was a rat race he didn't want to run in. He wasn't going to waste his time with some dipshit who wanted to see a million dollar home he had no intention of buying. Nor did he want to spend his golden years fighting over the pennies in a condominium sale. He'd seen that happen in the office.

McNulty read three or four daily newspapers, as well as every real estate newsletter, blog, and website that covered New Hampshire from the Massachusetts line to the Lakes region. He was always on the lookout for a particular sort of transaction, and for financing and development trends, while at the same time keeping a close eye on a handful of big players, including Mike Rivas. A few weeks earlier, when Rivas began construction near the intersection of South Willow and Route 293, McNulty made an offer on the vacant property across the street from the Granite State Mall site. For better or worse, McNulty was in the game.

As a rule, it wasn't easy to figure out what Mike Rivas was doing; he used a quartet of nondescript corporations to ma-neuver around zoning objections, water and sewer regulations, and other developers interested in the parcel, closing the deal be-fore most people knew it was Rivas's project. Six months earlier, while scrolling through a business blog on the *Derry News* website, McNulty found a post about a traffic study intended to measure the capacity of the intersection of Route 293 and South Willow. The name of the company paying for the study was El-Khoury Associates, Inc. of Manchester. That was Ellie Rivas's maiden name.

There were two aspects to McNulty's plan. After his offer was accepted in principle on the abandoned house, he took a lease option on the adjoining spare lot, an overgrown half-acre owned by the city. If the bank loan worked out, and the city would grant a reasonably priced lease for, say, ten years, Thom intended to knock down the old house and develop the site, leasing the land beneath five or six businesses. The location was perfect for this sort of operation—the gas station, Dunkin' Donuts, etc. would pick up customers coming and going from the huge mall across the street.

The other thing that could happen was that Mike Rivas, seeing the logic of the idea, could buy the entire parcel from McNulty, including the leasing rights, and develop it himself. In some ways, that scenario was the more attractive one—Thom would walk away with a substantial profit, minus the headache of securing additional financing for the site prep, and the hassle of arranging and managing the sub-leases. He could use that windfall to break away from Pro-Max and get into something bigger that he had his eye on, across the river in Bedford. But it all hinged on controlling the site, joining both parcels, and re-zoning them before someone else figured out his plan and topped the offer.

Thom had only middling credit, too, because of a semi-delinquent student loan; and he figured he'd have trouble getting a low mortgage rate on the bank-owned property. He'd already used two-thirds of the $15,000 he'd saved before the economy collapsed, to offer surety to the bank on the house and lot. He hadn't told Simone that he'd risked their nest egg, but was pretty sure things were going to work out. If the terms on the loan were acceptable, he'd have to tear the house down and pay a civil engineer to complete the site preparation; thankfully, engineers and plumbers and electricians were common on the rugby club, along with lawyers and surveyors and bankers. They were his trump cards.

In the light from the streetlamp, McNulty stood before the old house, its gabled peak and broken windows rising above him. As soon as 2056 South Willow Street had appeared on the bank's list of distressed properties, he'd arranged for a construction bond and made his offer. That same day, he filed for an improvement lease on the adjacent parcel of land.

Of course, Mike Rivas could step all over this plan whenever he wanted. Topping McNulty's offer on the house by ten grand could've been managed without a dent in the Rivas fortune, and one call to City Hall meant his lease bid was dead. Certainly, one of the brokers in Rivas's employ had already informed his boss that Thom McNulty had made an offer on the house, and just as surely, a mole in the assessor's office had called Rivas Development Corporation to inform them of Thom's lease application. McNulty was gambling that it was too unimportant to trouble Mike Rivas, or that he recognized the name and would allow his sons' rugby pal to snatch a few crumbs from the table. He'd soon find out.

Thom got back in the MG, and pushed off toward the lights of the highway. For nearly a half mile, the Granite State Mall ran alongside South Willow—a huge, darkened plain broken by mounds of dirt, piles of cinder blocks, and the silhouette of cranes and other gigantic earth movers. It was thrilling to look at, like the site prep for the pyramids at Giza; the type of project he'd always dreamed of undertaking.

Of course, McNulty's plan had been complicated by Simone's pregnancy—she was at twelve weeks, although neither of

them had known that until recently—and the cost of his wedding.
In the time he'd been employed at Pro-Max, Thom had pulled off
a handful of small deals to cover his overhead and living expenses, earning enough commission to leave his savings untouched
until now. Hodgie said he was a natural for that kind of work—the
sort of technical know-how, persistence, and charm it took to put
together deals between corporations—and that McNulty should
focus on that. But as long as Thom paid for his desk, didn't get
arrested, and joined in a few spirited choruses of "Black Velvet
Band" at the Rover, Hodgie let him do as he pleased. The old
prop forward didn't ask many questions, and everything had gone
smoothly to this point.

McNulty breezed along the stretch of Route 293 that
crossed the river, turning at the Bedford exit. Since they had found
out about the pregnancy, McNulty had been bunking at Simone's
apartment at Tauvernier Green. Her roommate had moved out in
October, and Thom had arranged to sublet his tiny apartment to
one of the guys on the rugby club. Simone quit working at the
Rover, and was teaching dance to eight- and nine-year old girls
over in Londonderry. It made sense to begin living together.

Soon there would be a new set of responsibilities and the
bills that came with that, but McNulty had more immediate con-

Jay Atkinson

cerns. He was tired and hungry and his shoulder hurt like hell. All he wanted was a shower, a piece of Simone's quiche, and the chance to lie down beside his girl in their king-size bed.

*

The door knock resounded within the interior of the house and, it seemed, the pit of Thom McNulty's stomach. He was standing just inside the gate that separated the Rivas's yard from the street. Rising above him was the stone edifice of the house, with its black shutters and window boxes and a lacquered front door, also black. Although the house was only a dozen blocks from the Irish Rover on Union Street, Thom hadn't visited the Rivas house in more than a decade.

Before the echo died away, the door swung open and Ellie Rivas was there, a petite, black-haired woman with lively dark eyes, her figure bracketed by two stone planters that held bunches of dried pink and yellow roses.

"A prospective customer and a handsome one, at that," Ellie said, extending her fine-boned hand. She smiled with her eyes. "Come in, Thom."

The foyer opened to a gallery on the second floor, which was draped in shadow. The main floor was quiet, except for the ticking of a grandfather clock that stood in the corner. The wainscoting, which smelled of oil soap, was illuminated by a row of windows somewhere beyond the gallery. There was also the smell of Lebanese cooking, the zaatar and turmeric and allspice that McNulty recalled from his youthful visits to the house. Somewhere out back, a piano concerto was playing on the stereo.

Ellie Rivas had perfect teeth, and her skin, the color of the wainscoting, was flawless except for the intricate lines that appeared beside her eyes when she smiled. "Jeffrey told me the news," said Ellie, leading him into the dining room. "We're very happy for you, Thom. Jeffrey says she's a wonderful girl."

"Thanks, Ellie," Thom said. "Simone is…"

There was a note of regret in his voice that McNulty hadn't intended, and as he trailed off, Ellie reached over and touched his arm. Thom's shoulder had gotten worse since he'd first injured it. He couldn't raise his elbow to his ear, and was limited to washing his hair with one hand. By instinct, he flinched at Ellie's touch.

"Sit for a minute," she said, directing him to a chair. Above them was an oil painting of two shepherd boys atop a hill, watching their flock of sheep descend toward a campfire burning in the distance.

Ellie's eyes were like pools of black ink. "It's not easy to start a family," she said. "I don't know much about your people,

Thom, but I came to this country with nothing but the clothes on my back. Same for Mr. Rivas—nothing." Ellie patted his hand. "In business, you start with nothing and then you build something together," she said. "It's the same as starting a family."

The windows were draped in burgundy damask that hung to the floor. Low winter light was coming in, advancing over the dining room table in an even plane, and glancing that way, McNulty caught the hardness of the merchant appearing for an instant within Ellie's gaze.

"Let's go look at some diamonds," she said, getting up from her chair.

Together she and Thom moved over to the table. McNulty was surprised to see a pile of loose gemstones lying on the table-cloth. There were enough to cover the bottom of a child's beach pail—octagonal stones, hexagons, squares, and rectangles; several with a number of tiny facets shaved into their glassy surface, and others so round and milky they looked like pearls. They were hazy inside, some of them, containing in their smoky vistas the geography of entire worlds only hinted at, while others were so transparent and smooth they magnified the rich thread count of the tablecloth lying beneath them.

There were stones as blue as arctic ice; rose-colored, lavender, and a pale fluorescent yellow; glowing that way in the arc of sunlight migrating across the table, the gemstones somehow holding and possessing the light in a way that seemed to come from inside the diamonds themselves, and not from the sun, still visible through the wavy glass of the window.

They were a marvel to behold, and Thom McNulty was surprised when he stepped back, not toward them, upon seeing the gemstones for the first time.

Ellie laughed. "It's all right. Pick one out for that girl of yours."

Before he'd known about Ellie's diamonds, McNulty had visited a handful of chain stores that peddled an array of huge, overpriced engagement rings. He therefore had a rudimentary knowledge of a stone's cut and weight and carat size; at least, he remembered some of what a clerk had told him. Probably it was bullshit.

"Just poke around and find one you like," said Ellie. "Every stone is first rate, in its own category."

"How do you choose the ones you bring in?" Thom asked.

"I have a partner who travels to Damascus to visit a gem dealer there. They've done business together for many years, and my friend buys a number of diamonds and sends a certain percentage of them to me."

McNulty leaned over the table, scrutinizing the pile of stones from eight or ten inches away. Ellie chose a half dozen stones from the assortment and placed them on a little rubber mat that she took from her pocket. With a gesture, she encouraged Thom to select a few and then handed him a jeweler's loop with which to examine them.

The one that McNulty liked wasn't the largest or the prettiest, though none of them were like the gaudy "bitches' headstones" at Diamond World, the so-called discount chain that occupied just about every shopping mall north of the Carolinas. To casual shoppers, those tacky sparklers shouted *new money!* and *trophy wife!* and *liposuction!,* none of which applied to McNulty, or Simone, for that matter. They were portable monuments to entitlement, arrogance and bad taste, with their inverted pyramid shape, bold facet patterns, and the trademarked "Fire of Happiness" that erupted within the stones when you turned them to the light. Even if McNulty could afford such a stone—some of them twenty thousand dollars "on sale"—Simone wouldn't want one, and God bless her for that.

Steering his finger through the pile of stones, McNulty extracted one that caught his eye. "That happens to be my favorite," said Ellie. "I noticed it when they first came in."

The stone was no greater in size than a small pea. It was not quite spherical, tending slightly to ovoid, and against the white fabric of the tablecloth the interior of the diamond had a peculiar cast to it—a faintly turquoise color. But when McNulty picked it up, turning the small, imperfect diamond to the light, it glowed with a more purplish tint, a kind of chameleon stone that was as small and exquisite as Simone herself. Illuminated from within by patterns of captured light, the stone was unassuming, elemental, and lovely.

McNulty recognized the diamond more than he selected it. This was Simone's engagement ring. "I'll take this one," Thom said, placing it on the mat.

Ellie picked up the stone and examined it through the lens. "It's marvelous," she said. "They are all of good quality, of course, but I don't think I've ever seen one so...how do I say it? So satisfied in being just what it is."

"I think Simone'll like it," said McNulty.

"She'll love it," Ellie said.

Thom removed a velveteen box from his pocket and handed it to Ellie, who snapped it open to inspect the gold setting Thom had purchased for five hundred dollars. In a matter of fact voice

Ellie announced the price of the stone. There was no question of haggling over it; particularly in light of the fact there wasn't another diamond in the collection that interested him, or would suit his fiancée half as much.

Ellie compared the stone and setting, proclaiming them fit for one another, and after deciding on when McNulty could pick up the ring, he peeled five one-hundred dollar bills from a roll in his pocket and handed them to Ellie, that being the deposit they had agreed upon over the phone. From what knowledge he had gleaned foraging through the chain stores, McNulty knew it was a fair price, though not a raving bargain, and besides that, he would rather his hard-earned money go to Ellie Rivas than some corporation headquartered in New Jersey. He was going to buy Simone a ring, either way.

Jeff hadn't mentioned it, but McNulty had understood that it would be a cash transaction. Ellie had a license to sell precious stones; he had seen a placard in the foyer that attested to that. But foremost among the aspects of the Rivas mystique was a reputation for playing a little outside the rules; maybe a few palms got greased in Concord, or an occasional malcontent complained to the *Union-Leader* about getting pushed around, but projects went through, and things got done. Personally, Thom had no qualms about that.

Ellie left the other stones on the table and, leading the way past the dried floral displays, ushered McNulty to the front door. Thom agreed to return the following Tuesday to pay the balance on the diamond and pick up the ring. He planned to give it to Simone that night.

Again Ellie took McNulty's hand in her smooth fingers. "You and Simone will be fine," she said.

For an instant, McNulty noticed someone passing along the gallery above them. He was back lit by a Tiffany lamp, half-glimpsed in silhouette. After the figure passed beyond his line of vision, McNulty detected the odor of cigars and some kind of balm or liniment. It occurred to him it was Mike Rivas; apparently Jeff's father wasn't in the mood for socializing.

Thom said goodbye to Ellie and, closing the door, went along the sidewalk to his car. The other houses of the neighborhood, mostly brick and set close together, were dark and still. Their uppermost windows reflected the late sun, but the withered rosebushes delineating the tiny lots were deep in shadow. Even here, a mile from the river, Thom could smell the water as it rolled toward the Massachusetts border and, finally, the Atlantic Ocean. Cold air pooled at his knees, creeping up the hill as the afternoon

Jay Atkinson

waned. Winter was coming.

*

By instinct, McNulty swung around when he emerged from the bank, tracking the motion of the girl's hips as she crossed Elm Street a block away. It was a bright, cold afternoon, the sky dark blue and cloudless, with dozens of people moving along the sidewalk and a fair amount of traffic passing on the street. Picking up the girl's trim figure amidst the welter of Elm Street wasn't something he had to think about—his eyes just fell on the most desirable woman, and he started after her before he even knew where he was going.

McNulty had just filed for his mortgage on 2056 South Willow, dropping it off in person though he could've done it electronically. He wanted to schmooze the loan officer a little; nothing major, just a pair of tickets to the Manchester Monarchs game on Friday night. Dan O'Riordan had given them to him, and if the tickets helped his cause at the bank, it was worth handing them over. Simone loved hockey and it would've been a cheap night out, but closing the deal was his top priority.

Now, McNulty was heading for his car, while keeping the girl in sight. Passing along the storefronts was a slender young woman in brown yoga pants and a tight-fitting black hoodie, a brown woolen scarf looped around her neck and a pair of designer sunglasses on top of her head. Although Thom saw his fiancée every day, it still came as a surprise when he realized he was following Simone. As he jogged across Elm Street, falling in behind her on the sidewalk, McNulty slackened his pace, congratulating himself on his taste in women.

Not quite good-looking enough to be a ladies' man—the tip of his left ear had been torn off in a rugby game, and his nose was askew—McNulty had navigated the local dating scene, such as it was, by utilizing his offhand charm and gift of persuasion. Getting a coed or secretary into bed was not all that different from closing a deal on a piece of property—attention to detail, a neat appearance, and a knack for conversation. But if scooping up a St. Anselm's girl at the Rover was akin to selling a time share on Loon Mountain, convincing Simone Allenby to go on a date with him was like developing the entire Manchester riverfront, or swinging a deal for the Abenaki to take back Concord.

When Simone first began working at the Rover, he made it a point never to be seen going home with a tipsy bank teller or adventurous divorcee. He had watched Simone's reaction when other rugby players had done that, and it wasn't pretty. In fact, once McNulty had zeroed in on Simone, he always left the bar

Jay Atkinson

early to do his skirt chasing elsewhere, over at the Back Room or the lounge at the Marriott. Watching Maloney and those guys slobber over girls at the bar, and then hit on Simone when they struck out, convinced McNulty to keep a low profile after rugby games.

Near the auto parts store, he caught up to Simone, but remained just outside her peripheral vision. Then he touched her arm. "Buy you a cup of coffee?" he asked.

Simone whirled around like she was going to square off with him. "Thomas Michael McNulty! I am going to kill you," she said, her blue-green eyes alight. She reared back, punching Thom on his bad shoulder.

"Je-*sus*," he said, his face turning crimson. "That freakin' hurt."

"Sorry, baby," said Simone, taking his arm. "But if you ever sneak up on me again, I'll hit you with a tire iron."

They walked together for a few blocks, drawing glances from passersby. McNulty wore black trousers, loafers without socks, a long-sleeved polo shirt buttoned to the throat, and a suede jacket. Simone clutched his arm and smiled up at him, matching his stride. For weeks after making her acquaintance, Thom had resisted the impulse to ask Simone out, deciding instead to remain friendly while keeping an eye on her interactions with the other rugby players. He usually stood at the bar with Dan O'Riordan because it allowed him the best vantage point—Simone in profile, moving back and forth as she poured Guinness and bantered with the customers. Maloney tried his routine on her the first night she worked behind the bar, acquiring a polite but firm *no* for his troubles.

A few other guys made a token effort, but none of them had any luck. The only time McNulty was the least bit worried occurred when Jeff Rivas came into the bar—a rare occurrence, with his schedule—and spoke to Simone in French. Her face lit up, as they exchanged a few dozen words. But after the surgical resident got his pint, drank it, and said goodnight to the rugby boys, Simone looked over at McNulty as if to reassure him, although at that point they'd barely spoken to one another. Every time she glanced at him, McNulty smiled, but he shook his head when she asked if he wanted another Guinness. Then he left a ten-dollar tip on the bar and sauntered out.

*

Right now, they were strolling down Elm Street, breathing the cold air wafting over from the Merrimack and gazing at the shop windows. Simone said that she'd felt a little nauseous after breakfast that morning, and had decided to visit a new organic cafe that specialized in homeopathic remedies.

"A little ginger root and chamomile, I'll be as good as new," she said, clutching McNulty's arm.

Simone had taken the bus, which gave her the opportunity to walk to the little shop and back again. Beyond her desire for a bit of exercise, their budget was very tight at present. The $1.25 bus ride was more economical than paying for gas, which had risen to almost four dollars a gallon. As a part-time dance instructor, Simone only brought in a couple hundred dollars a week. With no real estate closings in sight, McNulty had been skimming off his savings account; Simone had no idea he was about to drain it to buy her an engagement ring, and he didn't plan on telling her. Something always came up just when his financial situation seemed desperate, and McNulty believed that everything would work out.

On the next block, they ducked into a luncheonette for a coffee. A neon sign fixed to the window read *O'Connor's Lunch/ Breakfast All Day* in script that paled against the brightness of the afternoon. Inside, a slack-bellied gent in a paper hat leaned against the counter reading the *Union-Leader*. He looked up at McNulty and nodded.

Beside the cash register, a red-haired waitress was tallying up a handful of slips, punching the numbers into an adding machine. It was mid-afternoon and the restaurant was empty. Four tables occupied the main space, and a half dozen booths stood against the wall. With a gesture, the counterman indicated they could sit anywhere, and the two lovers slipped into the booth nearest the windows.

"I talked to my mother," said Simone. "She's going in for surgery on Tuesday, not Friday. Somebody else canceled, and they moved her up."

Simone Theresa Allenby was born in Valois, Quebec on Montreal's West Island, where her parents and younger sister Jocelyn still resided. Her father, Max, of Anglo-Irish stock, was a boat builder and carpenter, and her mother, the former Therese Dalphonse, was a French Canadian piano and dance teacher, who, in her youth during the 1970s, was an ardent Quebec separatist. As a teenager, she had occupied a roadblock where she and her friends would demand that English-speaking motorists, many of whom had been born in the neighborhood, produce their "Quebec passports." Her patriotic fervor died down when she met the strapping boat builder, Max Allenby, and married him, at the age of nineteen.

After graduating from Saint Thomas High School, Simone received a scholarship to study dance at Bennington College in Vermont, and later moved to New Hampshire with the intention of taking a Master's degree at UNH, while auditioning for a place in the Boston Ballet Company. Her first tryout went well, and she was chosen to dance in a production of *Don Quixote*. Less than a week after that, Simone found out she was pregnant.

"I'm going to leave Monday morning, and drive up," Simone said. Her mother, only 49 years old, had been diagnosed with ovarian cancer. "I wish you were going with me."

McNulty reached across to grasp Simone's hand. "I want to meet your Mom and Dad. But the hearing on my lease application is Tuesday, remember? Maybe I'll drive up on Wednesday. It'll take what—four hours? You can introduce me to your parents, we'll tell them our news, and if your Mom is doing okay, we'll drive back home on Friday."

"In two cars?" Simone shook her head. "It's crazy to spend all that money on gas. I have to teach Thursday night anyway, so I was going to head back early."

Simone's hair, which fell to her shoulders, was glowing in the sunlight. She patted it several times, although one long tendril remained, hanging over her face till the curled end touched her jaw.

"I should be there when you tell your parents about the baby," Thom said.

Simone tucked the wisp of hair behind her ear. "I'm not going to tell them," she said. "I want my mother to feel … and I don't really have a lot to tell—not yet."

The waitress appeared, setting down a cup of coffee for him, and herbal tea with a tiny pitcher of milk in front of Simone. "Cheers," he said, touching his cup to hers.

McNulty hadn't told Simone about the engagement ring, or his plan to ask her to marry him, though they got along so well she must have known it was coming. Still, he was a traditionalist, and hated the idea that Simone would be returning to Montreal for the first time in months, alone and pregnant, while he was busy with his real estate scheme. Things had been so hectic, McNulty hadn't found time to have Jeff Rivas look at his shoulder—he didn't have any health insurance—which at the moment felt like it was burning a hole through his favorite jacket.

"If the loan goes through, we'll close on the adjoining land in a couple weeks," said McNulty. For $200, he'd created an LLC called "Allenby Development" and filed his loan application under that name.

Jay Atkinson

"There's some extra money built into the loan," he said. "Thanksgiving weekend, we'll fly up to Montreal together, see how your Mom is doing, and tell your folks about their grandchild."

"Really?" asked Simone. She leaned across and kissed him, filling the air with her fresh, healthy scent. "Oh, Thom, I would love that."

Light was streaming in the windows, and a cavalcade of jaunty pedestrians waved to McNulty and his girl, or else tipped their hats. McNulty put down a ten-dollar bill for the waitress and kissed Simone goodbye, cradling her fragrant head for a moment. They parted, and Simone went off toward the natural foods shop and he crossed Elm Street, eyeballing the passing cars, timing it, his hips turned away like a bullfighter's, and then dashing across the open lane and onto the sidewalk. It was a mild day for November, the sky tall and deep and blue, perfect but for one tiny detail—McNulty's shoulder hurt like blazes.

Thom had a meeting with a builder whose office was on Union Street. It was the latest in a handful of interviews he had scheduled, aimed at finding a contractor for his project. He was looking for someone who was insured, so that Allenby Development wouldn't have to secure its own bond; at the same time,

McNulty didn't want any business associates who might try to take over, expanding the project with their own capital.

The first outfit he'd spoken with, Henry S. Gauthier Builders, turned out to be one of those fly-by-night operations that didn't bother to pull permits for most jobs. Manchester's Yellow Pages were filled with these French Canadian tradesmen—energetic little guys who had journeyed down from Quebec when the immigration laws weren't so tight, and lived in little pastel houses in Candia and Epping, building decks and porches and home additions at cut-rate prices. McNulty needed a licensed general contractor who would bring the project in on time and under budget, and keep his mouth shut. He was beginning to realize that finding such an outfit was easier said than done.

Preoccupied by these thoughts, McNulty failed to notice his employer, Bill Hodges, lumbering toward him on the sidewalk. In person, Hodgie was a wide, thickly built fellow, wearing a tweed jacket, an oxford shirt with a rugby club tie, and a scally cap pulled low on his forehead. His most dominant feature was a large walrus mustache, flecked with stiff gray bristles that resisted Hodgie's upward grooming. Generally, Bill Hodges was on very cordial terms with himself, as well as those he met along the way, with one hand in his coat pocket and the other holding a cigar, which had gone out.

Hodgie gave his distracted colleague a hard, jolting stiff-arm to the shoulder, knocking McNulty off balance. "Fuckin' *right*, Hodgie," said Thom, staggering against the brick façade of a lawyer's office. He leaned against the wall, gasping from the pain and cradling his bad arm. "Ohh, that hurts like fuckin' hell."

"You should keep your head up," said Hodgie, relighting his cigar.

Hodgie jingled the change in his pocket, rocked back on his heels, and drew on his cheroot, which he expelled in a wreath that encircled his head. "You look like you're up to no good," he said to McNulty. "Been rolling hobos under the Amoskeag Bridge?"

"I'm working," said McNulty. Tugging on his jacket, he took a couple of deep breaths. "You should try it some time."

"I haven't seen any checks with your name on them lately," said the old prop forward, laughing. His hand was freckled like a sea captain's and, using his thumb, he brushed the edges of his mustache and then flicked the cigar stub beneath a parked car. "Speaking of which, I got a phone call from a broker who works for Mike Rivas. He asked about you."

"Yeah, what'd he say?"

A good-looking redhead in her forties came sashaying toward them, and Hodgie smiled at her with all his stubby teeth, raising his scally cap and winking at McNulty as she passed. "Good afternoon," he said. "Fine weather we're having."

Hodgie turned to watch her, and Thom kicked him in the ankle. "Hey," McNulty said. "What'd this guy wanna know?"

"*Ouch*," said Hodgie, doubling up his fists for a moment.

McNulty shook his head. "Why was the guy calling you? C'mon, Hodgie."

"He asked if you worked for me, and I told him you did," Hodgie said. "Then he said he'd been talking to Hank Gauthier about a development thing you were working on. He wanted to know what you were planning to do with the property at 2056 South Willow Street."

McNulty frowned at Gauthier's indiscretion. "You can't tell anybody anything, especially a Frenchman," he said. "What'd you tell him?"

"Pretty much that it was none of his fucking business," Hodgie said.

Sirens were growing closer, and then a ladder truck screamed past with Maloney and another guy from the rugby club hanging off the back end. "So much for the element of surprise,"

McNulty said.

"I looked up that property in Multiple Listings after I got off the phone. What a shithole," said Hodgie. "I hope you're not thinking about living there with Simone and the baby."

"I'm thinking about a lot of things," said McNulty. "But that's not one of 'em."

"Fill me in sometime."

McNulty pushed off from the wall. "If it all goes right, you should see a good-sized check with my name on it," he said.

"That would be nice."

McNulty and Hodges leaned in, shaking hands and butting heads. "Hey, did you hear about the Old Red match last weekend?" asked Hodgie. In fact, McNulty didn't know a thing about how the club's final game had turned out; he'd forgotten all about it.

"We went down there with just thirteen guys," said Hodgie. "We played 'em shorthanded—they were ahead, but O'Riordan scored a try with a few seconds left to win it. But the ref disallowed it, saying he never touched the ball down. Right after the game, Old Red's coach said that the match was going to count in the standings. Van Valkenburg went ape shit. Fights, ejections. Dickie Tardugno punched out their coach. Broke the guy's jaw, and broke his hand in the process."

"Dickie played?"

Hodgie nodded. "We drove down together. He played; I didn't. Good decision by me."

McNulty watched as Hodgie went along the sidewalk, toiling on his bad knee. In front of Duke Cronin's Sporting Goods, the gregarious realtor hailed an acquaintance while reaching into his pocket for another long black cigar.

Having, after days of worrying, learned that Mike Rivas probably had a good idea what he was up to, and hearing from Simone that she'd be going to Montreal sooner than expected, McNulty hustled along the sidewalk, troubled about how he was going to spend the same five grand for the down payment on 2056 South Willow Street, and for Simone's ring. Meanwhile, his shoulder burned in its socket, and his path ahead was delayed by an assortment of top-coat wearing gentry, middle-aged women in bowling jackets, and the occasional military uniform. It reminded him there was a war going on.

McNulty took out his phone to call Jeff Rivas. He left a message, and a few minutes later, Jeff called back. McNulty explained the situation, asking if there was any way Ellie could finish the ring by the weekend, instead of Tuesday. He was planning to take Simone out to dinner Sunday, and wanted to give her the ring then.

Jeff said he'd check with Ellie. "My dad's not feeling well," he said.

After he hung up, McNulty thought about asking Bill Hodges to loan him five grand for the down payment on South Willow. It wasn't unheard of, and McNulty was pretty sure that his boss would have him sign a note and then lend him the money. But Hodgie was clever enough to recognize the logic of his plan and would try to insinuate himself into it, as any businessman would who was risking a chunk of his own money. Hodgie would also figure out that McNulty was planning to leave Pro-Max, which would not be good for his prospects if anything went wrong and the deal fell through.

Like most people, Thom assumed, his thoughts ran along definite channels. To certain individuals, he only said certain things; for example, he would never tell Ellie Rivas that he'd gone shopping at Diamond World, or let Bill Hodges know that his larger goal, beyond the construction of a strip mall, was to develop a million dollar retail-residential site across the river in Bedford. The world kept turning thanks to a delicate balance between withholding information and parceling it out. McNulty had a talent for that sort of thing; he was only going to make it as far as his imagination and his patter would take him, and he was smart enough to realize that.

But McNulty would say just about anything to one of the rugby guys. Only a handful of people knew about his old man, and most of those played for the rugby club; he had never mentioned his father to Simone. He had even told Maloney about him, one night at the Rover. Of course, there were rugby stories he wouldn't share with people from "regular life." That included the night one of his college teammates paid a whore in Mexico City seven dollars to put the head of a live chicken somewhere private, and then walk into a room where four or five of their UNH buddies had passed out after a night of drinking. One guy roused another, which incited the chicken, and the whore took flight around the room, the chicken flailing at her backside with its wings. She looked like some kind of sad, downtrodden angel on hiatus.

It worked both ways. One night at the Rover, when Van Valkenburg called somebody a "poofter," Jonathan Rivas, Jeff's twin brother, startled the assembly by declaring that he was gay. The silence lasted a couple of seconds. Then Van Valkenburg got up from his stool to embrace the fleet-footed winger. "That's all right, lad," said Van Valkenburg. "I'm a Presbyterian, and my dear old mum got over it."

Dan O'Riordan was the most well-liked fellow on the club; he was married to Tracey, a cheerful, blond-haired pediatrician, and they owned a little cape in West Manchester overlooking the river. But one Saturday morning, on the drive over to Portland for a rugby match, O'Riordan told McNulty and Dickie Tardugno that he'd been married once before, when he was eighteen, to a girl who was several years older. She was a stripper who worked at a bar in Massachusetts that was owned by the Hell's Angels. Six months after they were married, O'Riordan's wife was badly beaten in a hotel room on Route 1 in Saugus.

"It was probably some weirdo customer," said O'Riordan. He was quiet for a while, the panorama of southern Maine drifting by the car. "I started hanging around the strip clubs, talking to the girls, asking questions. One night after closing three dudes followed me to the parking lot with an ax handle. I got in a couple shots, then they gave me a good beating. Cracked my skull."

McNulty and Tardugno stared out through the windshield, not saying a word. The good-natured eight-man laughed, shaking his head. "I was just a kid. What was I gonna do? I drove myself to the emergency room, and told the doc I fell off my skateboard."

In front of New Hampshire Bank, Thom called O'Riordan

on his cell phone; on the other end of the line, he could hear the slap-slap of players running up and down a basketball court, and the sound of the JDC kids shouting at each other and laughing.

"What's up, dawg?" asked O'Riordan.

"I need to borrow five grand."

"When do you need it?"

"Yesterday."

O'Riordan covered the phone for a second, yelling at one of the basketball players. "No problem, bro," he said, returning to the call. "I get dibs on Simone, though."

While he was talking to O'Riordan, Thom's phone buzzed with another call. It was Rivas. "Come by Sunday," Jeff said. "Three o'clock. The ring will be ready by then."

McNulty clicked back to the other line. "That was Jeff Rivas," he said.

"I wanna talk to him about assisted suicide," said O'Riordan. "Tracey has my balls on her key chain and by tomorrow, you'll have all my money."

O'Riordan came through with the loan the next day, as McNulty knew he would. Late in the afternoon, they met for a beer at the Irish Rover, with rain pelting against the windows and Jack working solo behind the bar. After tapping the stout and waiting for it to settle, a pint of Guinness with a half-inch of foam was set before each of them.

"It's a work of art, Jack," said O'Riordan, taking up his glass.

Jack grinned. "I do what I can," he said.

A good listener and teller of jokes, Jack Doherty was the official bartender of the Manchester Rugby Club—a plaque above the cash register attested to that fact—and as near a part of the team as you could get without playing rugby. Guys often confided in him, and Jack had made a cottage industry out of counseling their girlfriends and fiancées when they strayed.

Now, looking at the streaks of rain on the window, Jack said, "If I could do anything half as well as I can pour a glass of beer, I'd be doing it, believe me."

When Jack dropped through the hatch in the floor to switch out the kegs, O'Riordan went into his pocket for a folded slip of paper and slid it over to McNulty. "Tracey asked me what it was for," said O'Riordan. "I told her it was my money, and that it was for you."

McNulty stored the check in his wallet. "I'll get it back to you in a couple weeks," he said, explaining that he was buying a diamond from Ellie Rivas with the money. "I'm going to ask

Simone to marry me."

"I can't think of a better person to ask," said O'Riordan, watching rain strike the window. He touched his glass to McNulty's. "Really, dude. She's a peach."

By Sunday, the rain had abated, leaving ankle-deep puddles along Elm Street. When Simone said she was going out for brunch with Zelda Reis, McNulty began to rouse himself from his Sunday morning torpor—he needed to shower, vacuum out the MG, and shine his dress shoes. There was plenty to be done before he'd ask Simone to marry him.

Emerging from the shower, McNulty said "Okay" when Simone called out that she'd be back in a few hours. Then McNulty, his shoulder a bit looser after the scalding hot water, crossed the hallway in a towel, hearing Simone's key in the lock on her way out.

McNulty retrieved the five grand in cash he had stuffed into one of his rugby boots, and thundered downstairs to the MG. He'd been busy all week with the bank financing for his project, and had promised Simone that he'd take her out—a romantic movie, dinner at the Black Brimmer, and a stroll past the old Amoskeag Mill buildings. There, beside the river, McNulty planned to show Simone the ring he'd purchased and ask her to become his wife.

Jay Atkinson

Going over Route 293 into Manchester, Thom fretted over showing up at the Rivas's too early and what he'd say if Big Mike answered the door. There is nothing people dislike so much as being forced to talk business while at home, but McNulty couldn't imagine how he could avoid it if Mike Rivas was around. He was better off asking for support than waiting to get out-gunned, which was a real possibility if Big Mike developed a hard-on for the adjoining parcel. McNulty's palms began to sweat just thinking about it.

On Elm Street, McNulty stopped to buy Simone a dozen roses, and then walked down to Brockman's to purchase a box of chocolates. The Rivas's were sticklers for punctuality, and Thom, killing time, saw that it was just past two o'clock, nearly an hour before his appointment but close to the time that Simone would be returning home. No doubt she would be surprised by his absence, and his phone would soon be ringing.

Gazing down the block, McNulty watched as Maloney emerged from the Red Arrow diner with a St. A's girl who looked about eighteen. McNulty saluted his teammate from a block away, pointed at his wristwatch, and ducked into the MG and roared off.

Driving toward the Rivas's, McNulty decided against calling Jeff Rivas to say he'd be arriving early. After all, it wasn't a social call; he was going to the Rivas's to give Ellie five thousand dollars. And as O'Riordan was fond of saying, it's always easier to ask forgiveness than permission.

The sky was clear and bright, and there was a freshness to the air that prompted McNulty to roll down his window despite the chill. His shoulder ached with every rotation of the little handle, and his scalp tingled from the sharp air that rushed in.

At the apex of Union Street, Thom parked the MG at the curb and went up to the door. The curtains were drawn in the lower windows, and the bulky gray monument of the house, looming overhead, was implacable and still, so tall against the sky it appeared to be leaning over him. McNulty banged the doorknocker three times, the portentous sound echoing within.

Stepping back, McNulty listened for any sound coming from within. There was neither footfalls nor voices. He craned his neck to glance in the side-window, but it was three panes thick. He waited another moment, and then heard what sounded like a command to enter, or some other exhortation, coming from within the house.

It was 2:20 pm. Hearing what he thought was Jeff, or perhaps Jonathan, for the second time, McNulty turned the handle and the door gave way. Since the voice that had called to him emanated from within the house, McNulty began traveling across the foyer, the gallery dark and silent above. The house was redolent of lamb and middle eastern spices; passing the dining room, he noted that platters of food had been arranged on the dazzling white cloth, and a silver candlestick held a burning taper.

Retreating a few steps, with a slight digression to his right, McNulty turned in, bringing himself to the foot of the table, at which, he now realized, the majority of the Rivas family was seated for dinner. There was a ravaged leg of lamb on a platter, surrounded by a tattered green furze. Occupying smaller dishes and bowls were an array of Lebanese delicacies familiar to Thom from the meals he'd eaten at this same table—hummus tahini; mezza, a side dish made with goat cheese, olives, and cucumbers; as well as stuffed white zucchini, known as cusa. These and other Lebanese dishes were eaten with the hands, swabbed out of their bowls with triangles of pita bread.

When McNulty had dined there as a teenager, the room was filled with the rowdy laughter of a dozen adolescent boys. Now, the figures arranged at the table were as silent as wax dummies. Jeff Rivas and his twin brother, Jonathan, were seated on the far side, by the windows. Each of Mike and Ellie's twenty-seven year old sons wore a sports coat, white oxford shirt, and school tie; their faces clean shaven, hair combed and shining in the candlelight. They had their heads angled downward, as if they had been praying, although it was obvious from the disarray that they were, by now, well into Sunday dinner. McNulty was taken aback when neither Jeff nor his brother spoke to him, or even as much as nodded, remaining frozen in apostolic postures while he stood there, mute. But then Thom looked toward the head of the table and understood why.

Big Mike was wearing a bathrobe and striped pajamas, his hair unruly and his face a ghastly hue. He was forty pounds below his typical weight, his shoulders reduced to the width of a coat hanger. His eyes glittering, Mike Rivas looked at Thom; his glance was a penetrating admixture of anger, fear, privilege, and humiliation. This whole episode spanned three or four seconds. McNulty felt rooted to the carpet, his jaw wired shut, unable to move or speak.

While thus engaged, a footfall sounded behind him, and looking round, McNulty was confronted by Ellie Rivas, standing there with the little jewelry box in her hand. She frowned in an involuntary way, beckoning to him, and McNulty excused himself and went out. Re-entering the foyer, he reached into his pocket for the cash, mumbling an apology.

Ellie was wearing a navy dress, heels, and a string of pearls. Her bare arms were covered in downy hair and when she opened the box—handing it to McNulty as she took the lump of cash—their eyes met, and after a second or two, McNulty looked away.

"It's a beautiful ring," Ellie said. "I think Simone will like it."

Then she counted the money, all of it in hundred dollar bills, from one hand to the other, wetting her thumb to speed the transfer. When Ellie was satisfied that it was right, she showed her visitor to the door. McNulty thanked her, and with a glance toward the dining room, where he could make out a portion of Jeff's shoulder and little else, he apologized once more for interrupting dinner, and went out.

On the stoop he took a couple of breaths, pocketing the ring and gazing over the housetops at the steep blue sky. After the warmth of the house, the chill took him full in the throat and McNulty hurried toward his car, which was parked beneath a giant elm tree. A variety of thoughts had been rushing through his mind when he'd entered the house for this awkward appointment. Whatever McNulty's original strategy had been, of negotiation, perhaps; of confession, appeasement, and dialogue; or maybe even just boldness—*this is what I'm planning to do, Mr. Rivas*—the question of a response to his modest endeavor had been rendered moot. Big Mike was beyond caring about any of that.

The wind came up, throwing grit against his car, and the empty branches of the elm tree clattered together with a dry, hollow sound. McNulty reached into his trouser pocket to wriggle his keys out, which sent a bolt of pain through his shoulder. Ignoring it, he unlocked the door, started up the MG, and eased down the hill toward the river. From this vantage point, he could see the entire city, all the way over to Bedford, where he knew Simone would be waiting.

Hoot

Heaving up her guitar case, Jami Jefferson pushed through
the heavy wooden door of the Bull Moose Tavern at five
PM, a time when working musicians in the Mount Washington
Valley were having a second cup of coffee. But Jami was determined to get on the list for the final hoot of the season; to that end,
she planned to be there when Jonathan went over the evening's
performers with Stan Hislop, who owned the Bull Moose and several other businesses.

A few years earlier, when Stan bought the tavern from its

previous owner, he began advertising a hoot on Tuesday nights, commencing at eight PM and running until the bar closed at midnight. The hoots began on the unofficial opening of the local ski season, typically the weekend before Thanksgiving in the upper valley, continuing until the only snow remaining in the area was on top of Mount Washington, six miles north on Route 16. Tuesday being an off night in the hospitality business, it seemed to Hislop an effective way to fill up the bar with professional and semi-pro musicians and their friends and admirers, who, as a rule, didn't drink as much as the skiers and snowboarders that packed the tavern on weekends; still, his net income on Tuesday nights had increased quite a bit in the past three seasons. And since the musicians used the hoot as an opportunity to perform with their friends, and to audition for Stan and other bar owners who attended, it had turned out to be a pleasant, economical way to conduct business in the middle of the week.

Stan noticed that bar traffic reached its height between ten and eleven PM during the hoot, when all the trios, duets, and solo acts who'd performed during the evening joined on stage for an old fashioned hootenanny. They'd huddle for a minute or two and then reel off a few numbers, usually old standards that everyone knew how to play, or, at least, they could strum along and harmonize on the choruses. During this raucous encore, the Bull Moose Tavern seemed to rock, pitch, and vibrate on its ancient foundation, the beer and whiskey flowed, and Sarah Dunston, the weeknight barmaid, frequently rang the bell that signaled a good-sized tip.

Jami Jefferson stood for a moment in the foyer, allowing her eyes to adjust to the dimness of the bar. Looming overhead was the head of a gigantic bull moose named Monty, its fur worn thin from being touched for luck so often, and one of its taxidermic eyes having been replaced by a Kennedy half-dollar. Jami wasn't very pretty but had an appealing, confident way about her. She'd passed age thirty a short while back—average height, an abundance of thick, curly brown hair, and a little chunky in the torso, but with the appropriate curves. Reaching up, she touched the bald spot between Monty's antlers and passed into the tavern.

It was the third Tuesday in April, and all the skiers and boarders had returned to Massachusetts and New York, except for the thrill seekers who enjoyed hiking up Mount Washington and skiing the headwall at Tuckerman's Ravine. Despite this exodus, Jami knew that every half-assed singer, songwriter, ukulele player, and bongo drummer in the valley would be crowding into the Bull Moose tonight, hoping to get on the list and expecting somebody famous to show up. For although the hoot had started as a "come one-come all" jam session for musicians of varying styles and abilities, it had grown more popular—especially since Del Keppler, the host before Jonathon, began organizing things. Over time, the down-home shivaree had grown more discriminating, and lesser known, out of town, or amateur performers were often left out.

Eight places on the list were reserved for specific acts, and on Tuesday evening around six-thirty pm the list was worked up, scratched out, and revised by Stan Hislop and the current emcee, Jonathon Kinsdale, lead singer for a well-respected band, the Mount Washington Trio. Arriving early would allow Jami a chance to be seen—and heard—just as Stan and Jonathan were composing the list.

Two birch logs were roaring in the fireplace when she entered the bar, the blaze large enough to take the substantial chill out of the room. The Bull Moose Tavern, located in Jackson Village, dated back to 1706. Originally a farmhouse, it consisted of a single-story building made from square timbers coated in pitch and fastened together with wooden pegs, in the style of the era. Built upon fieldstone underpinnings and suspended over a deep cellar that allowed for the storage of potatoes and other root vegetables, the construction also provided a defensible position in the event of an Indian attack. The tavern's first floor, measuring thirty-eight by twenty-two feet, featured a large chimney made of stones averaging the size of a cannonball. The chimney, hearth and bar, which had endured for three hundred years, were the central attractions of the Bull Moose Tavern.

Jami headed for the bar, which had the low ceiling, exposed timbers, and wide pine floors of the original building. To her left was the dining room and *maître d's* rostrum, both empty on a Tuesday, and above, on the second and third floors, were several rooms to let, which saw heavy traffic at the height of the ski season. Now, with spring approaching and snow melt creating a racket in the Ellis River, the rooms above the bar were empty.

The bar was quiet. A dour-looking man and his wife sat at a table by the windows, going over a trail map with the grim determination of military strategists. Behind the bar, Sarah Dunston paused in the midst of taking inventory and waved to Jami, saying something that couldn't be heard over the Willie Nelson CD that was playing.

Sarah indicated one of the stools at the bar, and then, since she was working alone, went out through the trap to wait on the couple by the window. Sitting catty-corner to the bar, the man had raised his hand like someone in a bingo game.

Jami had been back in town only a few days, but she and Sarah had run into each other on Sunday afternoon in the village. Jami had finished washing her clothes at the Downhill Laundromat—everything she'd taken to South America, and all the winter stuff she'd left behind. These had grown musty in her trunk, which she'd left in the back room at Baba Louie's, the bike shop where she used to work. Sarah informed her that tonight's hoot would be the last of the season, and Jami had spent two days trying to figure out who had her twelve-string, which had been passed around town in her absence.

"Hey, girlfriend," said Sarah, coming back to the bar. "First one's on me."

"Bourbon and water," Jami said. "Hold the bourbon."

Sarah laughed. "C'mon. You must be thirsty after all that…being gone."

Glancing around, Jami said, "I gotta get on the list tonight. Maybe put on my kneepads and get up close and personal with Stan, if I have to."

Sarah giggled. She and Jami were more allies than friends; in their own words, "two plucky broads" just trying to get by in the Mount Washington Valley. Sarah Dunston was a 36-year-old bottle blond with green eyes, a divorced mother of an eight-year-old girl, Julianne, and possessor of a mortgage and orthodontist's bills. She and her daughter lived in a little A-frame cottage off Route 302 in Bartlett. Because she had a kid, Sarah needed a steady job, two jobs in fact; she was the afternoon barmaid at the Bull Moose on Sunday, Wednesday, and Thursday; worked the Hoot on Tuesday night and did the cocktail waitressing on Saturday nights, where her tips during ski season might eclipse her other earnings for the week. Sarah also waited tables at lunchtime over at the Blue Parka Pub, which Stan Hislop owned half of.

When asked, Jami Jefferson liked to say she was "thirty-one and a half, single, and happy," with the sort of freedom to pick up and leave town usually reserved for the men who populated the valley. Jami called herself a "civilian brat," since she'd moved a dozen times as a child, following her dad, Harry, who worked for a company that made nuclear submarines. They'd lived in Norfolk, Virginia; San Diego, Honolulu, Baltimore, and six months in Reykjavik, Iceland, though Jami always referred to Portsmouth, New Hampshire as her home.

She'd attended school in Portsmouth, a many-spired, former whaling town at the mouth of the Piscataqua River. The Jeffersons' five years in Portsmouth was the longest they'd ever lived in one place, the most stable period in Jami's life, and though she'd been tormented by the sons of gift shop owners and lobstermen and electricians for her fluctuating weight and clunky eyeglasses, young Jami had sung in the chorale at Portsmouth High, gone on Saturday night forays to the Isle of Shoals, and learned to play guitar from a shaggy-haired folk musician who'd once performed with Tom Rush. She'd also lost her virginity to Rush's former sideman, at the ripe age of eighteen.

Without being prompted, Sarah Dunston brought out a salad, dinner roll, and a pot of herbal tea for Jami, who she knew was low on funds after her trip to South America. Back in February, Sarah had received a card postmarked Lima, Peru that depicted a fantastic, sprawling portion of that city, part architectural marvel and part horrific slum, across the bottom of which Jami had scrawled "I've been elected Minister of Frivolity and Merry-Making."

"Don't do that," said Jami, pointing to the free meal. "I ate before I came."

The barmaid sneered. "Yeah. What'd you eat?"

"Wild mushrooms. Pizza from Baba Louie's dumpster. All very filling."

Sarah laughed. "Eat," she said. "Stan isn't in yet, but I

doubt he'd care, anyway. He likes you."

Spearing a piece of cucumber, Jami asked, "When's he coming in?"

"He's been meeting Jonathan around six-thirty, quarter of seven."

"How *is* the prince of Route 16?" asked Jami, referring to the front man of the Mouth Washington Trio.

"Oh, Jonathan still suffers from terminal dreaminess," said Sarah, moving her shoulders a little. "We have to drive away all the snow bunnies, just so he can play his guitar."

For a moment, the only sound was the crackling fireplace, until Jami said, "It must be a great burden to him," and the women laughed.

When she had finished eating, Jami piled her dishes together, announcing that she was going out to "have a ciggy." Standing up to jounce her hair into place, Jami asked Sarah to keep an eye on her guitar case while she was gone.

"Did you like it down there?" Sarah asked, referring to her five months in South America. "Was it polluted, and stuff like that?"

"Peru is a very civilized country," said Jami. "They still allow smoking in bars. Hell, they allow it in church."

When Sarah's back was turned, Jami slipped a couple of bucks beneath her saucer and went out. The Bull Moose was a maze of crooked hallways and sloping floors, and after a twist and a turn, passing through a pair of doors, the scullery, and the old tack room, Jami descended a steep run of stairs, heaving open the door at the bottom.

Behind the tavern was a grassy rectangle hemmed in by oak trees, scrub pine, and wild blackberry bushes. To Jami's right, the yard was flanked by an old tennis court behind a chicken wire fence, as well as the parking lot, a half-acre of gravel dotted with a few cars. The lot was demarcated by birch trees and here at dusk, populated by a thousand fireflies.

As Jami wriggled out a cigarette and lit it, the blinking fireflies lent an understanding of the lot's dimensions that a surveyor couldn't have improved upon. Straight in front of her, Thorn Hill rose to its apex of 2,000 feet, so close it appeared to lean over the Bull Moose. It was the tallest among a cluster of glacial knobs that surrounded Jackson Village, each bristling with old growth timber, and as night came on, dressed in blue shadows that crept downhill. An owl hooted from somewhere, and a neighbor's inquisitive collie, or perhaps a doe, half-starved from the long winter, was rustling around twenty or thirty yards from where Jami stood.

Jami loved the valley, but wasn't sure how long she'd be able to afford her studio apartment in Jackson Village. She'd survived three years of tourist prices by working at Baba Louie's bike shop in the summer and fall; selling lift tickets at Mt. Cranmore in the winter; and playing out as many nights as she could: Bull Moose, Blue Parka Pub, Horsefeathers, wherever she could pass the hat, or pick up fifty or seventy-five bucks opening for the White Mountain Trio, Del Keppler, or Pickles & Bernie. Her first year in Jackson, she'd played a regular Sunday night gig with Keppler at the Pizza Barn for $250, an even split, but that ended badly, and Jami had been scrambling for gigs ever since.

In this economy, the ski areas and bars had entertained a smaller number of Massachusetts, New York, and Connecticut residents than in previous seasons. A lousy snowfall the year before, along with the migration of lift ticket sales to the Internet, had resulted in fewer seasonal jobs, and even before Halloween, when Luis laid her off at the bike shop, Jami had decided to leave for Peru. A nonprofit called "Guitars Without Borders" was offering five months employment, room and board included, plus air fare and a small stipend. So, having completed the online application and taken the bus to Durham for an interview, Jami was offered a position, whereupon she acquired a visa and sublet her apartment to Boxy Mitchell, the drummer in the White Mountain Trio, who'd recently broken off an engagement and found himself without lodging.

Despite their wanderings, Jami's father had never taken her to South America, and seeing it was a place she'd had little opportunity to visit, on November 1st Jami boarded a plane with her backpack and guitar case, hopeful that the economy and the demand for live music in the Mount Washington Valley would improve in her absence. Upon her return to Jackson Village, she'd been disappointed on both counts. Things had gotten worse.

Two pair of headlights reared up, as they veered into the lot ahead of Stan Hislop's convertible and Jonathan's shitbox VW bus. The sudden arrivals obliterated the fireflies as the vehicles crunched over the gravel, revealing a huge swath of the understory. Just as quickly, the headlights were extinguished, plunging the base of Thorn Hill into darkness. Jami flicked her cigarette away, following its ember toward the back door of the tavern, where she crushed it out with her toe and deposited the butt in a nearby coffee can.

Jami flew through the door and up the stairs, pausing in the ladies room, where she squirted breath spray into her mouth;

pushing up her bra, juggling her breasts, and pulling down the neckline of her jersey while studying herself in the mirror. This attempt at cleavage produced little visible effect, causing her to sigh. Then she fluffed her bangs and headed out to the foyer, where she rubbed Monty between the antlers for luck.

And now, vagabond Jami Jefferson, a new, improved version of the old Jami, sashayed into the tavern expecting to make a grand entrance, complete with the sort of nifty banter featured in old movies like "His Girl Friday." As a youngster, Jami used to stay up late with her dad, watching the screwball comedies of the 1930s on the late show. Whereas, Harry Jefferson could imitate Cary Grant's strutting cockney and the stammer of Jimmy Stewart to a T, his twelve year old daughter watched in rapt attention, imagining herself as Kate Hepburn or Rosalind Russell or Irene Dunne, a wisecracking sylph in a cocktail dress, or jodhpurs and a swallow-tail coat; someone who looked good in pants, an equal to the men, ready to give as good as she got.

It was more than their trim little bodies Jami envied; their beautiful smiles, long legs and narrow feet. She loved their sense of style and aplomb. If there was anything that beat getting off a real zinger at the expense of Cary Grant, it was doing so in a great hat.

But seeing, as she advanced beyond the fireplace, that Stan Hislop and Jonathan were already huddled at the bar, puzzling out the list, her face dropped; and Jami cast a worried glance at Sarah, who was loading the register with the fives, tens, and twenties that Stan had brought over from the White Mountain Bank.

"Look who's here," said Sarah, over the Johnny Cash song that was playing.

Jami took one last appraisal of herself in the cheval glass over the bar, and then she looked ahead to the targets, displaying her best, wide-eyed smile.

"Planning to knock over the general store?" she asked.

Stan was first on his feet. "We're a couple of desperadoes, at heart," he said, wrapping Jami in a bear hug. "Look at you—the littlest hobo. I'm amazed you could find your way back here."

"I left a trail of cigarette butts and Ambien," said Jami, extricating herself from Stan's embrace.

Stan Hislop was a square shouldered, blue-eyed man in his late forties, with a gray-blond crew cut, and a wardrobe consisting of plaid sport shirts, boat shoes, and khaki pants. He had the bluff, outgoing manner of a guy selling peanuts at a ball game, as well as a cheerful blond wife, and two blue-eyed children, "proving that the entire family is a Nazi experiment," as Jami liked to say.

Jay Atkinson

"Stan, the uber-mensch of the Mount Washington Valley."

Jonathan Kinsdale had swiveled around on his stool, and was grinning at Jami. "So—how was Bolivia?" he asked.

"I was to the left of Bolivia, as you regard the planet from your vantage point in outer space," Jami said. "I was in Peru."

Offering up a bewildered smile, Jonathan shook his head. "You got the continent right," Jami said.

Jonathan was a smooth-faced twenty-eight year-old, possessing a cleft chin and two Kennedys' worth of shiny brown hair. He was a capable guitar player with a baritone voice; an amiable fellow, if a tad dimwitted, in Jami's estimation. Jonathan was so good-looking that, as a coping strategy, Jami had literally stopped seeing him; whenever he appeared, Jonathan Kinsdale was nothing more than an empty place in the room surrounded by a dotted line, like a body that had been removed from a crime scene.

When they'd met, three years earlier at the farmer's market, Jonathan had been so friendly and handsome and eager, bursting with ideas for original songs, and innovative chord progressions and riffs—even dropping hints that he and Jami might form an upcountry version of the White Stripes—that she'd fallen for him in the first twenty minutes of their acquaintance. That Jonathan, who'd just moved to the area from Vermont and soon began dating every ski bunny, waitress, and female lift attendant in the upper valley, seemed less and less interested in reincarnating the White Stripes, came as a serious blow to the daydreams of Jami Jefferson.

From the beginning, Jami had been skeptical, having caught him flirting with a sexy brunette at the farmer's market. A week later, upon seeing him making out with a sinewy blond at the foot of the Cascades, Jami banished him outright—now he was just a blank spot in the wallpaper, the man who wasn't there—and when he sang and played his guitar, it was like listening to Chinese shortwave radio.

"So—how's the list coming?" asked Jami, indicating the paper on the bar.

She'd meant to deliver the line with the insouciance of Rosalind Russell, but there was an involuntary quaver in her voice that she despised. On his feet now, Jonathan stood beside Stan Hislop, screening her view of the paper they'd been writing on.

"It's a work in progress," Jonathan said.

Jami reached between them, snatching up the paper. "Let me doodle on it," she said, giggling.

Hopping away when Jonathan tried to retrieve the list, Jami spun around until she had her back to him. By the look of it, there was plenty of room for another act that night, maybe even two or three.

1.   Jonathan, with Bernie on steel guitar

2.   (Tom Masterson)

3.   Del Keppler and friends

4.   Pete Niceforo (?)

5.   Pickles & Bernie

6.   White Mountain Trio

7.

8.

9.   Hoot

"You guys made a mistake," said Jami, perusing the list.

Stan knit his brow. "What is it?" he asked.

"Del Keppler doesn't have any friends," said Jami, tossing the paper onto the bar.

And having, like her idol, Rosalind Russell, a keen eye for favoritism and hypocrisy, Jami began asking about each of the performers on the list, thinking that, at the very least, she could sit in with one of them, even if Stan explained the openings to her satisfaction. But all of her thrusts were parried by that blot upon the wallpaper, Jonathan Kinsdale, who noted, in each case, that either sidemen were not required, or a quorum had been reached; whereupon Jami said that it was possible, even on such short notice, for her to work up a set that would fit into one of the open spots.

In fact, Jami said, despite not having visited Bolivia, she'd written several new songs on her trip to South America, and could be persuaded to give one of them a debut airing at the Bull Moose, free of charge.

Jonathan held up his smartphone like it was the only one in the state. "We're almost positive that Pete Niceforo is gonna take the four spot, and I'm waiting for a text from Tom Masterson about number two," he said.

"Tom is number two, all right," Jami said. "Is he riding over on his deewee bike?"

Masterson had been pinched twice for driving under the influence, got divorced for the second time, and was often seen pedaling his mountain bike on Route 16, dressed in jeans and a leather jacket and lugging his guitar. He stood in front of the microphone splay-footed, strumming his battered acoustic and moaning like a constipated Springsteen; his act was so lacking in charisma that Jami usually left the room as soon as Tom Masterson began to set up. She'd rather stick needles in her eye than listen to him sing "Glory Days" for the umpteenth time.

While Jonathan stared at her with a bovine expression, Jami said, "What about seven or eight?"

Stan and Jonathan glanced at each other. "We're waiting on somebody," said Stan, unable to contain his grin. "A mystery guest."

"Okay, so that's one spot or the other. There's still an empty spot."

Each performer was allotted fifteen minutes, except for the hoot, which generally ran for twice that. Most nights, a brief intermission followed the fifth spot on the list, and if the hoot ended short of midnight, there was an unofficial tenth spot that closed out the evening, taking the revelers beyond last call, when the house lights came on and staff began putting up the chairs.

"We're saving two spots for this," Jonathan said. "He's huge."

"Huge, as in fat?" asked Jami. "Is it Meatloaf?"

Occasionally, the eighth spot was left open for a heavy hitter from Boston or New York who was playing a college gig over at UNH and wanted to see Mount Washington. Since the tavern only seated sixty-five people, these performers were never announced ahead of time. Still, holding two spots on the list was unusual.

"We're looking for a slot for you, Jami," said Stan, holding her gaze.

"Maybe you need glasses, Stan, because there's two right there."

Everyone knew that Stan Hislop didn't have a musical bone in his body, and it was also no big secret that Jonathan arranged for the various performers to show up, and had most, if not all, of the say over configuring the list. But despite his easy-going manner, which Jami referred to as "the stunned bumpkin look," Hislop was an astute businessman—owner of the Bull Moose, with an interest in another local watering hole, the Blue Parka Pub, as well as being a silent partner in Baba Louie's bike shop. In his own way, Stan had helped Jami out, recommending her for employment at the bike shop, and before the economy tanked, booking her for an occasional gig at the Bull Moose. Stan paid keen attention to every detail of his various concerns, if only to avoid the sort of fiasco that had occurred when Del Keppler was emceeing the Hoot.

To be fair, Del had founded this local institution by suggesting it to Stan Hislop, and over the three years of its existence, he remained its most well-known performer. But Del Keppler had always maintained a rather weak grip on his own concept;

he loved going on stage but never wanted to leave, often skipping over a tardy performer to give himself two slots, or crowding out the musicians at the end of the list.

Things got so bad that one night Jami whistled loudly from her barstool, saying, "It's called 'Hoot,' not 'Keppler'," which unleashed a bout of laughter and heckling from the audience.

Jami felt terrible about it the next day, in part because Keppler was such a talented musician—he'd toured with Earth, Wind and Fire in the eighties, playing bass guitar—but also due to her fractured relationship with him. They'd played together for a few months, ending three weeks before what Jami called Hoot Armageddon, and she was certain that Del believed her outburst that night was the result of lingering bitterness over the dissolution of their act. He was not mistaken in that regard, though Jami had little fondness for Del's habit of playing five-minute bass solos, or cutting into her vocals with a riff whenever the spirit moved him. Still, Jami had worked steadily after she teamed up with Del, who could play out every night if he felt like it, and she was sorry when that dried up.

Jami's was not the only voice registered in opposition to Del Keppler, who, despite his irreproachable musicianship, succeeded in alienating a large number of his fellow performers. People had complained for weeks about Del's attitude, giving Stan little choice when he fired him, installing Jonathan as emcee of the hoot. The miffed bass player stayed away for an entire season, but had returned to the lineup in November, right around the time Jami left for Peru.

From what she'd heard, Del was happy to just come in and play his set, often jamming with Pete Niceforo, a seventy-five year old trumpet player who'd once been in the NBC orchestra. And even Del recognized that Jonathan was a more suitable emcee—he played out five or six nights a week, knew everyone in the Mount Washington Valley who'd ever picked up a guitar, and had a modest, affable way about him. By all accounts, the hoot had flourished under his direction.

Jami could see this just by looking around. After Stan disappeared into the kitchen, and she'd helped Jonathan carry in his acoustic and electric guitars, amplifier, and two mic stands, Jami took up her usual position at the bar. Overhearing the lineup for that night, Sarah Dunston had comped her a large tumbler of bourbon, which she drank with plenty of water. By seven o'clock, the bar stools, tables, and hearth-side chairs were filling up. Plenty of young musicians were on hand, carting along their guitars and fiddles and banjos, including a kid in a pork pie hat with a Dobro, and a shapely blonde girl who wheeled in a Hammond organ. Several locals were in attendance, as well as a fair number of tourists, considering it was a Tuesday night in April.

A table of rugby players made a clamor by the door, beside an older couple in fishing waders who'd walked over from the Cascades. At the bar, a group of rock climbers who'd conquered Whitehorse Ledge were celebrating with shots of vodka, and Jami recognized a pair of ski instructors from Mt. Cranmore who were each married to someone else. The bar was so crowded that Stan re-assigned one of the waitresses from the dining room, who was delivering steak sandwiches and pizza to the buskers, climbers, and cyclists as fast as the kitchen could turn them out.

Glancing that way, Jami noticed Tom Masterson walk in with his guitar and bike helmet, whereupon he launched into a conversation with Jonathan, who'd been talking to a pretty young thing over near the bar.

Jami raised a hand to Sarah Dunston, rattling the ice in her glass. "Another dose of hemlock, if you please," she said.

Now fifty-one years old, Tom Masterson was a boozy, wheedling ass kisser who'd declared himself an institution after decades of mediocre performances at county fairs, old home days, and the occasional strip mall opening. When he sang, the cords that ran up his neck became so attenuated they looked ready to snap, and the tendons in his meaty forearms turned and twisted like snakes as he played his guitar.

To offset the laboriousness of his style, Masterson had decorated his guitar case with hundreds of stickers from places like Storyland, Clark's Trading Post, and the Flume, a gesture that he believed made him more fun-loving and accessible. His guitar case was lacquered with them, inside and out, insignia from the Eiffel Tower and Yellowstone National Park, and hundreds of destinations in between. His moniker was Travelin' Tom Masterson, a nickname he'd given himself. He'd revealed his marketing strategy over drinks at Mexico Lindo one night, sitting around with a bunch of performers drinking margaritas and eating taco chips.

"The kids love it," said Masterson. "They see the stickers and ask me about all the places I've been, going back to when I was in the Army."

Jami was busy scarfing down the complimentary chips and salsa after another gig-free evening. "Tom, you could hire a chimp in a tuxedo to hand out lollipops, and kids wouldn't piss on you if you were on fire," she said, pretending it was in jest.

The table erupted in laughter and Jami looked over at Masterson, batting her eyelashes.

Spotting her now, Tom Masterson flashed a smile that reminded Jami of the grimace on a corpse. In response, she wiggled her fingers at him and swallowed a mouthful of bourbon. Tom's arrival meant there was one fewer spot, and as he loitered there, chewing on the seat of Jonathan's trousers, Pete Niceforo limped through the doorway with his trumpet, and the last opening on the list disappeared.

All things being equal, Jami would never begrudge Pete Niceforo his set. He was as fine a horn player as ever she'd heard, an old pro, at home with jazz, pop, or the blues. Pete was a simple, good-hearted fellow, and of all the performers in the vicious game of musical chairs taking place in the valley, Pete was the most generous, self-effacing, and talented of the lot.

Pete's wife, Cassie, who was an artist, had passed away five years ago, and, tired of life in New York, he'd decided to winterize their cottage in nearby Bartlett, making it his permanent home. He sold his apartment on Manhattan's upper west side, a spacious two-bedroom with a loft that he'd purchased for $11,000 back in 1957, when he was playing with Skitch Henderson. That windfall, combined with his pension from NBC, allowed him to live year-round in the shadow of Mount Jefferson, where he could play music five nights a week, if he was in the mood.

As Jami stood amongst the crowd, doing the math on her diminishing chances, Pete hailed her from across the room. Soon he was laboring toward her on misshapen hips, wending his way through the crowd and sporting a denture-filled grin. Approaching his seventy-sixth birthday, Pete Niceforo was a short, squat fellow, with traces of orange furze stretched across his balding head, black-rimmed eyeglasses, and the complexion of a turnip. He wore a short-sleeved white shirt, bolo tie, and baggy pants cinched with a belt just below his chest. Pete had a distinct New York accent, as well as a habit of moistening his lips when he talked, in the rat-a-tat style of guys who'd grown up in Crown Heights.

"Hey kid, you look good, how was your trip? Listen, you like Chet Baker? I'm gonna play 'I Remember You.' You know the song? I'll play the first verse and the chorus, then I'll leave off, and you sing the second verse, the chorus, and I'll come in underneath for the final verse. Meet me right here on the changeover, and I'll give you the key. I'm gonna have a highball to prime the pump. Sure I can't get you something?"

With that, Pete winked at her, shuffling away to fetch his drink. He'd only play a couple of songs during his spot, but everyone wanted to collaborate with him. For most of the evening, Pete

Jay Atkinson

would be standing near the back of the stage, blowing hard or soft, jazz or pop, as the number required. He was very popular with the crowd, and with his fellow musicians.

Jami was excited, and though she'd barely even heard of Chet Baker, much less familiarized herself with his catalogue, she wasn't going to turn down a chance to sing. She had plenty of time to hustle outside, smoke a butt, and look up the words to "I Remember You" on her phone. She could even download Chet Baker playing the song from YouTube, if she hurried.

A minute later, she'd cleared the knot of people in the doorway when Del Keppler entered, carrying his bass guitar in its case. He was a tall, lean man, just turned sixty, with long arms, a cadaverous face, and sandy hair mixed with gray that swept back from his forehead, giving him the look of an angry clown.

Both in a rush to get someplace—Jami to have a smoke and look at her phone; Del to greet his admirers—and just as eager to avoid an awkward conversation, the former musical partners nodded, with Jami making for the backyard, and Del executing a left into the tavern.

Del Keppler was brilliant—that much everyone agreed upon; an accomplished musician, artist, rock climber, and computer gaming expert who'd written the program for Guitar Master, just one of several things he'd done that had turned to gold.

In his youth, Del had graduated from U. Cal Berkeley with a fine arts degree; in his twenties and thirties, he'd worked as a musician in Los Angeles and New York, recorded with Sly Stone and Harry Nilsson, and toured with Earth, Wind and Fire. By the time he was forty, Del had earned a master's degree in computer science from M.I.T., and, predicting the Internet boom ahead of just about everyone, invested his money in several online start-ups, unloading them at the height of the market. Now, he climbed on rock and ice 150 days a year, recorded bass parts for various producers at his home studio over in Glen, and traveled among the public houses of the Mount Washington Valley, promoting, promulgating, and pontificating on his favorite subject—Del Keppler, and his irrepressible greatness.

Even when they were playing together, and Jami was making three hundred dollars a week, in cash, beyond what she earned at Baba Louie's, she had a hard time defending her partner when local musicians got together. After a gig at the Pizza Barn, which Pete Niceforo, Boxy Mitchell, and Pickles & Bernie had attended, there was significant grumbling at the table when Del finally stop talking about himself and went home. For almost an hour, he'd dominated the conversation by detailing his latest achievements, including the bass part on a Sony commercial that Bob Dylan had recorded for Japanese television.

When the Pizza Barn door slammed shut on that frigid January evening, Pete adjusted his glasses. "Back in New York, I knew Bobby Zimmerman when he couldn't carry a tune in a bucket," he said.

"Still can't," said Pickles Armitage, a redhead with a marvelous set of pipes.

"Heck—listen. Del was vaccinated with a phonograph needle, but I suppose he's not a bad guy," said Pete.

Boxy Mitchell, the drummer for the White Mountain Trio, tapped out a rhythm with a pair of swizzle sticks. "Yeah, subtract the humongous ego, the condescending tone, and Bozo's old fright wig, and Del's a halfway decent human being," he said. "If he only knew when to shut the fuck up."

"C'mon, that's my meal ticket, uh, my mentor you're talking about," Jami said. "And we wouldn't be having this conversation if Del hadn't switched majors at Berkeley."

"From what?" asked Pickles.

"Mime," Jami said, and everyone laughed.

After a smoke, and feeling solid on the Chet Baker lyrics, Jami repeated her ministrations during another visit to the ladies' room, taking special care to poof out her bangs; and after rubbing the bald spot between Monty the Moose's antlers, re-entered the tavern. It was full to bursting—musicians, and bike mechanics, and tourists from New Jersey; hikers in woolen sweaters, and hipsters in little straw hats; locals, down-staters, and Massholes; gray-bearded hunting guides and dread-locked skaters who reeked of pot. Jami had never seen the hoot so well attended.

The seventy or eighty people in the room had their backs turned to her, facing the makeshift stage. It was a little platform, twelve by ten feet, flanked on one side by latticed windows and a baby grand piano on the other. Jami had missed Stan's introduction, since Jonathan was already up at the microphone performing.

Accompanying himself on acoustic guitar, the wavy-haired balladeer was halfway through "The Night They Drove Old Dixie Down," which Jami recognized as part of a two-song medley with "The Weight," a particular favorite of hers.

She stood to one side, following Jonathan's chord changes, the fretwork, when to pick and when to strum—imagining the song as a duet, her pure tone matched with Jonathan's baritone. But rolling into the choruses, Jami noticed that her erstwhile crush had no trouble reaching the most difficult notes. He could sing, the bastard.

Jay Atkinson

When Jami started for the bar, someone grabbed her by the hips and spun her around. "Miss me?" asked Boxy Mitchell.

"Like I miss cramps," said Jami.

Laughing, the two friends embraced, and while grinning at each other, Jami detected a familiar odor. "Got any weed?" she asked.

"Maybe. Whattaya gonna give me?"

Jami shrugged. "Whatever it is I caught from those sailors in Peru."

Bartholomew "Boxy" Mitchell was, as his nickname implied, a square, solid fellow, with a heavy beard, and a round, close-cropped head that he often covered with a wool hat. Boxy had learned percussion from Joey Scrima, a legend in the Boston indie scene, and was always drumming on something—his kit, the bar top, or, in this instance, pounding on Jami's shoulders with his thick, meaty hands.

Up on stage, Jonathan finished his set to applause, foot stomping, and whistling. It was always rowdy at the Bull Moose, a hard drinking bunch, with plenty of musicians sprinkled in, who supported and cheered each other on. When the noise died away, Jonathan introduced the next act, Travelin' Tom Masterson, and as the singer trundled up to the microphone, Jami caught Boxy's eye and jerked her thumb toward the exit.

"You sure you wanna clean the pig?" he asked, using their code for getting high. "You never do."

Jami eyed Tom Masterson as he mounted the stage and barked out, "Hello, Bull Moose."

Raising her voice over the opening chords of "Glory Days", Jami said, "either we smoke a bone, or I'm gonna steal Tom's bike and ride it off Cathedral Ledge."

They went out the back door and over to the tennis court, where spotlights outlined a mass of insects swarming in the air. The bristling hump of Thorn Hill rose up behind them, its shape made visible by the way it blocked out the stars.

Shaking out a few buds from a prescription bottle, Boxy filled the bowl of a pipe and handed it to Jami. Striking a match, he applied the flame as Jami inhaled.

"How was Peru?" he asked. "Did you dig it?"

Jami started waving her hands in front of her chest like a hummingbird's wings, her face turning crimson. "It was fuckin' awesome," she said, exhaling a plume of smoke. "I bought an Indian blanket for twenty bucks. Some of the kids I met had never seen a guitar in their lives, they were so poor. They live in cardboard boxes and shacks. But they love music."

Jay Atkinson

"Sounds pretty cool."

Jami coughed into her fist. "What've you been up to?"

Repacking the one-hitter, Boxy lit another match and took a sharp pull. "I've been playing some gigs over in Maine," he said, holding his breath.

"With the trio?"

Boxy shook his head. "I know this dude from Portland who started a band called The Undertow. Their drummer was on his honeymoon, and I filled in."

"How'd it go?" asked Jami, refusing a second hit.

It was good weed. Already Jami felt an expanding bubble of goofiness rising in her chest, and features of the landscape— birch trees, the tennis court, and parked cars gleaming in the weedy lot—took on a sharpness that hadn't been there earlier.

Boxy took another hit. "I played two sets a night for four nights—six hundred and fifty bucks. And I slept on this dude's floor, so expenses were minimal."

"That's killer," said Jami.

"It gets better," Mitchell said. "The Undertow's singer, this chick named Perri, is moving to Boulder, to go to the Jack Kerouac School of Discombobulated Poetry, or something. So I told my friend about you. Said you were down in South America on a tour, but were thinking of moving to Portland."

Jami laughed. "The quality of your bullshit is not strained," she said. "I don't know a fuckin' soul in Portland."

"The Undertow are killing it," said Boxy, lighting a cigarette. "They're already booked twelve nights in May, eight in June, and two shows at the Lobster Festival on July first and second, which pays really good."

"When's this chick moving to Colorado?" asked Jami.

"May first. They need a singer, dude."

Jami took a drag off Boxy's cigarette. "Hooray, hooray, the first of May," she said. "Outside fucking begins today."

"I'm serious," said Boxy. "I think you got the gig."

"Bullshit. They've never seen me play."

"Before I left, I downloaded one of your demos, and played it for them."

"Not 'Ellis River Serenade,' I hope. That disc sucks."

"No—'Highway Girl.' They fuckin' loved it, dude. They're paying eighty bucks a show, and you can get solo gigs, too. This dude has the thing wired."

"They write their own stuff?"

Boxy nodded his head. "Except Perri was the other half of the writing team, with my friend, Devin. So he needs a partner."

"Is he big in the pants?" Jami asked.

"What?"

"Just kidding."

Taking out his phone, Boxy said, "Open your email." The screen glowed with a keen blue light as Boxy scrolled through, attaching a file to an email. "I'm sending you three of the Undertow's songs," he said. "They play a sort of roots rock-ska fusion. A little folk-y, too. Devin's on lead guitar, steel, mandolin, and vocals. There's a bass player, drummer, and you'd be the second guitar."

Jami's phone pinged, and she opened the MP3 file containing a song called "Walking Joe's Cat." It had a distinct reggae feel to it—nice beat, a good hook, and everyone could play. They were tight.

"The singer's not bad," said Jami, holding her phone so they could both hear it.

Mitchell was drumming his hands on the top of the fence. "She's no Jami Jefferson," he said.

"Does she have big boobs?"

"I don't know. Maybe."

Using her forearms, Jami pushed her breasts upward, then rolled her shoulders to create a little décolletage. "Like this? Bigger?"

Boxy didn't respond, but Jami dropped her arms down. "That's a yes," she said.

"All you gotta do is sing a few songs for Devin, and you'll get the gig. They already know your stuff."

It was a pretty wild scheme, but Boxy had also tipped Jami on Guitars Without Borders, encouraging her to apply. Going to South America had been a mind-bending experience, a cross-fertilization of sound and ideas that had taken Jami's music into new territory—austere, vivid lyrics, and stripped down chord progressions; a fresh style that was charged with danger, hopelessness, and strength, all at once.

Jami had undersold it when she told Stan and Jonathan that she'd written a few songs in Peru. Laying up with her guitar, Jami had composed twenty-two songs, the best music she'd ever done. When she was writing, she'd heard some of it as solo stuff, but a good deal of the new material was meant to be performed by a band; at least, when she played it, Jami had heard the music in five parts, with backing vocals. At the time, she'd dismissed the notion that she didn't have a band to play it with, and just went on writing. But the Undertow sounded perfect for the music she was working on.

The neighborhood where Jami had lived was on the edge of San Cristobal, one of the most notorious *barriadas* in Lima. Spread over a dusty hill topped with a giant crucifix, San Cristobal was a teeming hive of shacks fashioned out of corrugated tin, crudely thrown together and haphazardly arranged. The hillside reeked of untreated sewage, rotten meat, smoldering fires, and heaped over garbage.

At the foot of the hill, where Jami rented a pension for ninety-five Nuevo Sol a month, about twenty-eight dollars, there was a market crowded with filthy stalls and bodegas; vendors hawking candles, cigarettes, sorry-looking fish, local produce, and other sundries; and a mishmash of cheap taquerias consisting of little more than a smoky brazier with a giant umbrella overhead. With four million people jammed into the *barriadas* surrounding the city, life in Peru couldn't have been more different from Jackson Village if she'd been living on the moon. Yet there was something about the people that reminded her of home—their work ethic, modesty, and cheerfulness, even when things were tough.

Despite the muddy lanes of the *barriadas*, the pungent odors, hazy vistas, and bursts of local music, all of which made a sizable impression on her, the majority of Jami's songwriting in Peru came out of the Mount Washington Valley—what she'd learned there, the people she'd befriended, and the contours of the landscape. The immediacy of the music came from her sense memory—the lovers, the heartbreak, dirt roads by the tint of the moon, and the Presidential Range ablaze with the orange and gold of October. It was as if she'd traveled halfway down the globe just to figure out what she already had, what she already knew.

Crickets thronged on all sides, hidden among the folds of Thorn Hill and alongside the tennis court. Hearing applause from inside, Jami and Boxy Mitchell headed for the back door, nearly colliding with some mountain bikers coming out to smoke a joint. In the tavern, Del Keppler was center stage while Jonathan and Tom Masterson accompanied him on guitar. Pete Niceforo was up there, too, holding his trumpet and a handkerchief down by his side as Del played a long solo.

"So you gonna think about this Portland thing?' Boxy asked.

"Day and night," said Jami. "I'll obsess over it, and get back to you."

Spotting a friend at the bar, Jami squeezed past dudes wearing bike shorts, and thin, muscular women in rock shoes bobbing to the music, along with rafting and kayaking guides spitting tobacco juice into plastic cups. What distinguished Del Keppler's style of playing wasn't its complexity; he didn't play fast, or in precise, shifting note combinations like some well-known bass players. Del's talent was expressed via simplicity; the space—or time, as it were—between notes; thumbing a dark note followed by an unexpected pause, then a somewhat lighter tone replaced again by that first somber note, all in succession. It was almost like a child's sense of music, except that when you listened carefully, the story he was telling was determined as often by the brief silences as the note patterns. It was like the simplicity of Piet Mondrian, or Georges Braque, two painters that Del admired; or like the climbing style of Reinhold Messner, who moved so casually, but with such economy and precision that he made even the most difficult ascents look easy.

Marooned between the fireplace and the bar, Jami caught herself staring at Del. Moving past her, Boxy whispered into Jami's ear. "Tell me you didn't bang him," he said, gesturing toward the stage.

"Maybe once," said Jami, looking away. "Okay, twice."

From the bar, Jami's friend, Luis Perez, who ran Baba Louie's bike shop, gestured with a glass of tequila in his hand. Jami laughed, waving off his invitation, but still came forward, smiling at her old boss.

Luis Perez was a soft-spoken Guatemalan, thirty-eight years old; a solid fellow with black hair, square white teeth, and the well-developed calves of the habitual mountain biker. Luis had arrived in the U. S. as a teenager, settling in the upper valley because it differed so much from the arid plains where he'd grown up.

Luis had been shot twice during the Guatemalan civil war, and if visitors to the bike shop persisted, he'd allow the curious to inspect his left forearm, where a piece of shrapnel was still embedded in the muscle. A bullet fired by the national police had ricocheted, split into fragments, and struck him in the neck, shoulder, and arm; his age and injuries allowed him to enter the U. S. as a political refugee, and he became an American citizen at twenty-nine.

"Down the hatch," said Luis, handing Jami a heavy shot glass.

"Bastard," she said, looking into the glass. The tequila blazed a trail into her stomach, reinstating some clarity to the general fogginess that came with smoking weed. "Man, oh man," Jami said. "That tastes like rotten kerosene."

For two years, Jami worked at Baba Louie's when the snow melted, which meant from late April to early November.

She ran the register, bantered with the tourists, and rode around on a unicycle to attract customers. But with the downward trend in bike sales, rentals, and apparel, Luis was forced to hire a year-round, full time employee who could also work as a backup mechanic and assembler, putting Jami and two other part-timers out of work.

"Looking for a job?" asked Luis, clinking his glass against hers.

"Was Magellan looking for Bloomingdales?" Jami said.

Taking stock of her circumstances upon returning from Peru, Jami realized that things were as bad as they'd ever been. Previously, she'd been able to stay afloat by working at Baba Louie's, selling lift tickets, and playing music in bars. But with gigs becoming scarce, and her bank balance ebbing away, Jami had discovered there wasn't any steady work to be had.

"I got a friend who's opening up a bike shop in Old Orchard Beach," said Luis. "Called me the other day."

Jami laughed. "Good luck with *that*. There's nobody in Old Orchard Beach except middle-aged Quebecers in banana hammocks."

"This guy owns a shop in Portland called 'Spokes and Bruises.' Doing good business in fixed gear, mountain, tri-bikes, and rentals. He needs people to work at the new place, so he's gotta fill a couple of jobs between the two shops."

Jami batted her eyelashes. "Have I mentioned how good-looking and charismatic you are?" she asked.

Pushing her hands away, Luis said, "He's probably gonna hire an assistant manager, too."

"Tell me there's health insurance, and I'll marry the guy," Jami said. "Hell, I'll marry both of you."

Adding in what Boxy had said, Jami felt the universe was mumbling something about Portland. She had about three hundred bucks left, and would be out of her apartment in a couple weeks. The sum total of her worldly goods amounted to an acoustic guitar; an old Fender electric that Del Keppler had given her; a cowbell, tambourine, one hundred ninety-six CDS, a fixed gear bike, an old road bike, a sleeping bag, futon, and a Navy duffel filled with jeans, sneakers, rock shoes, a half dozen sweaters, and a ratty gown straight out of an old horror movie. Jami estimated that she could move her entire life from Jackson Village to the Maine coast in three hours, if she could find someone with a truck.

Applause for Del Keppler broke up their conversation, and after telling Luis that she was also available for contract killings, Jami was called on stage, where Pete Niceforo was gesturing with his trumpet.

Boxy had set up his kit before Jonathan opened the show, and was sitting behind it with his brushes, ready to accompany Pete on the snare. When Jami got on stage, a little unsteady from the weed and the tequila, there was a ripple of applause, and Pete said, "Jami Jefferson on vocals, and Boxy Mitchell on percussion. We're going to do a Chet Baker song entitled 'I Remember You.'"

After Jami had listened to Baker on her phone, she'd copied two of the verses from lyrics.com, inking them onto her hand with a felt pen. Backed up by the snare, Pete began to play his horn while Jami stood nearby, patting the seams of her trousers to the beat. She smiled at the old trumpet player's acumen; the easy sense of style; his bristly chin, where he'd missed a few spots shaving, tucked into the collar of his dress shirt, and the way he kept time with one leather shoe thrust ahead of the other. It was something from another era, beyond styles and trends; it was a man playing a horn, nothing more, nothing less.

What Pete Niceforo was blowing was not an impersonation of an old classic, but a shiny, new version: his breath went into the horn in an idiosyncratic way and came out as his own story—a progression of sharps and flats that touched on what Baker had expressed, though reworked into something more personal.

Pete wore Chet Baker's song the way he'd wear his hat, at a different angle, on a different head.

Baker was a distinctive vocalist with a soft, plaintive, and tuneful phrasing, very intelligent and seductive. He was a slender handsome man with wavy dark hair, a prominent Adam's apple, and dark, mournful eyes. Until heroin ruined his looks and his talent, Baker was hounded by record producers, promoters, and touts; men and women desired him; movie directors wanted him for their big budget musicals, and starlets in New York and Los Angeles humped him half to death.

Jami had read all this on her phone. But when Pete lowered his horn to his left hip, signaling that she should pick up with the first verse, Jami skimmed past everything that she knew about Chet Baker, and closed her eyes.

> I remember too a distant bell
> and stars that fell
> like rain
> out of the blue

Here Pete moistened his lips, brought up the trumpet again, and blew a long tuneful phrase that created a bridge to the chorus. Jami glanced at her hand where she'd scribbled the lyrics, smiling at Boxy Mitchell as he patted his snare drum.

> When my life is through

> And the angels ask me
> to recall
> the thrill of them all

Jami had a sensuous, melodic voice, penetrating to every corner of the room without seeming to overwhelm the song. Just as it appeared she was likely to sing more forcefully, belting it out, she dropped into a lower, more intimate register.

> Then I shall tell them
> I remember you!

Boxy gazed into the distance, brushing his snare, and Pete blew a sequence of haunting notes that snaked around the room, between the gas station attendants and baristas and motocross racers, binding them all to one another and the mournful pitch of the song; throwing a series of notes up high, into the rafters, followed by a downward phrase that led back to Jami's reprise of the chorus.

> If they should ask
> I'll gladly tell them
> I remember you!

When she'd finished the last, trembling note, Boxy's percussion quit at the same instant, and Jami stepped off the stage to a fusillade of whistles and applause.

"You killed it," said Jonathan, heading over to introduce

the next guest.

"I try," said Jami.

As she turned, Del Keppler was there, his guitar slung over his back. "Just beautiful, man," he said to Jami, and to Pete.

Jami lunged back through the crowd at Jonathan. "What about the second-last spot?" she asked.

The emcee shook his head. "I got confirmation from our surprise guest," Jonathan said. "But come up and join us for the hoot."

Jami maneuvered around the room, accepting high fives and congratulations, then discovered some space by the doorway and installed herself there. Halfway through Pickles & Bernie's first song, Pete Niceforo spotted Jami and waddled over.

"That was pretty good," he said, wiping his neck with a handkerchief.

Jami leaned over to kiss Pete on the cheek. "If you were forty years younger, I'd take you up upstairs and show you a good time."

The trumpet player laughed. "If I was forty years younger, I'd be playing 'See the USA in a Chevrolet' and staring at Dinah Shore's ass."

Pickles Armitage was a well-endowed redhead with

a brassy contralto, and when she and her ex-husband, Bernie Schwartz, finished with "Mama, Don't Let Your Babies Grow Up to be Cowboys," Jonathan went on stage to announce a brief intermission. Boxy Mitchell and Jami and Pete Niceforo were passing through the kitchen by the time Jonathan finished, heading out for a smoke. Soon a handful of musicians had congregated behind the dumpster, a chance for them to catch up on the professional gossip and tell stories.

Cigarettes were doled out amidst the acrid smell of wooden matches and lighters. Just as Pickles, Jonathan, and Del Keppler, who didn't smoke, exited the tavern, Pete Niceforo lit one of his stubby brown cigars. Above him, hordes of tiny insects, massing in the light, formed a double helix that shifted and wavered in the air.

"How was Peru?" asked Niceforo, exhaling plumes of smoke.

Pickles Armitage puffed away like a teenager. "That's so exciting," she said. "You must have a shitload of stories to tell."

During intermission, Pete would relate anecdotes about Judy Garland, or the time he jammed with Miles Davis on the Isle of Wight. But, most often, it was Del Keppler who monopolized their chats, rhapsodizing about his work with T. Bone Burnett, or backing up George Clinton and the P Masters of Funk. When these monologues were delivered, the younger musicians, many of whom never had a paying gig, nodded and gaped and smoked their cigarettes, daydreaming of famous performers and far off venues.

Tonight, Jami had a story to tell, and when Del began pontificating on Muddy Waters, undoubtedly as prelude to his encounter with the old bluesman, Jami interrupted him. What Del was saying reminded her of an event she'd witnessed in Lima, and as Keppler attempted to continue his soliloquy, Pete Niceforo waved his cigar.

"Let the kid talk, for crissakes," he said. "Muddy Waters'll be here when we get back."

Jonathan and the others laughed, and Jami was emboldened to speak. It was a hot afternoon on the outskirts of Lima, two days before Christmas, and she was visiting friends in Keiko Sofia, a notorious slum not far from where she lived. The family consisted of Maribel Cortez, a stocky woman of thirty-five; her two sons, Tomas, who was eleven or twelve, and the younger boy, Ernesto; a three year old girl, Manuela; and the baby, Eugenia.

Through her employer, Jami had been providing guitar lessons to Tomas, and after just a few weeks, she'd grown close to

Maribel and the children. On her day off, Jami would buy a chicken or a few soup bones, and some candy for the little ones. Her Spanish was pretty weak and Maribel's English was nonexistent, but they managed to communicate with gestures and smiles, and Jami enjoyed strumming her guitar in their company.

On this visit, Jami sat outside their shack accompanying Tomas as he picked out "Streets of Laredo" on an old guitar the agency had provided. Maribel, with the baby slung over her shoulder, was inside warming tortillas over the fire, with a pot of beans simmering nearby.

Looking out from the hillside, which was crowded with shacks, huts, and lean-tos, Jami saw a black-haired young man crossing the highway that separated Keiko Sofia from the open-air market opposite. He was wearing a white shirt and black trousers, his hands thrust into his pockets.

Something about this fellow made Jami concentrate on him despite the hordes of women, children and starveling dogs ranging over the slum. When Tomas spotted the man ascending the garbage-strewn hill, he set aside his guitar and roused his mother from the shack.

Still carrying the baby, Maribel went out to their visitor, stopping his progress about thirty feet from the stoop. The man never once looked at Jami, or acknowledged the other people crisscrossing the *barriada* in all directions. Handing Maribel a small object wrapped in duct tape, the man pointed at Tomas, who stood outside the hut, and then gestured back toward the marketplace.

Beyond the plaza was a large hotel, its façade rising above the rickety stalls and pushcarts, a four-story building with two massive columns out front. The man looked at his watch, glanced around, and without so much as another word, returned the way he had come up.

Maribel gave Tomas the package, which he stuffed down the back of his trousers, and then pointed at the hotel, kissing him on the cheek before he set off. The market was roiling with vendors, hawkers, and mule-drawn carts, a frenzied hub of loud voices, rumbling machinery, and snatches of music emanating from the doorways of tacquerias and bodegas.

Maribel and Jami watched Tomas pick his way through the slum, hurrying to carry out his errand. In the early morning, before Tomas and Ernesto went to a makeshift school for a few hours, they sold candles or cigarettes beside the highway, trying to scrounge a few pennies. Taking the other children with her, Maribel did slop work in the kitchen of the hotel, and worked at a tacqueria in the afternoon, when her two boys had returned home. The family survived on one hundred fifty Nuevo Sol per month, about forty-five dollars.

Standing there, Maribel tracked the boy with a blank expression on her face. No money had changed hands, and it was pretty obvious that the terms were C.O.D.; if Tomas delivered the package without getting caught, Maribel would receive a dollar or two—money they couldn't live without. But in the short time she'd known the boy, Jami had become attached to him, and stood there worrying alongside his mother.

Though he hadn't been playing guitar very long, Tomas was a natural mimic and had a penchant for theatricality. Before he knew how to play chords, Jami had taught the boy how to impersonate Pete Townsend with his great, windmill strokes; showed him how to duck walk like Chuck Berry, and stare into the distance while picking out a riff, like Jack White of the White Stripes. And when Tomas learned to play something that resembled what Jami had demonstrated on her own guitar, the boy's face would explode in a smile, his dark eyes gleaming with delight.

"Elvis Costello," he'd say, taking Jami's little straw hat and setting it on his own head. "Brang, brang, brang," Tomas said, pretending to play his guitar.

At the bottom of the slope, Tomas clambered over a ramshackle fence, glanced up and down the highway, then darted across and vaulted the fence on the other side. No sooner had his feet hit the ground when a taxi, barreling along the access road, struck the boy head on, slamming him to the pavement. The taxi driver never hesitated as he sped away.

Maribel uttered an involuntary cry, unslinging the infant and handing her to Jami. Without another word, she ran off down the hill.

Jami paused in relating the story, her throat tightening. "Oh, my God," said Pickles Armitage, huffing on her cigarette. "Was he hurt bad?"

Tomas died before Maribel could get there. She knelt beside him, waving her arms in panic and grief, hugging the boy to her chest. Seconds later, her son still lying on the ground, Maribel climbed back over the fence, ran across the highway, and came staggering up the hill.

"What on earth for?" asked Pickles. "That was her little boy down there."

Maribel arrived at the shack, her eyes wild and her clothing and hair deranged, struggling to catch her breath. Beckoning to Ernesto, she flung herself down, sobbing in little gasps, and shoved the duct-taped package into the boy's hands, pointing back toward the hotel. Before he left, Maribel clutched her younger son to her breast, stroking his hair and whispering to him. Nodding in response, Ernesto rushed down the hill and Maribel took the baby and went into the shack.

"That's just—that's awful," Jonathan said.

Jami took a drag on her cigarette. "I took one look at that old guitar leaning against the hut, and cried like I was five years old," she said. "But Maribel was all done crying. Ernesto got back a little while later with some money and gave it to his mother."

Nobody spoke, and Jami flicked her cigarette onto the ground. "Later, Maribel went back down to see about Tomas' body. She bought a can of milk and dried beans for the children. After supper, Ernesto picked up his brother's guitar and I showed him how to hold it and strum a little."

Boxy Mitchell and Jonathan went inside to prepare for their set, and Bernie poked his head out the service door, looking for Pickles. Del had wandered off somewhere. The crickets started up again, while Jami lit another cigarette and Pete Niceforo puffed on his cheroot. The other half of Jami's tale seemed to descend from Thorn Hill as they stood there smoking: her abiding guilt; the sense of futility attached to her efforts in Peru; everything that had been lost that day.

It all weighed on her, until she said, "I should've done something to keep Tomas from going down that hill."

Pete looked at her. "Look, the only useful thing I can say is, put it into your music. Even the sad, horrible things. Everything. Anyway, that's what I always tried to do."

Going back inside, Jami heard the White Mountain Trio segue from "Mexicali Blues" to an original tune, "Crawford Notch Express," which marked the end of their set. When Jonathan and his band left the stage, there was a delay before the next act, and a rising hubbub spread over the tavern. Rumors had circulated all night about a special guest, coupled with wild speculation about who it might be.

At the moment, Stan Hislop and Jonathan were conferring near the stage, followed by Stan picking up the mic with a big grin on his face.

"Hi, everybody," Hislop said. "We have a special addition to the last hoot of the season. This performer is a legend in the Mount Washington Valley, a hometown guy who made it big. So it's my great pleasure to introduce a singer-songwriter-comedian you've seen on TV. Ladies and gentlemen, the Bull Moose Tavern is proud to welcome...Rusty Sprague!"

The room exploded with whistles, cheers, and applause, but no one approached the microphone. Glancing around, Stan looked at Jonathan and made a palms up gesture, shrugging his shoulders. The applause continued, blotting out Jonathan's reply to Stan, who left the stage and came toward him.

At that moment, the window behind the stage was yanked open and a dark-haired man with a guitar climbed through it, waved his hands in the air, and bounded over to the microphone. "Last time I was here, I skipped on my bar tab, so I have to avoid Stan," he said, and everyone laughed.

Stan shook his fist in mock anger. Plucking his guitar, Rusty Sprague said, "Hey, Stan, is there a statute of limitations on a chew-and-screw?"

"Not at the Bull Moose," said Hislop, prompting more laughter.

In person, Rusty Sprague was a stumpy, eager-faced man with a shock of dyed black hair and tiny bloodshot eyes. To camouflage his bulk, which had increased in the years since he'd quit the valley for LA, Rusty wore baggy pants, black hi-top sneakers without socks, and a loose fitting black dress shirt, unbuttoned halfway down to reveal a platinum medallion figured in his birth sign, Aries, the ram.

"It's great to be back in the valley," said Rusty, playing his guitar up around his neck, flamenco style. "Where, if you're out of work, you can steal a fishing rod and catch a trout for supper. Last week, I was on The Tonight Show, and I talked about how much I miss the local grass-fed beef. Back when I was playing dumps like this, I'd drive into Bartlett after last call and run down a cow. Throw it in the back of the truck, and eat steak for a month. Hard to explain the big, rotting cow's head in my trash, but you get by, somehow."

Members of the crowd jostled one another and laughed. Over at the bar, Jami huddled with Sarah, drinking another glass of bourbon.

"He's supposed to be a comedian, but nobody ever really laughs at his jokes," said Jami. "Doesn't he have that little voice in his head that says, 'I'm not funny?'"

Most of Rusty Sprague's act was a mixture of furious guitar playing and scatological humor—explaining that he was rich enough to marry an attractive woman who was twenty years younger, but how sex at his age was like "sticking a marshmallow into a mousetrap," and so on.

Another bit, greeted by howls of laughter, was the music that was playing in his head after a snowmobiling accident.

"I refuse to pass on from this world listening to 'Spirit in the Sky'," said Rusty.

He picked up the tune on his guitar. "Goin' up to the Spirit in the Sky/that's where I'm gonna go when I die. When I die and they lay me to rest/I won't hafta take the Breathalyzer test." He looked over the crowd, settling on a familiar face. "Sing it with me, Tom Masterson."

"That's kinda funny," said Sarah, leaning on the bar.

"It's pathetic," Jami said, tossing back her drink. "What a sellout."

Rusty Sprague was sweaty, swarthy, and short; needy and neurotic and full of false brio and brashness. Still, it was hard not to notice his talent. He was skillful on guitar, capable of playing a few bars of just about anything shouted out by the crowd, and he possessed a smooth tenor voice, something worthy of the big band era. Near the conclusion of his set, truncated further by his late arrival and the hoot's format, Rusty Sprague waved his arms and hushed the room.

After referring to his recent appearance on a bill with the comedians Ron White and Lewis Black, a show called the Black, White and Rusty tour, Sprague slowed down his guitar playing and said, "I know I've been lucky: had all the right breaks, and much less talent than some of the people in this room." He saluted Tom Masterson, who looked down at the floor, glanced back up, and laughed as Sprague indicated Pickles Armitage, who stood nearby.

"Not you, Tom," he said. "Pickles."

Sprague went on. "I'm just a kid from Intervale who practiced hard because he was too fat to get laid." He twanged a string on his guitar. "And I'm grateful to all of you for giving me my start. For letting me have this dream of a career."

Rusty picked out the opening chords of "Streets of Laredo," an old hoot favorite, back when it was held at the Blue Parka Pub. Gesturing to Del Keppler, Pete Niceforo, Jonathan and the others to join him, Rusty told Boxy Mitchell to occupy his drum kit. Strumming along, Del, Jonathan and Rusty conferred for a moment, and then Del stepped to one side, nodding his head.

Rusty Sprague motioned Pickles over beside him, directing her ex-husband to the other microphone as he smirked at the crowd. Bernie hung his head in mock shame, and went over beside Jonathan and Pete. Still picking his guitar, Rusty located Tom Masterson over by the fireplace and waved him toward the stage.

Pointing at his own chest, Tom mouthed the word "Me?", which made everyone laugh.

"Sorry, Tom," said Rusty, over the mic. "But we're not gonna do 'Glory Days' for the millionth time."

At the bar, Jami leaned back with a drink in her hand. Looking that way, Jonathan beckoned to her, flashing his crooked grin and pointing his guitar in that direction.

Jami shook her head and yelled, "No fuckin' way."

But Jonathan sidled over to Rusty, whispering something while the comedian put his hand over the mic, creating a squelch of feedback.

"Paging Jami Jefferson," said Rusty, in a low voice. "Jami Jefferson—we want your body."

Several people began calling for Jami to go on stage, as the other performers extended the opening bars of "Streets of Laredo". Rusty Sprague began to chant her name, and the audience picked it up. "Jami! Jami! Jami!"

Feigning weariness, Jamie slung the old twelve-string over her shoulder, and joined Pete and Jonathan at one of the microphones.

Just as the first verse was about to roll around, Sprague ducked over to Jami and said, "Take the second verse and the chorus. " He returned to the other mic; Jami glanced over and he nodded, winking at her.

A trumpet, bass, drum kit, and five guitars can make a lot of music; enough to knock dust from the rafters and cause the old pine floor to warp beneath the weight of the revelers. At the edge of the stage, Rusty took the lead, singing the first verse in his half-serious, half-bullshit voice, with Jonathan leaning over to harmonize on the last line.

> As I walked out in the streets of Laredo
> As I walked out in Laredo one day
> I spied a young cowboy, all wrapped in white linen
> Wrapped in white linen and as cold as the clay.

Everyone but Pete, Del, and Boxy Mitchell joined in the chorus, and then Jonathan stepped back from the mic, giving Jami room for her guitar. In a sweet, mellow tone, she sang:

> These words he did say as I slowly walked by.
> Come sit down beside me and hear my sad story,
> For I'm shot in the breast, and I'm dying today.

On the next chorus, the hoot was in full swing: Pete Niceforo blowing contemplative phrases at the ceiling; Del Keppler laying down a powerful bass line; Pickles shaking her ass and her tambourine, and Rusty playing a Mexican style rhythm on his guitar. All of the old grudges were forgotten, as Pickles and Bernie harmonized on the same mic, and Del jammed with Tom

Jay Atkinson

Masterson and Jonathan; and the volunteer fire fighters and bike mechanics and tradesmen shouted out their gleeful approbation, whistling and stamping and cheering.

By mutual assent, the other performers moved to the rear of the stage, ceding the two microphones to Rusty and Jami Jefferson. Playing their guitars in unison, they looked into each other's eyes and sang.

> 'Twas once in the saddle I used to go dashing
> 'Twas once in the saddle I used to go gay
> First to the card-house, and then to the Bull Moose,
> Got shot in the breast and I'm dying today

Pete took the next verse as a horn solo, then the wrecking crew swung back into old school honky tonk, bringing the cooks from the kitchen and the extra barmaid and waiters right to the edge of the stage where they cheered along with the patrons.

Rusty signaled to the others, and the music grew slower, more subdued, and he and Jami lowered their voices and sang the final chorus.

> Oh, beat the drum slowly and play the fife lowly
> And play the dead march as you carry me along;
> Take me to the green valley, there lay the sod o'er me,
> For I'm a young cowboy and I know I've done wrong.

While the band continued to play, Rusty gestured toward

his duet partner and the audience whooped and cheered until Jami took a bow. In turn thereafter, Jonathan waved to the crowd; Del grinned, nodding his head; Boxy smashed his high hat a few times, and Tom Masterson and Pete and Bernie registered the applause by smiling and pointing to Jami and Rusty Sprague. Passed over for the duet, Pickles maintained her good cheer, holding Jami's arm aloft, and accepting a buss on the cheek from Jonathan.

Unhitching his guitar strap, Rusty said something in Jami's ear; and with a thumbs up to the crowd, stepped between the other musicians, lifted the window sash, and exited the way he'd arrived, into the darkness of the side-yard.

The applause went on, punctuated by whoops and hollers. Gradually the other musicians left off playing their instruments and exited the platform, where they were congratulated and hugged by friends and strangers. Some of the performers, Boxy Mitchell foremost, began disassembling their equipment and packing up. While Jami was standing by the bar, feeling a little disoriented, Sarah Dunston approached, extending her right arm for a high five.

"That was fuckin' awesome," said Sarah, handing her a glass of Wild Turkey. "What did Rusty say to you at the end?"

Jami drank half the whiskey. "He said, 'See you in Hollywood, kid'."

"He must think you're very talented."

"He probably needs someone to clean his pool."

The lights blinked on and a mass of patrons were leaving, but there were still twenty minutes until last call and Jonathan asked Jami if she'd like to play one of her new songs.

"Does a bear like to shit on a golf course?" she asked.

All that remained on stage was Boxy's stool and high hat, an amplifier that belonged to Tom Masterson, and a single microphone, located stage left. Jami had torn her blouse right after her duet with Rusty Sprague, catching it on a metal bracket attached to the bar. Now, while Jonathan tweaked the sound board, she went over and asked Sarah to lend her something to wear. The barmaid handed over a long black jacket with velveteen lapels; it hung down to Jami's knees, and matched with her black jeans and boots, took on the appearance of a preacher's frock coat. On a whim, Sarah also loaned her the black, wide-brimmed hat she'd worn to work, and dressed in this garb, Jami drank the rest of her whiskey.

"Somebody just told me about a cheap apartment," Sarah said. "Over in Bartlett."

Jami finished her drink, banging the glass on the bar. "I'm

moving to Portland," she said.

"Why you gonna do that?" asked Sarah.

Jami shrugged. "Papa was a rolling stone," she said.

By now, more than two-thirds of the audience had left the tavern. Somewhere near forty patrons remained, not a bad crowd for 11:30 on a Tuesday night, but with the disappearance of so many people, the room looked empty. Gazing out from the stage, Jami recognized a couple of faces, and slinging her guitar by its strap, she leaned into the microphone.

"Hi, I'm Jami Jefferson," she said. "I'm probably gonna suck, because I just got back from South America and haven't played my stuff in front of an audience in, like, six months." She tuned her guitar for a moment, then added, "Thanks for sharing, Jami."

A few people laughed, and there was scattershot applause. Someone yelled, "Go for it, Jami," and, looking over, she waved to a guy she knew, a rugby player who was visiting with his wife, a lovely blond girl. Jami also noticed that the booze and weed had brought out a smoky quality in her voice that sounded good over the mic.

"I'm gonna sing something I wrote when I was away," said Jami, strumming her guitar. "It's called 'Highway Girl'."

Whenever she got up to sing, Jami recalled a bit that Harpo Marx had contributed to "A Day at the Races," an old movie that she'd watched with her dad when she was a kid. In it, Harpo wanders through a barnyard in a crushed top hat and a long baggy coat, tootling on a piccolo. A troop of black children, who are performing chores, shooting dice, and skipping rope, begin following the curly haired mute, waving their hands in the air, and singing, *"Who dat man?"*

Soon the entire neighborhood is dancing along with this pie-eyed piper; men, women, and children jumping, leaping, tumbling, and singing in a great chorus. Grinning at them, Harpo coaxes the group to new heights of improvisational whimsy, accompanying them on the piccolo, and other times gesturing to them and swaying along in blissful appreciation.

Jami never understood why she identified so powerfully with this antic, androgynous misfit, in tattered clothes and reduced circumstances, who later in the scene daubs half his face with axle grease and performs a spastic minstrel number with Groucho and Chico. Now, as she began playing her guitar, Jami realized that it was Harpo's ability to move his audience—transforming them into participants—that so appealed to her. Jami had often thought of Harpo and his colorblind enthusiasm when she was walking through the slums of Keiko Sofia.

As soon as Jami struck the first chords of her song, Boxy Mitchell, who'd been talking to a little brunette by the fireplace, headed for the stage and what remained of his drum kit. Taking his sticks from his pocket, Mitchell sat in front of his bare high hat, crossed the drumsticks in a narrow X, and, holding them in his right hand, struck the top cymbal with the butt of the sticks while pumping the foot pedal on the offbeat.

Across the way, Del Keppler, listened to the opening bars of the song with a quizzical look on his face. At that moment, Jami edged closer to the mic and sang the first verse.

> Buses, ferries, & freight trains
> It was all the same to Kerouac
> From French Lick to Bangor, Maine
> I'm goin' & I'm never comin' back

The tune had a rolling, country-folk melody, underscored by a subtle Caribbean rhythm that Boxy picked up on. Before Jami finished the verse, Del had climbed onstage, brought his bass guitar around, and plugged into Masterson's amp. Watching Boxy Mitchell and tapping his foot to the beat, the old axe man laid down a simple line that completed the percussion, thus solidifying the song's platform.

Wish I could take you with me
There's only room for my guitar
Time comes, I go swiftly
Just me, the road, and a car

By the chorus, Jonathan had ambled on stage, and was strumming along on his guitar. The improvised quartet gathered momentum, and she sang:

I'm a Highway Girl
I'm a Highway Girl
Get a car/go 'round the world
I'm a Highway Girl

Jami had written this song in Lima, gazing at the clutter of the slums. Now, she sang it like a woman who had $273.45 to her name; an expiring lease; an old Nissan, and a vaguely formulated plan to leave the Mount Washington Valley and start fresh, someplace else.

So long, good-bye, adieu
I'm gonna give it a whirl
But I'll remember you
I'm a highway girl

Fronting the little band, Jami changed the tempo of the song. People who'd been standing at the bar or sitting along the wall began gravitating toward the stage.

Luis Perez was still there, and the rugby player and his

wife. In front of the stage was a divorced carpenter from Fitzwilliam who was Sheet-rocking a couple rooms upstairs, and had decided to stick around for a beer. Nearby, there was a blond-haired guy who used to frequent the Pizza Barn when Jami was playing there. Jami hadn't seen him since October, when his brother died of cancer.

By the time she repeated the last verse, the fire fighters and mountain bikers and builders, Luis Perez and Sarah Dunston and Travelin' Tom Masterson, were all singing along.

> I drove along the mighty rivers
> & the waves lapped the shore
> Don't call cuz I won't answer
> You won't see me anymore

They took it around in a big circle, the two guitars meshed together, and Jami hit the chorus again, smiling over at Del and Jonathan like she had a terrific secret.

-END-

Jay Atkinson

Acknowledgements

A lot of the fiction I write grows out of my observations as a journalist. I go looking for a certain type of story, and often end up finding two of them. The first kind of story is comprised of the facts, and the second incarnation illustrates the deeper meaning of those facts. My story, "The Tree Stand", which opens this collection, arose when I was walking along a dirt road in New Hampshire to scout a lake. I keep myself busy writing outdoor narratives for magazines, and on that raw November day I was searching for a remote spot for a pond hockey story I was hired to write when the weather turned colder. An out-of-work carpenter who lived nearby and was selling his house originally mistook me for a realtor, and we struck up a conversation. It was the tail end of a severe economic downturn and the carpenter, a low key, friendly guy, told me about his impending divorce and the difficult market conditions that had thus far prevented him from selling their house.

In a quiet voice, he shared a number of personal details, and his recitation of those facts soon transcended their literal interpretation. It was a story of gritty persistence tinged with regret and an equal measure of resolve, along with the sort of reluctant compromises—Hobson's choices, really—that a significant percentage of human beings must accept in order to get by. Over the next few years, I heard or experienced stories about other working class people confronted by similar choices, and all those details led to the bartenders, building contractors, club owners, cops, farmers, fire fighters, realtors, rugby players, struggling musicians, truck drivers, and waitresses who fill the pages of this book.

University of West Alabama English professor Joe Taylor is a hard-working and hardnosed editor, writer, and publisher. I am indebted to him. For although I grew up in Massachusetts—and spent five happy years in Canada, first at Acadia University in Nova Scotia and, after I graduated, sticking around to play rugby in Ontario—my writing owes more to the Southern Gothic tradition than it does to the northeastern intelligentsia. I grew up among blue collar people, and so recognize and feel compelled to explore their lives, loves, dreams and hardships in my work. Joe Taylor gets that, in spades.

My teacher, friend, and mentor, novelist Harry Crews, once advised me to "write about your boys up north." I studied with Harry at the University of Florida graduate program in Creative Writing, enrolling in his fiction seminar for seven consecutive semesters.

Jay Atkinson

Over that time, he kept returning my failed stories, often saying: "Burn 'em. Fire is a great refiner, son." (Eventually he admitted he liked one sentence I'd written—one—in a story entitled "A Small Penance".) A decade after I left Florida, I finally began to grasp what Harry was teaching in that cramped, windowless room. I produced a novel entitled Caveman Politics based on my rugby experiences in Florida, and have since published eight more books. I would never have gotten close to that sort of output if not for Harry's patient instruction, and—despite his "gonzo cracker" reputation—his sincere affection for my son, Liam, and me.

Joe Taylor has published three of those books through Livingston Press at the University of West Alabama: a novel entitled City in Amber; a previous story collection, Tauvernier Street; and now, The Tree Stand. He knows all about Harry Crews, and in many ways, I believe Joe understands that I'm carrying on that same sort of regional tradition. Taking Harry's direction, I often write about my home ground on the Massachusetts – New Hampshire border. I'm grateful to Joe Taylor for helping me do that, and for all his efforts in keeping Livingston Press alive.

My agent, Sharon Bowers of Folio Literary Management in New York, was a big supporter of this book from the start—in an era when publishing literary short stories is as rare as seeing a snow leopard in Central Park. Sharon sent the collection to Joe, they talked, and he agreed to publish the book. Sharon's enthusiasm for my quixotic endeavors is remarkable, and I fully intend to tackle a future project that helps to keep her children in shoe leather.

In pursuit of both kinds of stories that I write, I'm often in the company of my rugby/ outdoor adventure pals and their families: Chris and Tanya Pierce, along with Kaya and Willem; "Surfer John" Hearin; Mike Zizza and his wife Lorna, and Anthony, Sofia and Anna; Ken "Bubba" MacIntosh and his wife, Karalyn Gauvin; Paul "Big P." Godbout and his wife, Krystyna; Doug Langdon, Jackson Spellman and his wife, Kristi; Randy Reis, Greg "Duke" Cronin, Jason Massa, John "Big Country" Prieto, Kevin Moore, and Thom Pollard; my good pal, Spencer Cackett and his family, in Australia; Frank Baker and his wife, Brandi and their boys in LA; Brad Hayman, Todd Hathaway, Frank "Francois" Kelly, Steve "DUMA" Johnson, Tom "Reggae" Rege, Lyle "The Vulture" Jones, Julian "Hollywood" Bristow and his wife, Astrid; Matt Medina, Lee "Burgers" Bartlett, Damian Maguire, Marc "Psycho" Murray, Bill "Short Bus" Bishop and his wife Linda; Skip Barry, Bob Poirier, Bob Bishop and his wife Mandi; Glen and Amy Hollingworth, and their daughter, Ella; Dave and Tammi and Sarah Wilson; Scotty "the Body" Souza and his wife, Brigit Ryan and their kids; Fred and Deb Roedel; Pat Connolly, his brother Jim Connolly and Jim's wife, Marianne; Tim "Big Sully" Sullivan and his wife, Lauren

Boyle Sullivan; Dan "Original Sully" and his wife, Lisa; Mark and Sharon Maloney; Tom Turner and his wife, Maura; rugby pal Stew Dunlop, owner of the Wildcat Tavern in Jackson, New Hampshire, and Sue "Sporty" Holt, who keeps Stew in line; Paul Male, Nick Murphy, Bill Good, and the legendary Chris Vale from my seasons with the Boston Rugby Club; and all my "right honorable" Vandals Rugby Club mates scattered around the globe. I am also indebted to my University of Florida rugby teammates, including "Surfer John" Hearin, "Stormin' Norman" Litwack, Dave Civil, Ken "Wee Wee" Alabiso, Noel "Osama" Carpenter, Carlos Ballbe, Conrad Merry, Frank Merry, Mike May, "Boca Scott" MacDonald, Matt Allen, Robert "O'Shaughnessy" Kaplan, Brian "Free" Friedman, Greg "Psycho" Taylor, Mike "Yes! Yes!" Siskin, Dave "AWOL" Farwick, Ken "Burr" Farrington, coach P. J. Van Blokland, and my dear UF friend, Dr. Karen Koffler; and from my sporting days in Canada, Bill "Dag" Fullerton, Scott "Scooter" Riddell, Ron James, Ed Handler, and Drew and Sheila Cooper. You are all family, and I trust you in all kinds of weather.

To my hockey pals, including my childhood and high school teammates Rick Angus, Dave Frasca, John Kiessling, Gerald and Gerard Comtois, Gary Ruffen, Ken Schelling, Curt Goulet, Rich Zacharias, John Sabbagh, Paul Trussell, Jim MacDonald and his wife, Lisa; Chris Cagliuso and family; Paul Healey, Brian Martin, Dennis Dube, and all the rest; along with Brian Duffy, his wife Jan, and their children Jake, Ava, Ella and Carter; Mark Machera and his family; Chanel Moreau, Russ Phippen, Livia Lawrence, Breena Lawrence, Noah Page, Erek Croteau, Elliot Perry, and Evan Doria-Yahiaouia; in the Methuen Fun Hockey League Skate & Read program, all the Yirrels and Moreaus, and the Kees; the Baez family; the Collettas and Wordens and Pages and Perrys and Binghams and Bates and Conways and Fotinos and the Doria-Yahiaouis, et al, thank you for your friendship and your sporting efforts on and off the ice.

I am grateful to my Boston University colleagues, Bill Mckeen, Greg Marinovich, Lou Ureneck and David Lyons for their ongoing encouragement and support. Also, special thanks to writer/Valdosta State University journalism professor Ted Geltner, along with his wife Jill and their children. Ted is a great sounding board for projects I am working on or considering, and I can only hope he takes my crackpot advice related to his work as seriously as I do his thoughtful suggestions. From my home ground, Bob and Linda Sheehan, Carmela Pagnoni, and Glenn and Marianne Gallant are always reliable in a pinch; also, Krista McLeod, the director of Nevins Memorial Library; Lisa Napoli Rosenberg, Jane Kelly, Dina Cottone, Andrea Doherty, John Goodwin, Gene Kee, Joe McCain, Jr., Dennis Febles, and Mark Donahue, and his wife Maureen. Thanks to Jim Gallagher for sharing his many insights into hunting deer with a bow. Family friend Dan Murphy is a close reader of my work and has offered valuable feedback and encouragement going all the way back to my 2007 novel, City in Amber. I am lucky to have his sage counsel and friendship.

Thanks to my friend and creative collaborator Joe Klementovich, one of the best outdoor photographers on the planet. Writers Chuck Hogan, Neal Bascomb, Pete Fornatale, David Daniel, Steve O'Connor, Paul Marion and Joe "Dutch" Kurmaskie are on speed dial when I need literary help with something, and my Boston University students, particularly the varsity athletes and the returning "customers" who take more than one of my classes, are bright, talented, funny, helpful and caring. Good on ya, Zeynep Ann Cavusoglu (she designed the cover of this book!); Mei Coble, Patrick Curry, Shane Bowers, Dominic Vidoli, Mark Cheremeta, Francesco Montali, Ryan Lee, Evan Morrison, Erin Sullenburger, Domenick Fensore, Thomas Jarman, Francesca Morales, Dan Dellechiaie, Adrian Thomas, Brittany Chang, Erika Banoun, TJ Butzke, Jack Brickner, Emma Longo, Charlotte Howard, Suzanne Crow, Melena Rodriguez, Audree Damiba, Lauren Fox, Maya Bhat, Hinsley Casenet, Ulrika Brameus, Matt Curtis, Talia Cresci, Quinn Barton, Siena Giljum, Matt Rouleau, Kalani Kwan, John Spaulding, Aidan Walsh, Lincoln Currie, and Robert Mastrosimone, among many others. I'm proud of our association.

I have dedicated this book to my siblings – Jodie, Jill, Jamie and Patrick. I love you all very much and appreciate all you do for me and for Liam. Cheers for my son Liam, the smartest guy I know despite being a Philadelphia Flyers fan. Also, my nephews and nieces, Matt and Katelyn Berry; Nick and Michaela Sparks; Owen and Reese and Shane Bower; and my brothers-in-law, John Berry and Jay Sparks. And to my longtime friend, Virginia Elinor Maple of Caribou, Maine: No diggity no doubt.

Jodi Hilton

Called "the bard of New England toughness" by *Men's Health* magazine, **Jay Atkinson** has published two novels, a story collection, and five narrative nonfiction books. His latest book, *Massacre on the Merrimack: Hannah Duston's Captivity and Revenge in Colonial America*, received the 2016 Massachusetts Book Award Honors in nonfiction. Among his other works, *Legends of Winter Hill* spent seven weeks on the *Boston Globe* bestseller list; his memoir, *Ice Time,* was a *Publishers Weekly* Notable Book of the Year and a New England Independent Bookseller's Association bestseller; and his rugby novel *Caveman Politics* was a Barnes & Noble Discover Great New Writers selection and a finalist for the Discover Great New Writers Award. *The Wall Street Journal* called Atkinson's *Memoirs of a Rugby-Playing Man* a "hymn of praise for the rugby game" and an "exhilarating book." A former two-sport varsity athlete at Acadia University in Nova Scotia, Atkinson teaches writing at Boston University. He studied with Harry Crews for 6 consecutive semesters while in the graduate writing program at University of Florida. Moving across different genres, Atkinson's body of work reflects a keen interest in the power of the landscape.